LIARMOUTH

LIARMOUTH

◆

A FEEL-BAD ROMANCE

JOHN WATERS

Farrar, Straus and Giroux
New York

•

Farrar, Straus and Giroux
120 Broadway, New York 10271

Library of Congress Cataloging-in-Publication Data
Names: Waters, John, 1946– author.
Title: Liarmouth : a feel-bad romance / John Waters.
Description: First edition. | New York : Farrar, Straus and Giroux, 2022.
Identifiers: LCCN 2021057148 | ISBN 9780374185725 (hardcover)
Subjects: LCGFT: Humorous fiction. | Novels.
Classification: LCC PS3573.A8174 L53 2022 |
    DDC 813/.54—dc23/eng/20211203
LC record available at https://lccn.loc.gov/2021057148

Designed by Abby Kagan

Our books may be purchased in bulk for promotional, educational, or business
use. Please contact your local bookseller or the Macmillan Corporate and
Premium Sales Department at 1-800-221-7945, extension 5442, or by email at
MacmillanSpecialMarkets@macmillan.com.

www.fsgbooks.com
www.twitter.com/fsgbooks • www.facebook.com/fsgbooks

1   3   5   7   9   10   8   6   4   2

LIARMOUTH

1

❖

Marsha Sprinkle has always been glad she's self-employed. She's her own boss and that's the way it must continue to be. She can't imagine having regular office hours, punching time clocks, or paying taxes. Fellow employees are impossible for her to picture unless she can dominate their every move. Marsha is better than other people. She knows that. Smarter, too. Maybe not about the needless crap they tried to teach her in school, but about important stuff like how to put things over on other people who think they have the right to speak to her before being spoken to first. The ones who make unashamed eye contact as if it were their God-given right to invade her privacy. Marsha just feels everybody else on earth is . . . well, too familiar. Common. No one has the right to know her.

She knows she still looks good. Forty years hasn't dented her sexual magnetism. Not that it matters to her except when she can use her appeal to punish. To trap. To enslave the clueless men who actually believe they will one day penetrate her. Thrust their filthy member into any of her openings above or below the waist. Especially into her own mouth, the oral cavity that refuses to tell the truth unless it is whispered privately for her alone to hear. Marsha won't even imagine sex. All that moaning and thrusting and humping with another human. Sweating. Drooling. For what? That's what Marsha wants to know. For what?!

Oh, she knows how to walk the walk, thrust out her natural-born tits and effortlessly swivel that still-well-rounded behind while ignoring men's panting gazes, just to frustrate them, torture the lamebrain bastards who even for one moment think they could invade her insides. Like the moronic Daryl Hotchkins, her crime partner, her fake "chauffeur," her sexual slave, who actually agreed to work for her if he could have sex with her just one day a year. That's right. Once. Every 365 days and not one more, and Marsha made sure Daryl understood this. Divide all that lust time up hourly and you sure as hell get a low minimum wage, yet Marsha feels she is *still* overpaying Daryl. It has been a long haul to Marsha Sprinkle's vagina, but today, Tuesday, November 19, 2019, *is* that day, the end of his one-year journey. He doesn't know it yet but there'll be a detour. A dead end. Marsha Sprinkle is no man's used-up calendar.

But first things first. It's a workday and she has to concentrate. She has always felt safe in whatever foreclosed McMansion they've squatted in. "Squat" is a word she dislikes, so homeless, so housing crisis. Daryl knows how to fool the neighbors, showing them fake leases he's typed up and jerry-rigging the electricity so these rubes pay for not only their own home's power but Marsha and Daryl's, too. They aren't squatting, they have taken charge of a house no one else could control.

Marsha likes how impersonal the interior design is in this "starter castle," as she once heard a real estate agent refer to her current unlawful occupancy. She needs empty rooms around the ones she deigns to inhabit, voids she'd never enter but needs to know are there, sadly existing but not benefiting from her presence. And of course, the countless other giant bedrooms with full baths are the perfect dumping grounds for the thirty or so rifled-through, picked-clean suitcases she and Daryl have appropriated from the baggage-claim carousels at Baltimore/Washington International Airport.

The ridiculous cathedral ceilings give Marsha the required headroom respect she needs to feel one with the house's vacant hauteur. Rich yet possessionless, fancy but hardly to the manor born, a style no one could call their own. The overpriced and oversize furniture left behind had failed to flip this white elephant of a house, and that suits her just fine. It can't compete with her. She'll never let the plush sectional sofas, the neoclassical mirrored tables, or the ludicrous Mediterranean chandeliers forget that she's the boss. Marsha is like a McMansion herself: too big for the land underneath it, defying both nature and the environment, and daring *anyone* to move inside . . . her.

Marsha hates anything old. Antiques. Vintage. Collectibles. It's all dirty to her. Used. Stained with other people's fluids—children's tears, unwanted sperm, stray mucus, even unrequired food. Nothing smells here. Odors are an unwanted invasion of her superiority, an interruption to her focused life. She has never worn deodorant in her life. Why would she? Her underarms smell like nothing. Nothing at all.

The walls are bare. Freshly painted—she can tell because there are no telltale smudges around the frames of the art-work she had immediately taken down. How dare some pa-thetic painter try to ruin her self-perfection with any form of competition? The cool circulating breeze of the air condi-tioner is still set at sixty degrees despite the chilly fall morn-ing. Marsha is always too hot, even though there's not an extra pound on her well-maintained body. She's never really hungry. That would be weak. Oh, she knows she needs fuel. Why do you think they invented crackers? That's all she eats. Not the cheap ones. No Ritz or saltines for her. The good ones. From Eddie's on Charles Street. Or Graul's in Ruxton. Imported. They turn to waste quickly and quietly. In. Out. Little pellets that leave no trace or mess. She remembers to flush the already-clean water in the house's toilet several times a day just so it will be pristine enough to receive her regularly scheduled but oh-so-spare eliminations with the proper hygienic welcome.

Daryl is always assigned the bedroom farthest from hers. Here he can take cold shower after cold shower as he waits day after day to fulfill the lust she knows he feels for her. He's in a good mood this morning, thinking about his pie-in-the-sky supposed payday. Daryl doesn't need much in life, just stealing and her "crazy cave," as he once so vulgarly called her private parts. He's from the Erie Canal area in New York, so what do you expect? Marsha may be from a similar blue-collar neighborhood in Baltimore—Dutch Village, it was ri-diculously named—but those so-called "townhouses" that boasted "sliding glass doors" and a pool are nothing more to her than McSlums, and she got out early and never looked back. She may be a criminal, but she's a classy one now, a mastermind if you really want to know. Daryl is nothing more than a common thief, and without Marsha planning their "actions" he'd be out on the streets, where he's gonna be today anyway. Furloughed. Fired. Whatever you want to call it.

Daryl's not bad-looking. She realizes that some lesser mortals might go for his trim thirty-five-year-old hillbilly build and his long brown hair, which he often wears up under a chauffeur's cap whenever they're doing a job. She's heard a woman or two comment on "what a cute little butt he has," whatever that could possibly mean, but his cocky assurance alone is enough to make Marsha gag. She's seen him buttoning up that uniform shirt over his swimmer's-build chest that somehow is both scrawny and muscular at the same time, and OK, he does have that flat stomach with a trail of light brown hair going all the way up to his annoyingly always-hard nipples, but all Marsha sees is a landing pad for his filthy little spermatozoa that would like to crawl up inside her and make her pregnant. Not again. No, she gave birth once and has been paying for it ever since. He may think he's going to invade her body with his confident erection filled with future colic-infected, learning-disability-stricken children, but he's got another thing coming. And it's not gonna be her.

Here he is now. Plodding down the white, unstained carpeting on that ridiculously grand circular staircase. Marsha ignores the bulge in his pants as she slips on a saucy but elegant blond wig over her naturally . . . well, who knows what the real color of her hair is these days? Does it matter? Not when she's wearing this hairpiece she's never worn before that came out of that monogrammed suitcase on carousel number four from United Airlines. There's always a treasure trove of disguises in strangers' suitcases. Maternity outfits, padded bras, falls. All ready to seize. Identification papers and personal items, too, that enable Marsha to avoid the terrible truth of everyday life. Like Daryl's disgusting unit aimed her way, rearing its ugly head. He had violated the third wall of decency by once mentioning he was circumcised. As if she cared! There it was, showing itself off unashamed through the too-tight polyester pants of the chauffeur uniform they stole off a hanger in the back seat of what *had* to be the last stretch limo this side of prom night, parked outside the Prime Rib restaurant years ago. He likes to brag how the pants "still fit" as if this were some sort of erotic news bulletin. She pretends she doesn't notice the leer of anticipation in his eyes as she quickly slips out of the expensive white silk pajamas freshly swiped from an Alaska Airlines bag and into an understated periwinkle-blue Gucci suit that lets the world know she means business. In this case, business class, British Airways. Flight 217. Heathrow to D.C. Direct. Last Christmas.

"Ready?" Daryl asks impatiently at the front door. It's early. 6:00 a.m. early. Usually he's a lazy bastard, so she knows he's anticipating getting his work done in the morning so he can have the whole afternoon ahead of him to pounce. On her. Oh, she's ready, all right! Just you wait. For plans he can't even imagine. As Daryl electronically opens the door to the ridiculous five-car garage outside, Marsha grabs a snappy winter-white wool jacket she swiped off a luggage cart outside Dulles Airport and slips it on. She's headed north. It might be chillier.

Marsha schedules ahead. Today is also the last day for

their black town car they had leased on a credit card they'll of course never pay. She'll give Daryl one thing. He does know how to build a chain of false identity by stealing junk mail from mailboxes and using those preaddressed mailing labels the March of Dimes sends out without asking if the residents want them or not to get new credit cards that can be maxed out in the first thirty days before Mastercard or Visa catch on and cancel. There's nothing else in the garage besides the limo. No garden equipment, no lawn mowers. Marsha doesn't mow her lawn, she moves. She's gone. Gone without wind.

Daryl can be a good actor, too, and he takes his chauffeur role seriously. You can never tell who might be watching. Realtors. The neighbors. He pulls out the car and drives it up to the front door for his "client." Marsha regally steps out of the house. It's nice out. Not that she cares. The only time she notices the weather is when flights are canceled. Just as Daryl leaps out to open the back door, Marsha opens her own lying mouth for her first "practice" lie of the day, but she doesn't get a chance. A large horsefly accidentally flies directly into her oral cavity before she can speak. Outside in the air, this creature doesn't seem that big, but from inside her mouth it feels like that giant flying reptile Rodan she once saw in a movie on cable. Her jaws are no match for this frightening pest, who, temporarily blinded in panic, begins biting her tongue with its tiny bloodsucking mouth. But Marsha is ready for any curveball nature might throw her. At first she considers spitting out this invasive monster, but then her reflexes take over and her snapping-turtle-like tongue, hidden behind her freshly glossed lips, rips the unwanted tormentor from the roof of her mouth, and with one bite of her cavity-free teeth, the execution of this pesky intruder is complete. Yes, she swallows.

"Hurry it up!" she snaps to a confused Daryl, who's not sure what he just saw. Knowing how she hates his "nosy questions," he just helps her into the back of the town car and closes the door behind her without the thud he knows could easily get on her nerves. They pull out of the driveway and glide through "Happy Hollow," their ridiculously named development of McMansions. Hollow it is, but there's nothing "happy" about it. All but one of the eight oversize houses sit empty or foreclosed by the banks. Expensive portable residential basketball hoops stand alone like giant floats in driveways, abandoned by their former families' athletic children, lonely for even a single ball to swish through their nets.

Only one couple is left besides Marsha and Daryl, and wouldn't you know it, they have a dog. Its name is Frederick, Marsha knows from hearing the blowsy woman who lives there yell its name every time they drive by, and then out comes this idiot creature, bounding toward them, giving chase. Is the dog so dim-witted that it actually believes their moving limousine is another dog? Apparently so. Slobbering, barking, jumping up, falling back down with its pencil dick fully exposed, racing forward and again jumping back up and smacking its ignorant head on their backseat window, it acts as if it's just seen Satan. Actually, it has. Marsha doesn't blink. Not even once. Frederick! she thinks. What a stupid fucking name.

Finally, they're in the real world. A place Marsha distrusts outside the aorta of classless wealth where she knows how to hide. Of course, Daryl drives at the exact speed limit so as not to attract "county-mounties," as he calls the police. Marsha is glad to be using gasoline, harnessing energy, baiting the environment. Daryl knows she likes to take Falls Road all the way into Baltimore City on the way to the airport, avoiding trucks whose drivers she's convinced are always looking down from their cabs onto her passing crotch. She debates stopping at Whole Foods on the way to pick up some of her favorite upscale crackers (their own brand of organic multiseeded flat-breads are quite yummy) but decides against it. That horsefly has left a bad aftertaste in her mouth.

Instead, she touches Daryl icily on the back of his jacket and says in a misleadingly friendly voice, "You know you're going a little bit bald in the back." "What?" answers Daryl with alarm as he rips off his cap in a panic and looks in the rearview mirror. "Just a little," she lies, feeling the adrenaline she always gets from untruthful statements. "You can't see it from the front," she continues, greedy for thrills, "but I noticed it yesterday. Don't worry," she adds with a dig, "you can always wear hats to cover it up." "I'm not balding," he sputters in narcissistic paranoia, turning his head to the left and the right, trying to get a fuller picture in the reflection. What a fool! Every day she lies to him and every day he believes her. It's not even a challenge anymore.

The "commute" to work, as Marsha thinks of their twice-monthly drive to the airport, is fairly uneventful. Daryl dares not even turn on the radio because he knows music troubles Marsha. It's too cheery and upbeat and all the huffing and puffing and strumming that goes along with instruments hardly seems worth the effort. Silence is better. Silence is about her.

They pass the Roland Park neighborhood, and Marsha

chuckles out loud over all the memories she has of ripping off that much-loved supermarket on Roland Avenue where longtime faded-gentry families sign the bill on house credit. Customers there may think they're better than Marsha because she hails from Dutch Village, but who's the fool now? The shoppers who carelessly shouted out their account numbers to the trusting clerks for the world to hear as their groceries were bagged and charged, or Marsha, who wrote them down and used them herself the next time she shopped there? Oh, those were the days!

Time passes by quickly when you're having fun. Suddenly, they've turned onto Martin Luther King Jr. Boulevard, in Marsha's opinion the most direct route through the city to the airport, no matter what the clueless GPS dictates. Marsha's preferred route always overrules what any ridiculous navigating device has to say. She knows every escape route there is, and no computer is going to help her in that department.

Despite the poverty, despair, and rage of this neighborhood, Marsha likes it here. No snitches. At every red light are squeegee beggars, often aggressive, who squirt car windows with soap and then dare drivers not to give them money to clean it off. Marsha usually tells Daryl to give them a few bucks. She respects their line of work. They're scammers, too. They're not lazy. They have jobs! They're here every day on the same corner at the exact same time. In costume. Marsha's convinced there's a pimp who controls the whole scene, putting the hungry "actors" through hair and makeup every morning, feeding them, giving them signs with well-written, heart-wrenching messages, handing them borrowed or rented real-life babies or skinny stray dogs for props and dropping them off every morning and picking them up every night before pocketing all the money.

She'd better have a cracker. She's got a few of those Haute Cuisine brand Basil & Sweet Pepper ones in the otherwise empty pocketbook she plans to ditch in baggage claim after her on-time arrival. They're still fresh in the baggie. Crisp. Almost sweet. Easily passed through her small intestine and colon toward the tiny wave of muscle contractions she has learned to control to assure a painless, speedy ejection.

Daryl doesn't really get nervous before one of their heists. It excites him to feel good down there and evil up top. As he turns onto Russell Street, the exit that leads to the Baltimore-Washington Parkway, he remembers Hammerjacks, the long-gone heavy-metal club that was razed and replaced with a football stadium, where Daryl got his criminal feet wet for the first time, before he met Marsha. That night Marky Mark, the stud-muffin white rapper, played, long before he became Mark Wahlberg. Even Daryl was shocked at the pubescent girls who were sexually awakened and encouraged to be excited in a lewd way by their horny mothers who brought them there on one of those all-ages-admitted concert nights. Daryl almost felt heroic when he swiped a bad mom's wallet from her purse underneath her chair. Didn't she deserve it? Hadn't she just swilled down two sloe gin cocktails and bought a third for her underage daughter? The wallet was just sitting there, his for the picking. No wonder he got a hard-on. Theft was sex, wasn't it?

Finally, he had a vocation. His parents might have been divorced but that didn't stop both of them from nagging about him getting a job. His father, Bruce, was on lifetime disability from losing a leg in a freak accident at his job in a steel mill, but you couldn't call that a career, could you? Even his mom, Betty, who had been fired from the gift shop at the Erie Canal Discovery Center for drinking on the job, had the nerve to suggest he seek employment. Fuck that *and* them.

He left the club, fully aroused in a new way. He didn't try to hide it, he just adjusted his rod in his pants so it rested upward, just below the buckle of the old Sunny's Surplus belt he'd worn for years. He was a loner with a boner, he chuckled to himself. A new superiority was throbbing all through him.

And then he heard it. A loud crash. The Number 22 bus had pulled away from the stop, and another driver in a car trying to get around to turn had collided into the side of the transit vehicle. Finally, Daryl had the nerve to do what every like-minded criminal in Baltimore knows they must. Run and get *on* the bus for insurance claims. Get a "suitcase," as some of the old-timer grifters still called phony neck injuries, marrying the word "suit" as in law with "case" as in court. "Suitcase," the all-purpose secret word for fraud.

Amazingly, his erection still held. It was a little painful going up those first bus steps, but so what, it felt even sexier doing a second scam before he'd completely gotten away with the first one. The lucky few passengers on board were already going into their cries of "whiplash," holding their necks and moaning out loud. He limped to an empty seat and held his knee as if it had been painfully slammed in the impact. Even the bus driver was faking injuries as he called into his dispatcher to report the accident, exaggerating the speed he had been going to make it sound worse. Daryl knew he was surrounded by fellow swindlers and felt, for the first time, part of a community.

Then she got on. Last to board. She looked different from

14

the others. That parentheses-shaped hairdo curtained each side of her angry face like a stage. Made up not to attract but to intimidate. She glared at Daryl, who glowered back and then spread his legs to show her who was boss. Marsha ignored his ridiculous genital display and moved to the empty seat right next to him to show her lack of apprehension as the Maryland Transit Administration accident investigator got on board and everyone went into full injury mode, holding their "aching" backs and whimpering in phony pain. Even Marsha joined in, which shocked Daryl, who hadn't realized she was on his team. Here's a real cool cucumber, he thought, as he stood up to get past her and fill out the report first, before the others' lying testimony became redundant to a skeptical transit authority claims adjustor. Daryl made sure he paused just for a second with his crotch right in front of Marsha's seated face. What he didn't realize was that while the lump in front of his pants was still there, the lump in the back—his wallet—was not. Marsha had just stolen it.

He was pissed for nine long years. And then he saw her again. In Nordstrom at Towson Town Center. She looked kind of the same, only meaner. Her hair was different, but whose wasn't? His was long now, a little greasy but it looked cool. He could tell by how women looked at him. Women who were nothing compared to this hot tamale. His cock practically jumped out of his drawers, springing to attention at the memory of her brazen pickpocketing. Who cared about his old wallet? She could have it for all he cared as long as he got to have her now. He'd better wait, though. He was on the way to the manager's office wearing a pair of new-enough Nike tennis shoes with a rip in one of them that he'd stolen at a gym and planned on claiming had been torn on the escalator when he got his foot stuck. It was usually good for a hundred dollars or so—managers would pay that just to get rid of you. But you couldn't pull off this scam with a hard-on showing.

She was taking a coat off a mannequin right in the store. Did she fucking work here, he wondered in amazement as he did a U-turn at the top of the escalator and went back down to investigate. It was her all right. She was boosting! Slicing off the security tag with a box cutter and brazenly putting the coat right on in the store. At that moment, their eyes locked. His criminal cock jumped involuntarily. Almost in respect. She looked down and recognized it. Him *and* it. The bus scammer and his signifying penis. The duo that didn't seem to fear her. We'll see about that, she thought as she turned on her heels and went up the escalator. Daryl followed in an awed trance, his dick pointing the way.

He couldn't believe it. Both he *and* Marsha were going to the manager's office to scam. She barged in first and didn't even bother to close the door as she filled out the job application forms with what must have been a phony name and bogus contact information. He had to hand it to her. Who would suspect her of thievery if she was supposedly seeking employment while wearing the coat she was stealing? As she exited, she ignored him, which made his penis feel challenged from rejection, but what could Daryl do? He had to go right into his "I just ripped my tennis shoe on your faulty escalator" spiel with the manager, who actually believed him for once. *Two* hundred bucks they gave him! A record high. Maybe this vixen was his lucky charm!

Outside she was waiting. In a town car, no less. "Get in!" she ordered from behind the wheel through the passenger-side window. He did. That was the day they stole the chauffeur's uniform. The day of their first airport luggage theft. She needed him without his penis; he needed her with it. They were a team, but their needs couldn't have been more different.

2

◆

Daryl and Marsha take the airport exit and go into full travel-fraud mode. He drops her off at the upper-level departure check-in door to Southwest Airlines, one they both favor because it's located next to where passengers from arriving Delta flights exit. She waits for him to open the back door and steps out without making any eye contact with those nosy, tip-hungry curbside baggage skycaps, who she suspects have some kind of luggage scam going themselves. Marsha, in character, politely thanks Daryl as he painfully bends with his still-hard unit to retrieve her carry-on suitcase from the trunk. He puts it down on the curb and extends its handle with a click. At least the props have been tuned, she thinks, relieved. The wheels had better not squeak. She has been known to fine Daryl for such inexcusable grievances. Marsha has filled this eventually-to-be-abandoned suitcase with reject clothing from past hijacked suitcases so it doesn't feel empty if some misguided gentleman attempts to help her during the check-in process she'll pretend to be part of. Daryl bids her a professional goodbye for the world to see but manages to give Marsha a knowing leer before re-entering the car and pulling out. As if, she thinks. Marsha will never become "one" with anyone, especially not him. Not today. Not tomorrow. Not ever.

Marsha's not checking in anywhere except other people's luggage. But for now, she has to be careful, bide her time. No attracting attention until the Delta Flight 1411 they've targeted lands at 8:15 a.m., which according to the Flight Tracker app on her phone will be four minutes early at Gate D11. To blend in, Marsha takes a spot at the end of a long, snaking Southwest Airline check-in line knowing she'll never get to the counter before the Delta passengers without luggage to claim will exit, file past her, and, without realizing it, let her know that theft time is about to begin.

Marsha likes Delta flights because that airline guarantees the luggage will be delivered to baggage claim in twenty minutes or you get 2,500 bonus SkyMiles. She has long realized she has to swipe coach bags because top-tier passengers get down there first and their bags come out right away, but coach passengers, emptying overhead bins, bottle-necking behind stroller families and wheelchaired fliers, take forever to deplane and find their way downstairs. By that time, Marsha and their bags are both history.

Today's plane is a red-eye from Las Vegas. Good. They'll be groggy. Marsha likes flights originating in warmer climates. The checked-in suitcases usually contain winter clothes their owners never wore the rest of the year. Many of the garments still have the dry-cleaning tags attached. Clean. No stains. Uncontaminated by sexual parts.

She's also not one to waste valuable lying time. "Did you hear?" she suddenly says with false alarm to the harried family who has just appeared behind her in line. "It's *snowing* in Atlanta!" "You're kidding!" wails the dad. "I know," says Marsha, "I bet our flight gets canceled." "Oh no," yell all the customers around her who have overheard. As they begin making panicked phone calls to whoever was picking them up, Marsha chuckles to herself. Lying is like working out; you have to do it every day to stay in shape. It's almost a calling.

By now, Daryl has pulled into the covered short-term parking lot where all the meet-and-greet drivers leave their vehicles. After 364 days of delayed ejaculation, he knows he's in danger of a "retrograde" orgasm where the sperm enters the bladder instead of emerging through the penis. He hasn't gone through all this for some "dry orgasm." No thanks to his own load shooting back up inside him. Hasn't he fucked himself enough working for Marsha? If he gets to blast off only once a year, he wants his sperm count to go through the roof and hit the stars. And in the center of that galaxy is you-know-who. Today's the day. He feels like Cape Canaveral.

Marsha can always tell when the first Baltimore passengers begin to exit the terminal for baggage claim. Their voices are so loud! With that appalling Baltimore accent! If she could manage to eradicate it from her speech, why couldn't they? "Geow down-ee movin' steps," she hears an older woman yell to her husband ahead of her as if there were any other place to go. "Moving steps"? Marsha hadn't heard that term in decades, but that's Baltimore for you. Nothing changes. Another arriving passenger has on an OCEAN CITY, MD hoodie. God, can you imagine going there, she marvels to herself. But that cinched it. Here was the flight from Vegas to Baltimore. She waits until a larger group of travelers comes through from another arriving flight and joins them without anyone being the slightest bit wiser.

Down the escalator she goes. Playing a coach passenger doesn't come easily. She is first-class all the way, but every flight to Baltimore was business at best no matter what they called it, so Marsha reluctantly accepts this humiliation. Besides, coach being crowded always works to their advantage. But there could still be trouble. Like that time they almost got caught in the Philadelphia Airport when they had overstayed their criminal welcome and done six separate baggage thefts in a month. She had told Daryl that was enough, but "no," he had said, they weren't "heaty." One more couldn't hurt. Wanna bet?

Another escalator had saved their lives that day. Marsha had just blended in with a gaggle of passengers on their way down to baggage claim, dressed way down in a tracksuit with running shoes, when she heard, "Hey! Hey!" from behind her. Two security guards who must have somehow recognized them from security tapes were coming toward her. Stepping off the last step, she saw Daryl in the distance with the other chauffeurs and their signs, but it was too late to warn him. She immediately pretended her carry-on prop suitcase was stuck in the claws of the escalator and jammed it sideways, causing an immediate pileup of descending passengers. Some shouted, others fell, a few lucky ones jumped right over her bag and landed still standing, while other more foolhardy ones, like the cops, leapt over the handrail halfway down and didn't meet such a happy fate.

Daryl instantly realized it was time to split and hightailed it out of there in the commotion, as did Marsha, ripping off her Chanel raincoat and salt-and-pepper wig and throwing both into an empty baggage cart that lazy airport workers had foolishly left for travelers to use free of charge. Snaking her way to the parking garage in a complicated roundabout route they had rehearsed twice, she knew they'd escape. He was already behind the wheel, motor running, holding a fresh red wig and plain-colored jacket that wouldn't clash with the tracksuit she was still wearing. The box of getups they always kept in the trunk of any vehicle they were using had come in handy more than once, and Daryl made sure it was always freshly stocked. Marsha jumped into the back seat, put on her new disguise, and held her head as high as any natural redhead would dare. They peeled out, bagless but uncaught. Time for a new location. Baltimore, here we come. Again.

But today, all is going smoothly. There is Daryl waiting at the bottom of the escalator to baggage claim as he should be. Oh, he thinks he is funny. A real card. Today his little chauffeur sign reads BARBARA MACKLE, which is a private joke between them that she is sick of sharing. Barbara Jane Mackle, as she was better known in 1968, is today almost totally forgotten but was once a twenty-year-old Miami heiress who had been kidnapped for ransom and buried in a box for three days before being dug up and rescued. For some reason this true-crime story delights Daryl, so she lets him blather on about it whenever they have to make small talk. Today will be the last day she'll have to hear this crap. She'd like to bury his *penis* in a box and let it smother to death.

Marsha nods to him as one does when you find your driver, and he immediately takes her fake carry-on luggage and pulls it along smoothly to carousel number two, where

Delta flights' bags are usually delivered. "Carousel"? Who thought up that misleading term? It's not some amusement park ride, Marsha thinks angrily, as she sees some idiot child sitting right on the rim of the luggage circulator while his parents totally ignore his blatant disregard of safety. Can't they read the sign right in front of them! DO NOT SIT OR PLAY ON BAGGAGE CLAIM MACHINERY, it says in plain English. God, she abhors children. What a curse on all women! She has only one, thank God, but what a freakazoid loser she is! Just the sight of this arrogant little brat gives Marsha flashbacks to childbirth. What a disgraceful experience it was for her. Every day since she has tried to be a bad mother to her daughter, but that revenge has still never been enough. The child, now a woman, somehow lives content with her own flaws no matter how often Marsha points them out. But now is not the time for regrets. She's got luggage to steal. All she can do is fantasize about this little bastard in front of her getting his pants caught in the rubber slats and being dragged around by the rollers in the conveyor belt howling his apologies. That'd teach him.

Marsha hates it when she has to wait for luggage. She must have misjudged the twenty-minute promised delivery time because here she is with at least ten other passengers and still no bags. This is the most dangerous window of time, when families greeting their arriving loved ones take cell phone pictures that can later be used against her. Finally, she hears those lazy baggage handlers pull up to the loading area. Nobody's really looking at her except for that fucking kid. He's not playing on the carousel anymore. No. He's just staring at her.

Little Timmy is tired. Cranky. He has been wedged in the middle coach seat for the last four hours, and he is hungry, too. No snack for him because he's allergic to peanuts. He hated that lady flight attendant. The one who stopped him from sneaking into the business-class lavatory and made him go all the way back down that long aisle filled with dumb adults who now knew he had wiping issues. His little underpants were riding up his butt, and no matter how much he tried to wiggle them down by fidgeting, they remained stuck up there, causing a rash he knew would eventually spread.

Look at that rich bitch with a chauffeur, Timmy thinks, as he sees the first baggage with the PRIORITY label go past him. Just 'cause she's got money why should she get special treatment? She's obviously too dumb to drive—why else would she have a chauffeur? Maybe if he stares at her long enough, she'll die.

What the hell is that brat looking at, Marsha angrily seethes inside. Aren't all children cursed invaders hell-bent on ripping open your genitalia the way her daughter did? Babies are Satanic. All of them. Baby Jessica in the well. The Lindbergh Baby. Even Baby Jesus himself. And now this grown-up baby moron in front of her.

Suddenly the carousel is filled with coach luggage, some bags sliding down over others so you can't even see the tags. Marsha knows what kind of suitcases to pick. Large black ones without any identifying ribbons or personal markers that overly paranoid travelers sometimes place on their checked bags. There's one. She points to it and Daryl obediently picks it off the conveyor belt.

Little Timmy sees Daryl's hard-on through the material of his uniform, and his hatred of all grown-ups soars to a new level of childhood fury. Suppose his own parents saw it? Suddenly he worries this bad man might be able to see his own little pee-pee. It wasn't hard now but sometimes it got that way in the morning and it scared him. Did that make him like this man? Dirty for life? He ought to punch that man's peter right in the mouth! That'd show him!

Christ, what's that kid looking at? Daryl thinks in alarm. "Take a picture, it'll last longer!" he wants to yell, but what the fuck! Who cares about a fruit-loop kid when you're concentrating on not busting a nut? The carnal knowledge of Marsha, that's what he has to focus on. He's got it all planned out. It will be soon. He's waited a year; he can hold off for another twenty minutes. They'll exit the airport unnoticed as always with their freshly stolen luggage and glide right over to the Hilton, located just 1.4 miles away. And then you know what! Pay dirt! Who cares who gets the Hilton guest points? She can have 'em for all he cares.

Just as Daryl begins to wheel away the freshly stolen bag with Marsha dutifully following him, a man rushes over and taps her on the shoulder. "Excuse me," he says with some agitation, "that's my suitcase you have there." "Oh, you're kidding," Marsha sputters, ever the actress. "I'm so sorry, they all look alike." "You could have checked the claim tag," he argues back weakly, relieved that his missing luggage has at least been located. Yeah, right, Marsha thinks, who checks the baggage tags? They don't even bother to have a security guard outside each baggage-claim area matching the bags to your boarding pass sticker the way they did in the old days. Why, she wonders. Surely, she is not the *only* suitcase thief working in airports!

"I'm really sorry, sir," Marsha stammers with faux embarrassment. "It was really my fault," Daryl adds as he hands over the luggage to its rightful owner. "I'm the one who should have checked the tags." "It's not your mistake," Marsha argues with noblesse oblige, "I'm the one who pointed to it." Turning to the easily fooled victim, Marsha continues the scam. "What an idiot I am, sir. I'm so happy you were alert and notified us about the mix-up. Imagine if I had taken it home!" Yeah, just imagine. The contents would be looted then fenced and the other personal items they couldn't use or sell would lie discarded in squatter McMansion bedrooms unclaimed forever.

"Timmy, stop it!" his father barks when he sees his son digging his fingers into his butt and staring at that lady with the chauffeur. "That's disgusting!" adds his mother as she swats his hand away from the seat of his pants. "I can't help it, it itches," he whines, relieved that his little tinkler hasn't hardened like that dirty man who's picking up another suitcase that rich witch pointed to. Doesn't she notice that filthy bone in his pants? It's practically a third leg for God's sake.

"Excuse me," the fellow Las Vegas passenger announces to Marsha with exaggerated politeness, "that's *my* bag you just picked up!" Daryl jumps to the rescue again. "I'm so sorry, ma'am, all these bags look alike," he pleads. "I have this *exact* same suitcase," Marsha stammers in believable astonishment. By now, all the Las Vegas passengers are down at luggage claim, and Daryl should know better but he grabs another one off the conveyor belt and Marsha looks back at him in fury.

"I see you!" Little Timmy yells at the top of his lungs, and the still-waiting baggage claimers look up from the carousel and turn to him in confusion. "They're stealing luggage!" he bellows like the kiddie crime-stopper hero he is in his mind. "Hey mister, hands off my bag," a pissed-off air passenger yells as he charges over to Daryl menacingly. "It's all a mix-up," Daryl tries to reason, "her suitcase is the same size, same color!" But because of Little Timmy, the passengers are beginning to see the true picture. Maybe he could go on *America's Most Wanted* and tell his story. It's still on, right? Is there a reward?

"Mayday! Mayday!" Marsha thinks. She was gonna ditch Daryl in the garage where she had that other car parked but now all plans are off. The crowd is turning on them. They're caught. Daryl looks to her in panic. He can't really run with a full hard-on and any sudden movement would be dangerous. He's close. Oh, so close. He concentrates on the most unerotic thoughts imaginable; jail food, HIV testing, square dancing, dead movie-star vulvas; anything to keep from coming.

Suddenly Little Timmy runs from the crowd and punches Daryl in his crotch. That's right. As hard as he can right in the boner, and then he has the nerve to jump back and laugh. "No, this can't be," Daryl thinks as he feels his penis begin to explode involuntarily. No squeezing of his prostate can stop it. Suddenly, like a geyser from hell, his prick begins to shoot out a giant load of pent-up semen. A year's worth of cum right here in his pants, just minutes away from launch time at the Hilton hotel. He staggers backward, flailing, convulsing, ejaculating, in double, triple, quadruple orgasm in full view of the approaching security guards and the rubbernecking crowd. He can't help but bellow out moans of animal pleasure that now Marsha will never be able to hear.

She's gone. Where *is* that wench? She can't leave him now! Not on their day of intercourse! The crowd is backing away in full repulsion. The charging TSA cops are stopped in their tracks as they see the gooey white liquid pooling down onto Daryl's shoes and spilling over onto the airport floor. A lady in a wheelchair vomits. So does her attendant. On her. Little Timmy's parents try to cover his PG-13 eyes, but he pulls their hands away. He wants to see this discharge of filth. This is what adults do. In secret. At night. Right in their own homes while children are sleeping.

Daryl realizes through the last spasms of overdue ejaculation that now is his only time to flee. That scat-rat of a kid is making weird laughing hyena noises as his appalled parents try to silence him. The crowd is backing away, unsure of which way to run. Marsha has seemingly vanished into thin air. It's now or never. His crusted pants are cold, clinging, and sticky, yet he makes a break for it. What else can a man do when he's just shot a year's load in public at the airport?

3

◈

Marsha's already in the ladies' room. Off comes the blond wig straight into the trash can. Same with the purse and her winter-white jacket. She combs her own Jean Seberg–style short brownish hair with her fingers and slips on a pair of librarian's reading glasses with thick clear lenses she always carries just in case. There. She's somebody else.

It's quiet. Too quiet. The only time she welcomes the sound of a stranger's urination and, better yet, defecation is when she's about to reach over a stall and grab a pocketbook or coat and run. She crouches down to look under the stalls and bingo! There's a set of legs in two different booths. As swift as lightning, she reaches over to snatch whatever may be hanging on the hook on the other side of the door. Some airports have gotten wise to this trick and moved the hanger lower, out of reach, or removed them altogether, but not Baltimore/Washington International. She feels a coat and just as she's about to pull it off, *bang!* The woman presumably sitting on the toilet hits her hand with something hard, probably an aerosol can of air freshener. "I'll break your god-damn neck, motherfucker," the lady threatens, and, while Marsha is impressed with her victim's readiness against the odors of human waste inside a public restroom, she knows she's trouble. In one last-ditch effort, Marsha reaches over the other occupied stall and hip, hip, hooray! Another coat. The woman inside is already trying to grab it back but, mid-excretion, she is no match for Marsha's sticky fingers. She's outta there.

Daryl makes it out the front door. Still no fucking Marsha. Still no fucking hard-on. Day one. The sperm count must begin again. She'll get hers no matter how long it takes. He hops on the first shuttle bus he sees. Long-term parking. There's only one other passenger on board. A man about forty years old with a suitcase clumsily repaired with duct tape. He looks kind of strange. Peroxided blond with a re-ceding hairline, dark goatee mixed with gray, some kind of harelip scar. Wearing a sixties vintage thrift shop suit that actually fits him quite well. What's with this fuck? He looks down at Daryl's cum-stained pants and smiles. Oh great. Daryl smiles back. What else can he do?

With her short hair now showing, Marsha feels vaguely French, and this stolen brown Timmy Tuff coat is long enough to cover her identifiable blue suit. Up the escalator she goes to the departure area just to confuse her trackers, but she gets stuck behind a brain-dead couple who obviously don't know the rules about standing to the right to let hurried passengers through on the left. Marsha is in a hurry at all times and feels the general public should be attuned to her schedule and her schedule only. People standing right are losers, cowards, undecided voters, while those on the left are winners, role models, and leaders. She breathes down the necks of the unfortunate couple blocking her escape and the man politely nudges his wife or whoever she is to let Marsha pass. "Thank you," she mutters as she dips down and nimbly swipes the wallet out of the lazy, unambitious, slow-moving, passive woman's open handbag and quickly walks off the escalator on the second floor. She aims for the door and not once makes eye contact with the great unwashed public.

The long-term-parking shuttle bus pulls into the endless lot of row after row of vehicles. The cheapest place to park at the airport. Here's where you meet the losers, Daryl thinks, and he is definitely talking to one of them right now. "They call me Ritchie Highway," says the creep with the battered suitcase, one that neither he nor Marsha would *ever* steal even if it were the last left on the carousel. Daryl sees two separate police cars cruising the lot, stopping to talk to passengers who were let off before them. He knows who they're looking for. Him.

Marsha exits the airport and wouldn't you know it? Not a cab in sight. Just clueless relatives dropping off confused un-frequent flier family members or smug passengers thinking they're oh-so-modern hopping out of Uber vehicles. Marsha hopes to never have to use such a service! No thank you to some unemployed bum with too much time on his hands behind the wheel of some about-to-be-repossessed midsize sedan. A driver that can actually rate her! Can you imagine such a thing? What ever happened to the customer is always right? That's what she'd like to know.

"I'm Clark Avenue," says Daryl, continuing the courtesy-van introduction charade by using the address of his first child-hood home without bothering to add his middle name like in that porn-star name game he can never remember the rules to. "Looks like you had a little accident down there," says Ritchie with a slight leer. "Yeah," mumbles Daryl angrily, re-membering the payday long promised by Marsha now spent in his underpants, clinging, caking, probably hatching jock itch and wafting the odor of wasted desires. "This you?" asks Ritchie as he stands up to get off at Station B in the parking lot. "I don't have a vehicle," says Daryl in a lowered voice, suddenly paranoid the bus driver will hear him. "Good," whispers Ritchie in pervert happiness, "I'll give you a ride."

There's a fucking taxi. It's about time. Marsha is not waiting in any cab line downstairs. That's for amateurs. Up here on the departure level, drivers know they can somehow snag a rider who, like them, thinks fast and knows how to butt ahead in life. She gets in and per usual for Baltimore, the interior smells like half a cold-cut sub left over from Harry Little's, which closed a decade ago for Chrissake. How can that be when the driver has one of those pitiful Christmas-tree-shaped deodorizers hanging from his rearview mirror that makes any vehicle reek like a freshly scrubbed latrine? "The train station," she barks. The driver, who looks kind of like a junkie Barry Manilow, looks up at her in the rearview mirror and says in an angry voice, "In Baltimore?" "No, Bangkok!" she thinks to herself before answering affirmatively in as neutral a tone as possible. And why, pray tell, do these drivers think passengers want to look at snapshots of their families clumsily Scotch taped to the dashboard? How these Middle Eastern–looking people could possibly be related to this Baltimore cracker, she can't imagine, but mixed marriages are off the charts these days. Anything is possible, she supposes. One thing she knows for sure. She wishes she could be wearing one of those face-covering burkas all the women had on in his sun-faded picture. Perfect way to disguise herself for what she is planning. A certain amputation.

Ritchie Highway hasn't asked Daryl any questions, just told him to get in the truck bed and then covered him up with a tarpaulin. When he drove to the pay station, handed over his ticket, and forked over the cash, there wasn't a peep from the attendant. Peeking through a tear in the waterproof cloth, Daryl saw another cop pulling up with lights a-flashin' and siren blaring but they sure as hell didn't see him.

"I guess I should tell you I'm not gay," says Daryl, after they'd pulled over about a mile up the road and he'd moved to the passenger-side front seat of Ritchie's seen-better-days Silverado pickup truck with the words HEE . . . HEE . . . HEE . . . hand-stenciled on the door exterior. What the fuck that means Daryl hasn't the foggiest. Probably some secret homo code. Who cares? He's got bigger things on his mind. Like escape. And his new "friend" seems decent enough for a deviant. Ritchie didn't even look down with lust at Daryl's crusted manhood back there when he changed alongside the road out of his hardened boxers and befouled chauffeur's uniform into a pair of tighty-whities, a vintage multicolored Nik-Nik shirt, and red blue jeans (they still make them?!) that Ritchie had offered up from inside that ratty suitcase. And hey, they fit! He even was decent enough to part with some Dude Wipes and let Daryl clean up his spent penis all by himself. His new unprivate part may be stymied, but it is still fierce, righteous, and unafraid, weary yet wary and ready for a whole new orgasm. But this guy isn't getting it. Marsha is. Where is that fucking Marsha?!

In the back of the cab, looking through the wallet she just nabbed from the slow-moving escalator traveler, that's where she is. Outraged to see it contains eight dollars! Who would go to an airport with only eight dollars? A mousy go-go dancer no one tipped? A tone-deaf street musician who can't sing a note or play any instruments? And now Marsha has to pretend to be *her*? What even is her name? "Frieda," she reads off the driver's license. "Frieda Collins."

I'm wiser than you, Frieda, Marsha says to herself, much wiser.

Suddenly the driver pulls off on the Westport exit from the Baltimore-Washington Parkway. "Excuse me," says Marsha aggressively, leaning forward and getting a full blast of pine-smelling deodorized front-seat air, "this is not the exit for Amtrak." He doesn't answer and continues driving a little too purposefully for Marsha's comfort. Is this fucker deaf?

These rich people sure are something, the cabbie thinks. Do they really think they know how to get around "Smalltimore" better than he does? A guy who grew up here in "Bumberg" and never wanted to leave? "Mr. Peanut Himself," as he is known with a certain amount of respect on the downtown streets of Baltimore, doesn't need no GPS or whatever that shit is called, he knows where the Amtrak exit is—he used to cop right outside of Chip House, that sober-living center near there. But you aren't going on any train trip, lady. I'm not even an illegal hack. I stole this cab!

"Can I ask you something, Clark?" Ritchie suddenly blurts in a voice sounding as serious as a heart attack. Clark? Who the fuck is Clark? Daryl tries to imagine. Oh, that's right. You're Clark! That's your new name, remember, moron? "Uh . . . sure," he answers with a certain trepidation. "Tell me," Ritchie purrs as they pull up to a row house in the Irvington neighborhood with a goddamn wishing well in its small weed-filled lawn, "do you like to tickle?"

"We gotta stop," Mr. Peanut Himself growls, not showing the slightest acknowledgment of Marsha's upper hand as a paying customer. "We're not stopping anywhere!" she orders in sudden concern as he swerves into an alley. An alley! Marsha has never stepped foot in an alley in her life. Even back in Dutch Village, she had refused as a child to take out the trash as her parents had demanded because "out" was back in an alley. Alleys are for sanitation workers and abandoned broken refrigerators with the door still attached that starving children suffocated in looking for food, but not this girl. She is out front!

"Is that you?" Ritchie asks with distracted surprise as he glances up to the TV from the "tickle table" Daryl is restraining him on with reluctant dominance, inside the so-called laughter dungeon hidden in Ritchie's dilapidated row house. Daryl can't really deny it because there he is right on Channel 11 News in airport security footage fleeing the airport. Marsha, too. She's not even looking for him! He can't hear what investigating reporter Jayne Miller is saying because the sound is muted so freakazoid Ritchie can hear his shitty music (who on earth would ever buy the soundtrack to that Elvis turkey called *Tickle Me*?), but it's not hard to figure out with the news ticker reading LUGGAGE THEFT: A GROWING MENACE underneath. "We all gotta make a living," Daryl says with a shrug as he puts the final feather handcuff around Ritchie's wrist. Christ, he thinks as he looks around at all the creepy framed Tickle Me Elmo portraits hanging on the walls, what a con man has to do to hide out from the police these days.

"We'll see who is giving commands," Peanut Himself thinks as he slams on the brakes, turns to his "fare," and pulls out a small untraceable ghost gun he traded just yesterday for an eight ball of coke. He's jonesing and he wants money now. "Gimme your wallet," he snarls, proud of his Baltimore accent, one that a Miss Fancy Pants like her had better understand. Marsha thinks, Of *course* these foreigners in the photograph aren't his family. This junkie looks like he's never traveled anywhere except to Lexington Market to cop heroin. Out of the corner of her eye, she sees a police car cruise by looking for drug sales, but she's pretty sure they didn't see her. Should she call for help? Old Smackhead might shoot her. She can't die here. Not in an alley. Not on a fake street with no name.

"Tickle trade" is a rarity in the "giggle community," as it is sometimes called, and Ritchie knows this. Yet here one is— the perfect specimen. Clark, or Daryl, as he now knows is his real name from the TV, has made it quite clear that he will tickle, but not be tickled. For pay of course. Five hundred dollars' worth of food stamps. Daryl will go for the feather duster, even the electric toothbrush, but no bottoming for him. Ritchie's fine with all that role-playing. This guy's a real tickle-top, he thinks dreamily, and Ritchie's ready to give it all up in tickle-torture ecstasy.

Ritchie himself *used* to be more versatile. He would be tickled or do the tickling, but that was before he was arrested for "breaking and entering and tickling" that hot sanitation worker he'd followed home on trash day. That changed everything. Yeah, he'd hidden in the bushes of his house, but who was that hurting? When the garbageman finally dozed off and Ritchie crawled in the window, all he wanted to do was make the guy laugh. Is that a crime? Even the prosecutor at the sentencing hearing had admitted the Maryland correctional system offered no treatment for tickle offenders. Parole was no joke either. It was tough to be forbidden to be anywhere within five hundred feet of laughter. But that was then, and this is now. He's served his sentence and is ready to get his funny bone tickled again.

"I only have seven dollars," Marsha argues in a supposedly embarrassed voice. A lying voice of course. She actually has eight dollars, but that one-dollar difference makes her feel like she has the upper hand. "Seven dollars!" Peanut Himself bellows in outrage. "That won't even buy me a bologna sandwich." Marsha knows it actually *can* in Dutch Village, or at least it used to, but before she can argue the point, he rips open the back door and yanks her out with surprising strength, considering his puny, track-filled arms. "We're going to the money machine," he announces as he pops open the trunk to reveal a gagged and terrified Afghan man who must have been the original driver. "Isn't Baltimore exciting?" Peanut asks with a chuckle. Then he grabs her wallet. The cabbie runs for his American life.

What's so fucking funny, Daryl wonders as Ritchie laughs hysterically while he runs his fingers across the soles of the guy's feet. It can't tickle that much! Now I at least get what HEE . . . HEE . . . HEE . . . meant stenciled on the side of your truck's door. Those same words are tattooed on the underside of your feet. OK, you're a tickle freak, but do you really think our whole deal here is romantic? You've got little votive candles lit all around like we're on some kind of honeymoon. Go ahead and giggle all you want because I'll be the one getting the last laugh. Sure, I can use those food stamps, but my *real* fee is gonna be the truck you drove me here in and I saw right where you hung the keys, buddy.

"Do my knees . . . do my knees," Ritchie begs between spasms of laughter. What's with this guy? Is he a fucking adult baby? Daryl picks up the feather duster that's laid out on velvet like some kind of S&M shit and uses it lightly on the back of this wacko's knees. "Hahahahahahahahah," screams the tickle bottom with a volume that could wake the dead. Daryl just wants to get this over with and prays he'll yell the "safe word," whatever that means. He had just nodded his head when Ritchie tried to explain it was "squirm." Safe from what, though? Who was supposed to yell it? Him or Mr. Giggles? "Squirm"? "Worm" was more like it! That's what Daryl feels like yelling now. In the most unsafe way possible.

Marsha looks back into the trunk. It is dirty but there is enough room for her to lie down among the oily rags and the one pair of jumper cables. Maybe she could use that donut-wheel spare tire as a pillow? "You had *eight* dollars," Peanut Himself rages, rifling through her cash, "not seven." "Sometimes bills get stuck together," she argues back feebly, but he's having none of that. "Get your lying ass in the trunk," he seethes, pointing the jerry-rigged firearm at her that she's sure he has no idea how to use safely. You don't lie with your "ass," you lie with your mouth, she'd like to point out to him, but grammar lessons at this stage seem pointless. You'd think there'd be some homeless types around to notice but all Marsha sees is a rat running by with a shredded Fudgsicle wrapper in its mouth. She wishes she were a rat. They're smarter than people. "All right! All right! I'll get in the goddamn trunk!" *Bang!*

It's dark, but as he pulls out, Marsha refuses to panic, even though she quickly realizes the emergency trunk release has been removed. At least there are a few inches of room for her to turn side to side. She's been in a trunk before, driven back across the U.S.-Canadian border by Daryl after that job at Montreal Airport had to be aborted when they were chased by security.

She guesses Daryl might think it's a funny coincidence that just this morning he had used the name Barbara Jane Mackle as her alias and now she herself was buried . . . well, not in a box like Barbara but in a car trunk, close enough. Marsha remembers Daryl reading aloud to her the part of the book where Barbara, once rescued, told the authorities she kept her sanity by "thinking happy thoughts," so Marsha will, too. Daryl's shriveled prick. Her daughter's about-to-be-missing cash savings. The death of her mother's dog. And the happiest thought of all? Her ex-husband's expression when she cuts off his sexual appendage.

❖

40

Daryl picks up the electric toothbrush he had been told to use, and Ritchie goes nuts, blubbering and gurgling in horny tickle-torture anticipation. Suddenly the next-door neighbors start banging on the wall. "Quiet!" they scream. Daryl freezes but Ritchie just begs, "Keep going, daddy!" OK, he'll try. He's hungry and Marsha never ate anything but those fucking crackers, so he had to fend for himself. He knows a market right near Marsha's daughter's house that takes food stamps and never asks for ID, so after this ordeal, he'll go there and kill two birds with one stone. Buy some potted meat and wait for Madame Pay Day just in case she shows up on the run.

On goes the power button. Daryl caresses underneath Ritchie's armpit lightly with the brush and it sure does the trick. Ritchie starts thrashing, howling in erotic laughter, tears of humiliation rolling down his cheeks. "Shut the fuck up!" one of the same neighbors shouts, this time with a real fury, banging on the sidewall separating the decaying row houses. But Ritchie's too far gone in erotic delirium to care.

Daryl turns his head away in disgust and there she is right on the TV screen. Marsha herself. Today. With him. Another angle of that same security-camera footage. They look good together, don't they? And look at her figure! But she's on the news now, not in the next room. Take this job and shove it. That's what he's gonna do all right. Into you-know-where!

Peanut Himself is in the city now, she can tell, because he's stopping but not that often, which means he's driving north on Calvert Street, a route all thieves know is the best escape due to the timed green lights for traffic flow. She's feeling around in the dark for something to use as a weapon. Jumper cables? Well, they *do* have those jagged clips to connect to a dead battery and what a perfect way to think of her captor. A dead battery. She'll make him jump for sure.

The fucker is slowing down, then turning left—going into the more gentrified "hood." OK, she's ready. Hidden like a rattlesnake ready to strike inside a Synanon enemy's mailbox. One clip to the right, the other to the left. A new kind of road service. She's got a hot shot just for him.

Peanut Himself knows this money machine. It used to be in a nice neighborhood. A gay bar called the Eagle was right up the street and once attracted old guys who dressed up like bikers and spanked each other's fannies. Peanut could rob somebody outside of there every night and no one complained. But it's gone now. Reopened by some young rich kids as a restaurant that serves vegetarian food. Eccchhhhhh.

And the hookers! Well, back in the day it was all trans girls still packing their original equipment and there's nothin' he liked better than smoking a rock and getting fucked in the ass by one of them with their tits hitting him in his back. But they're gone, too. Got respectable. Old Carrot Bottom. Ah, there was a gal. Got the surgery and now she's the manager of a Trader Joe's. And Feral Street, God, what a bod, what a rod! Bunch of do-gooders from a group called Baltimore Safe House "rescued" her and helped her start anew, off the streets. Guess where she works now? H&R Block, right up the street. And they know! And don't care! It's normal now! What's the world coming to?!

Bang! Bang! Now the neighbors are pounding on the front door. Daryl's got to get out of here. He turns up the speed of the electric toothbrush and Ritchie goes into the last spasms of tickle hilarity, but his arm reflexes involuntarily and his elbow slams into Daryl's face, knocking him back and over-turning two of the votive candles.

As the fire spreads to the feather duster, the irate neighbors break down the door and come crashing through. Daryl is still too stunned from the elbow blow to his head to stop the flames from igniting the rug and the power strip where the TV is plugged in. When the nosy Filipino couple from next door sees the fire and the tableau of Ritchie howling in triple orgasm, they freeze. Ritchie yells out the safe word, "squirm," and loses consciousness. Maybe he's had a stroke? Laughed himself to death? Is that even possible? Daryl's not sticking around to find out. He grabs Ritchie's truck keys off the hook on the wall and runs past the horrified complainers, who are now trying to extinguish the flames with Ritchie's old fire extinguisher that is way past its service date. Oh yeah, the food stamps. He runs back in and grabs them off the table. The last thing he sees before leaving is a close-up of Marsha's face on the TV right before it explodes.

Marsha hears Mr. Peanut Brain, or whatever his name is, fiddling with the stolen keys, trying to figure out *again* which one opens the trunk. Here goes. She's ready. *Ka-klick!* The trunk pops open, and even though she's blinded by the sudden sunlight, she still can see his big ignorant head like a moron moon in the middle of a solar eclipse of stupidity. Before he knows what hits him, one jagged rusty alligator clip of the jumper cables clamps onto his cheek with such force that a squirt of blood flies out and narrowly misses staining Marsha's outfit. The other spikes his right eye like a claw machine picking up a cheap prize. His pupil pops open faster than a week-old grape tomato, but the blood doesn't spurt, it just puddles down like an overpriced curtain in one of Marsha's fancy McMansion squats. He screams louder than Wilson Pickett ever did, but without the joy.

She hates the aftermath of violence. She really does. It's messy. Masculine without privilege, fueled by adrenaline, not intelligence. It attracts police attention, complicates escape, and announces itself vulgarly. Besides, red is a color that stands for law and order. Not exactly Marsha's politics. Mr. Peanut is sure a Planters one now. Planted right on the ground, writhing in pain. He'll need more than a monocle to see through that eye in the future. And a cane won't be of much help to that cheek wound, will it? Marsha looks around. There's one scary-looking homeless lady off her meds wearing a BALTIMORE, I ACTUALLY LIKE IT T-shirt who might have seen Marsha in action but she's minding her own business, laughing to herself like the lunatic she is. Marsha gives her a thumbs-up and, feeling a little puckish, pops into her mouth the last half of a leftover cracker she had stored in her bra alongside her *real* ID, just in case she needs it. She walks away with as much dignity as possible in such a situation.

4

❖

"We don't serve no food-stamp customers," snarls the snippy little white boy clerk behind the counter at the Overlea Convenience Market. All Daryl's trying to do is settle for his purchase of a chicken salad wrap (whatever the hell that is), some fancy bottle of dumb water shit, and a little package of two Berger Cookies that he always thought were overpriced and stale-tasting even new. This place *was* once OK. He was here with Marsha in the past because her out-to-lunch daughter lived in the neighborhood and they had broken into her van and stolen not only a whole bag of quarters she carried for parking meters but her E-ZPass, too. Would Marsha come back here today? Maybe. He hoped so. He'd fuck her right in front of everybody if he had to! Anyway, this place *used* to take food stamps—even for toilet paper! Plus, they carried *real* soda, Royal Crown to be exact, and that wasn't easy to find, even then. But now? Oooh-no! They have to pretend they are rich or something. "Since when did you stop taking perfectly good food stamps?" Daryl asks as that old familiar rage starts building inside him. "Since they switched to a food-stamp card with a PIN number, dumbbell," the smart-aleck employee answers with an attitude. How's Daryl supposed to know food-stamp rules? He's not on the dole. He works for a living. Stealing suitcases is a hard job. A trade, really. A craft this bumfuck clown could never ever master.

"Section Eight shoppers like you, who don't like our new décor, usually go up to the Joppatowne Royal Farms," the arrogant little prick adds with a superiority that begs to be smacked out of him. How dare he say the word "décor" to Daryl? Right here in Overlea?! Who does Mr. Fancy Pants think he is? Richie Rich? Just as Daryl is about to reach across the counter (and boy is this little pussy gonna wish they still had that old ghetto plexiglass protection), he sees local news anchor Denise Koch on WJZ-TV here in the store. Christ, how long has she been on? Since *Charlie's Angels*, he bets. She still looks pretty foxy. But not as sexy as Marsha looks now on the screen in that old airport security footage the station dug up from how long ago? Five, six years? Lookin' all hot-to-trot in that wrinkled linen suit he can see her visible panty lines through. She'd just say that was his filthy imagination, but he's not imagining the first stirring of old faithful down below in his pants. Damn! Look at her moist, lying lips in that close-up of her at LaGuardia during those airport construction problems when it was easy to snatch suitcases even curbside because passengers were so confused on where to meet their drivers. She's gotta be going back to this neighborhood, Daryl thinks hornily, rubbing his dick. Where else could she go but her daughter's? Yeah, they hate each other. He knows that. But still. They're family. Fucked-up. But still family.

"Hey, creep, hands off your cock," yells the new guy at Overlea Convenience Market, and before Daryl can look away from the medium shot of Marsha the news just cut to—the one that shows her cleavage—the clerk grabs a Taser from under the counter and shoots Daryl right through his pants and into his balls. Daryl doubles over in electrified-crotch agony, and when he tries to break his fall with his outstretched arm, he lands right on his wannabe hard-on. No, dear God, he thinks, tell me it's not possible to fracture your own penis! But it is, Daryl. It is.

Marsha stands at the corner of Guilford and 21st. Peanut Himself's cab is way too hot to risk using again. She needs fresh wheels, and she needs them now. It was easy to find a corner to herself in this neighborhood. The only hookers left were natural-born females and these johns weren't interested in them. Every once in a while, one who hadn't heard would pull over, but as soon as they sensed cisgender private parts, they'd pull off. Marsha has to pretend to be old-school pre-op if she ever wants a trick to stop. She tries imagining transitioning into another classy woman while still keeping her own cuckoo's nest below. She'd be Martha Stewart. Now, there is a lady *and* a criminal. Marsha would undergo surgery any day if she could have Martha Stewart's head switched and transplanted onto her neck. She'd be even more grand then. Yessirree. "Marsha Stewart," she'd call herself. There's a tasteful trans name if there ever was one. Same initials, too.

Marsha looks through a couple of trash cans and finds an old wig. God knows it's probably infested with lice, but once she shakes them out, she realizes they are dead, so technically it's safe to wear. Fashion doesn't come easy when you're on the run. As she slips it on, she sees it's at least her own color, brown, and the shoulder-length sheitel style favored by married Orthodox Jewish women who cover their own hair for religious reasons is one she's never been photographed in by the authorities. Had a hooker wig-snatcher been loose in a Hasidic neighborhood where this style is still seen? Only in Baltimore, only in Baltimore.

She had found a stained tablecloth under a porch earlier and tied it tight around her in a way that actually looked like a sexy wrap dress. She'll have to keep her own shoes on but those airport cops are all straight men and they never know how to properly describe a woman's footwear anyway. She takes a small twelve-ounce bottle of Dr Pepper out of another garbage can and wedges it inside her delicate undies. After a little adjustment, it looks like her "package." She sticks out her thumb.

Daryl reaches down and grabs the Taser barb left in his balls and tries to pull it out in one quick, painful movement, as if he were ripping a bandage off a cut. But this little fishhook is no fucking bandage, and it doesn't come out that easily. So, he grabs it again and yanks it up just to get the jagged little head out from under the sensitive skin of his once-filled testicles. His shaft hurts like hell. It's bruised. Swollen, too, and he's horrified to see it's now bent and crooked. As they say in Baltimore, broke. Went up.

That little dart was like a bullet and he doesn't want the punctures to get infected so he pours the last drops of beer from a discarded can on his injury. Damn, that stings! But beer is liquor, isn't it? Alcohol is alcohol when it comes to disinfecting. Nowhere to buy peroxide when you're hiding under a bridge with a bunch of homeless guys. But wait a minute. These guys don't look like *Bud the Chud* types. Which means they're sex offenders. Yep, he sees a couple of them have their puds in their hand, pounding away. Oh great! Just what he needs. More perverts to come between him and Marsha's vaginal payoff. Especially when he's got injured balls and a goddamn broken dick.

Marsha can't believe this preppy fuck of a man who claims to be straight just offered her twenty-five dollars to blow *her*! Parked in an alley off Cathedral Street! In his goddamn gunmetal-gray Volvo that has to be at least three years old. She adjusts her Dr Pepper penis inside her finely stolen underpants just to keep him excited until she can get hold of his car keys. Christ, he's wearing a wedding ring. This Brooks Brothers blowhard has a wife, and oh my God, there's a Gilman School sticker right inside his front dashboard window. He's got kids, too. There's even a lacrosse stick in the back seat. Wonder if his family knows he's been cruising for Adam's-apple Annies up and down Cathedral Street on the way home from Legg Mason every night? That's right, he's a stockbroker and he doesn't even try to hide his work folders lying right on the floor on Marsha's side of the car. And now this old-money asshole is playing with himself through his pleated khaki pants. In front of her! Mr. Bull Market may want to go down, but this to-the-manor-born bastard must have been born yesterday. Marsha's like the stock market—she's going up. And he's gonna pay. Aileen Wuornos had the right idea!

Now that it's out in his hand, Daryl realizes he needs a splint for his poor cracked penis, but where do you get medical supplies when you're down here? He sees one guy, roughly his age, who's not that ratty looking. He's not talking to himself, either. Just sucking on a Popsicle (do Good Humor men come down here ringing a bell?), watching an old portable TV that looks like it was left over from the seventies hooked up to a portable battery-powered station. Daryl slowly and evenly walks over to him, trying not to chafe his exposed private parts. Oh Christ, this guy is masturbating! To *The Simpsons*! Marge, to be specific. Oh well, Daryl's got his own cock out, too, maybe this guy will be sympathetic? "Hey, buddy," Daryl yells in a bro-like voice, hoping a little humor will break the ice, "can you lend me a hand?" "Hey, it's the luggage guy!" the whacker yells back with criminal respect. Christ, that old security footage must have been on every channel, Daryl thinks, but maybe here it will be a plus. He'd like to point out that he's not "the luggage guy," he's the luggage master, Sexcalibur himself, who's first in line for Marsha Sprinkle's royal tunnel, but decides to keep these basic truths to himself.

"Can I have that Popsicle stick when you're done?" asks Daryl as civilly as possible considering the fact he's approaching another presumably heterosexual man when both of them have their penises exposed. "Looks like you broke your boner," the *Simpsons* wanker answers with a good-natured smirk as he slurps off the last hunk of flavored red ice from his frozen treat and hands it over. Daryl doesn't see anything that amusing about his fractured member but accepts the piece of pink-stained birch, slaps his injured dick down on it, and wraps the whole package up with an old piece of shredded denim he found that was probably a pant leg cut off by one of the freaks here to make a pair of shorts. Securing the ligature with a discarded string of used dental floss that somehow got tangled in his shoelaces, Daryl looks up from his makeshift cast and thanks the guy. "Want me to sign it?" asks Mr. Jerkoff, trying not to be an actual jerk. "Why not?" reasons Daryl. "We're all in this together." Marge Simpson's number one fan whips out a black marker from a dollar store bag and writes the word "Pudding" on the compress with as little pressure as possible. "Pudding"? That's his fucking name? Jesus! Daryl reaches down and painfully lifts up his now autographed, bandaged penile package and drops the wounded family jewels back down inside his new Jockey shorts that the tickler pervert gave him. Good. He could use some support.

Marsha has no clue what the private-school-dad-john is talking about when he mentions "muffing" her as foreplay. Between pants of lust, he explains it's some sort of "entering" into the twin pockets within the male groin located between the scrotum and the testicles. Even if Marsha *did* have a penis, nobody is picking her "pockets," no matter how much cash they have on hand. Especially in a parked vehicle! She grabs him by the expensive haircut and shoves his head down toward her crotch as he moans in power-surrender pleasure. But when she hikes up her makeshift dress, he's in for a surprise. The Big Surprise! Dr Pepper! She grabs the plastic bottle and dick slaps him across the face with it. He's such a wuss that he's knocked out from the first strike. A female out-of-work prostitute who's been loitering for hours rushes over to help her sister in crime. They drag him out of the car and together insert the entire bottle of Dr Pepper into his mouth sideways, a much bigger female joystick than he had hoped for. They go through his wallet and split the $120 between them. Marsha lets the lady hooker pull off his wedding ring to keep as some sort of romantic booby prize. They drag the unconscious body over to a trash can with some address spray-painted on it (a lot of good that did the original owners) and lean him up on it. Marsha gets creative and grabs the lacrosse stick from the back seat and props it up on him to complete the tableau. The jobless fille de joie slips on the ring and marries herself in some sort of twisted ceremony of self-delusion as Marsha gets in the car and peels off. Next stop, a family visit. Daughter dearest, here I come! To rob you again!

5

Poppy Samuels is bouncing on one of the two mini trampolines that make up much of her office at the Bouncy-Bouncy Trampoline Fun Park. She's dressed as always in a one-piece tracksuit, this time floral, and her brunette hair is kept short and simple for minimum jumping upkeep. She always feels the most relaxed, healthiest, and, yes, happiest when she's midair and free from the financial troubles of running her privately owned business that *used* to be quite lucrative until those idiot International Association of Trampoline Park officials shut her down. Was that unfortunate children's birthday party that ended with three injuries, two of them serious, really her fault? Hadn't those young folks refused to follow the posted rules anyone could see? And what good's a parent-signed liability waiver if the court ignores this valid contract? Why was Poppy responsible for some oaf of a child jumping on top of another one, fracturing his leg? Shouldn't her errant parents have been keeping an eye on this delinquent who was wearing shoes while trampolining, despite warnings? Why is the other kid's bruised pelvis Poppy's fault? And don't even start on the birthday boy, the one who supposedly broke both arms after tearing through one of the older, worn trampoline nets and landing on the concrete floor below. How was Poppy negligent just because she had innocently forgotten to put the OUT OF ORDER sign back on that over-priced piece of equipment after cleaning up from the *very* busy Saturday night before? Poppy ran Bouncy-Bouncy all by her twenty-two-year-old self. She can't do *everything*.

Despite the largest single-jury verdict against a commercial trampoline park in the United States (and Poppy plans to get back not only her gigantic fine but her attorney's fees, too, once this injustice is finally overturned), her most loyal customers refused to jump ship. Like a defiant speakeasy in Prohibition, Bouncy is up and running, illegally. Luckily her landlady, Miss Betty, also known as Leepa, the two-hundred-plus-pound gymnast whose idea of "All You Can Eat and Bounce" night really took off, has been a loyal customer from the beginning. Leepa immediately embraced Poppy's idea of disguising the place with a fake storefront to fool the authorities and keep it open. When the chips are down, extreme jumpers stick together, and today is their first fundraiser.

"This Volvo drives pretty well," thinks Marsha as she cruises out of the city in the car seized from her potential molester. She should have been on the show *To Catch a Predator*, the women's version. Yes, where she's headed is kind of near the dreaded Dutch Village, but she can go another route to avoid even a glimpse of her past. She's exhausted but not defeated. Her plans may have been interrupted but she's back on track and Operation Ditch Daryl has already been a success. Now for the next step.

As she stops for a red light, she's relieved. Almost nothing can happen except getting carjacked, and what are the odds of that considering what she's been through today? But then, out of the corner of her eye, she sees some man, another goddamn *man*, frantically gesturing to her from his vehicle. With a certain amount of irritation, she rolls down her window a little, but not far enough for any wildlife to fly in and invade her mouth. "Excuse me," he whines, "I'm kind of lost. Can you tell me how to get to the Owings Mills mall?" Well, that's a first. A male without a GPS asking for directions. Usually, they'd rather die than admit they don't know where they're going. Of course, Marsha does know where this now-demolished mall once was. She has fond memories of the Saks Fifth Avenue that used to be there—especially its rather naive Returns Department she scammed several times. Even if the mall *was* rebuilt and reopened under a different name fairly recently, why should *she* tell him how to get anywhere? Had they had the pleasure of an introduction? Is he offering any kind of fee for this information? "Sure," she answers sweetly, "turn right up here on Joppa Road and go about three miles until you hit York Road and make a right and just follow that and you'll see it right on the left." "Thank you so much," he shouts cheerily as she even waves him to cut in front of her to make the turn. Of course, these are the exact wrong directions and just that fact alone makes her feel better, more intellectually advanced yet practical and, yes, prettier.

❖

Poppy's rigged the place so she never really has to stop bouncing. She can fly up and down and then project herself to the far left and land on a larger mat in the main tramp room and then hurl herself to the left wall, ricochet back to the main springboard, and then, with one final burst of adrenaline, jump up to the specially designed ceiling tramp with a super-duper SkyBoard brand of springs where she uses her hands to propel herself back down in a front full somersault, landing on the Bouncy-Bouncy landing pad with grace. It's quite an entrance.

Her customers are thrilled to be leaders in the radical trampoline movement, and today they've put their money where their feet are—right here in the clandestine recreation center. What other tramp park, especially one of this size, has hosted Drag Competition Bouncing Nights? Campolina, as she calls herself proudly, has been fearless about getting the word out in the gay community, and Poppy owes her big-time. Some of these queens really flip their wigs doing back somersaults! It's a diverse lot here at Bouncy-Bouncy and Campolina's generous cash donation proves her dedication.

Vaulta, a six-foot-tall Caucasian female bouncer who has been unfairly rejected from Olympic tryouts, can do a mean "full twist" despite having only one arm (it was her business how she lost it; no one has ever asked). She had organized supporters for other legal fundraisers in the past, but now that the chosen few had gone underground, it was her own cold hard cash that was paying the electric bills. And God bless Springboard Sam and Double Back Barbara, that African American couple who had never revealed their real names but were once a yodeling musical duo who performed while trampolining under the name "The Twitching Tonsils." They stayed even after the "tramp troubles," as that fateful party night of shame became known in the trade. Despite being labeled "safety scofflaws" and "gravity conspirators" by the authorities, they aren't afraid of frivolous lawsuits any more than Poppy is. "Having an altitude" is something all tonight's guests were proud of. They are a movement in the making.

Marsha cruises Belair Road slowly and turns off on a street that looks vaguely familiar. Bouncy-Bouncy used to be *somewhere* around here. Of course, on their coded Facebook announcement she spied on once, they really don't give the exact address for their ridiculous fundraiser. She's been there before, the time she boosted the wallets out of Poppy's customers' handbags on "Talent Day." Talent! Oh yeah! An idiot on a trampoline who juggled! Real talent! And don't even get her started on those two yodeling air tumblers! I mean really.

Marsha's not even sure what Poppy's business looks like on the outside these days. She knows there's been some legal trouble, so at least that ridiculous sign with the cartoon children springing up in the air like rubber balls must be covered up. She remembers some kind of low-rent convenience store on the corner and this looks like it could be it, but it's now all fixed up. Maybe you could *finally* purchase a good box of crackers in the neighborhood! A lawn-mower shop called Mower Mania. Could that be it? Probably. What a cheesy name to hide behind! That daughter of hers will never learn. She must pay. Pay through the teeth for polluting Marsha's birth canal.

Wouldn't you know it? Some whacker-fuck stole Daryl's already stolen car right when he was under the bridge. Hot-wired that Tickler's piece-of-shit truck just when he was giving himself first aid on his dick. Now what? How will he get back to Poppy's? How will he fuck Marsha on this rightful day of pay? He's now standing on the entrance ramp to the Baltimore Beltway that was luckily nearby, even though walking to it was a real pain in the dick. He's holding a sign saying ANYWHERE as he hitchhikes in his "homeless" disguise; a dirty hoodie he found back in the encampment with the words MOLE PEOPLE printed on the front and a ripped lampshade on his head he's wearing as a hat. His crotch bandage treatment gives a ridiculous bulge to the same pair of red jeans, now covered in grime. He definitely looks very different from the chauffeur he was seen as in those airport surveillance videos on TV. No one in their right mind would *ever* pick him up, though. Even he is starting to realize this, so when the first car to pass pulls over with a screech to the side of the road he can't believe his good luck. He runs as fast as he can with a busted dick and punctured balls up to the passenger side of the junker with several dents and looks in to see a very creepy man with rotten teeth, dressed in a hunter's camouflage outfit, leering at him from behind the wheel. Daryl's not sure what damaged sexuality this guy is, but he knows a freakazoid when he sees one. One thing he'd like to know: Why, oh, why is he such a pervert magnet? He gets in.

"Want some hooch?" asks the creep-o, two minutes into the ride, but even Daryl knows not to accept liquor offered up by a stranger from inside an old peanut butter jar. "No thanks," says Daryl as he painfully adjusts the splint inside his pants, which makes his crotch stick up in an almost comical way. Well, "comical" if you weren't Daryl. "I'm Jimbo and I'm lookin' for some homeless action," the driver announces without the slightest bit of embarrassment. "You're in luck," teases Daryl, spreading his legs to shift the splint to an even more vertical angle. "Crusty crotches and drifter balls, that's my specialty," says Jimbo, drooling. Daryl thinks fast, grabs a rusty can opener he sees on the floor, and holds it up to Jimbo's neck. "Detour ahead," he announces, suddenly all business. "Please don't kill me, I'm on disability, too," begs the bum fucker. "Yeah, well, I'm a hetero hobo," trumpets Daryl proudly, "and we're on a very different route."

"Stop this ridiculous bouncing!" shouts Marsha over the din of multiple springing elastic coils as she barges her way into the main trampoline area of Bouncy-Bouncy. Poppy is happily hurling herself upward as her fellow acrobatic fanatics spring up and down like crazed jack-in-the-boxes, showering her with ten- and twenty-dollar donation bills. Poppy is just going into a "lazy-back, easy-back" somersault when she spots her mother. The sight of Marsha used to trigger panic attacks in Poppy. Now her system just shuts down. She faints.

"Watch your wallets," yells Vaulta midflip as the rest of the disciples—and really, what else could you call them— leap to Poppy's unconscious side to form a protective shield around her. As Marsha tries to approach their cash area, Leepa grabs up the alms each time she lands. "Mrs. Sprinkle," Campolina says with as much civility as you can muster while doing a "stomach drop" wearing a sparkled minidress, "you know Poppy doesn't want you on the premises."

"My daughter is out of her mind," Marsha announces matter-of-factly, ignoring the rebuke as Vaulta attempts to get a coming-to Poppy to take a sip of a high-energy drink. "We're *all* crazy for trampolines," argues back Leepa before she pulls off a flawless "full-twist, straight-front" somersault. "We are raising money to continue our journey of trampoline resistance," adds Vaulta, cradling Poppy's head in her arms.

"Well, you won't get far up in the air," counters Marsha as she tries to push through the bouncing followers toward her daughter's stash. "All causes begin with marches right here on the ground and that's where you belong!" "There's no time for public protests when you are fighting for your financial life," pipes in Twisted Billy, an Asian newcomer, who had turned over his entire life savings of $340 before Marsha intruded. Because of his young age and double-jointed talent, he can jump with his legs and his arms wrapped around him like a pretzel and does so as a defensive move that renders Marsha speechless for a second. "Trampoline park upkeep funds don't grow on trees, you know," adds Vaulta as she bounds up from Poppy and completes a "hand-and-knee turnover" and, with amazing dexterity, considering she has only one arm, scoops up the last bill, which is stuck in a coiled spring that still needs repair. With what she thinks is a magician's sleight of hand, Vaulta passes the cash to Campolina, who stashes it with the rest of the donated kitty in a Bouncy-Bouncy water bottle, one of the few marketing items Poppy had manufactured and still owes money on. Marsha thinks these low-echelon tumblers may not realize she sees the proceeds getting stashed under the side deck of a nearby damaged trampoline, but she wasn't born yesterday. She was scamming three-card monte games even *before* she got out of Dutch Village. You can't grift a grifter. That's one thing Marsha knows for sure.

"Bounce," whispers Campolina into Poppy's ear as she starts to do exactly that herself. "Jump," orders Leepa quietly but firmly as she too begins moving upward in defiance of Marsha's attempted feet-on-the-floor domination. "Up-el-ey-ee-ooo," yodels Springboard Sam to his leader in a repeated sharp shift and pitch as he lands next to her. "Downy-ay-ee-ho," warbles back Double Back Barbara in a sudden falsetto alpine voice as she propels herself upward with a new musical combativeness. "Blast off!" shouts Twisted Billy as he launches his irregular limbs upward with a grace only he can achieve.

Poppy begins bouncing, at first slowly, but then building in speed and confidence, gaining altitude with each leap, jumping higher and higher, almost as if this strenuous exercise could propel her out of her mother's orbit forever. "I say no to static abuse!" she yells as her fellow jumpers join her in a chorus line of leapfrog-like ballet. Up and down they go in confident moral superiority, but Marsha never loses eye contact. Her features may freeze in the face of lunacy, yet her fingers are darting with the speed of light until she finds the hidden bank of money right there below them. They're still bouncing like idiots when she runs out the door. She can hear their shouts of outrage when they discover her theft just as she rounds the corner to Belair Road. Their pain is nothing compared to what Marsha's was like at childbirth.

6

◈

Daryl likes being behind the wheel again even if this wreck of a jalopy is beneath his standards. It's a Ford. He never liked a Ford, always preferred a Chevy if he was not driving a town car. That vagrant-hawk probably has so many out-standing warrants against him he'll think twice about re-porting his vehicle stolen. But you can never be sure how these wack-a-doodles think. All a mentally healthy man like Daryl can do is concentrate on promised pussy, and he sure as hell hopes that's what's waiting for him at Poppy's.

"Help," he thinks he hears a voice call in some kind of prerecorded announcement from inside the dashboard. How could that be? Was it some kind of Bluetooth issue? A GPS malfunction? He's surprised there even is a satellite system in this crap-wagon but thar she blows, right there on the floor where you can't even see it properly. *He* should be the one recording those directional voices. "Go left, asshole," his version would say. Ha! "Turn around, scumbag." Just imagine the driver's reaction! "In three hundred feet, kill yourself." He could make a fortune with this funny shit.

"Help," he hears again, but wait a minute, is it coming from beneath his car seat? He looks down and sees his impaired dick is stirring in his pants. Hey, that's a good sign. Maybe. But where is that squeaky voice coming from? "Let me out," he hears, and this time he knows for sure it's coming from his peter. Is he losing it? His crotch moves again, painfully, more aggressively, as if it had only one shot to be heard. Looney Tune time or what? But yes, he just heard his own penis talking to him. He fumbles with his zipper, swerving back and forth between two lanes. Hey, he'd better be careful. Suppose his own tool started babbling to the cops?

Poppy swerves the Bouncy-Bouncy van up to the front door of her clandestine jumping center in full fury. The driver's seat has been customized so that she can bounce in place while driving, sort of like an adult version of a child's bouncy chair that usually doesn't attract much attention yet lets her feel that up-and-down motion she requires in her daily life. But today she couldn't care less if the neighbors see. She's never been this pissed. She looks both ways for the dreaded process servers and honks the horn to signal all is clear. Vaulta opens the door jumping in place, as is the whole gang behind her. This is war. Marsha Sprinkle must die!

Poppy "hops" the whole van up and down in lowrider non-cholo, solo fury, still proud that she figured out all by herself how to install the hydraulic lift kits to each wheel that allow the vehicle to jump as high as four feet. Bouncy-Bouncers rush out militantly chanting a cover version of that classic rap song "Jump Around" by House of Pain, which Springboard Sam and Double Back Barbara have reimagined as a bluegrass call to arms. Campolina even adds a fierce falsetto horse-braying sound effect from atop a pogo stick she sometimes uses as a mode of travel when she's feeling more theatrical than usual.

"Shotgun!" yells Vaulta, and at first some of the jumpers are confused, thinking Poppy might be so angry at her mother that she is arming her followers, but then they realize Vaulta's claiming seniority seating here at Bouncy-Bouncy. The entire back of the van has been stripped and the cushions have been replaced with wall-to-wall minitramps that allow the passengers to feel the emotional comforts of extreme up-and-down movements. Vaulta gets the springiest one up front right next to Poppy, and, yes, she's a little tall for this privilege but even today, filled with rage, she remembers to dip her head each time she propels herself upward.

Poppy peels out. The springs of the vehicle, never allowed to wear, keep the suspension system in tip-top form so the wheels of the van move up and down excessively. Many riders might find this uncomfortable, but the Bouncy-Bouncers would never complain. In fact, their minibus launches upward and lands back down in a vibrating bounce. *We'll sit still when we're dead, Marsha Sprinkle!!!*

Marsha has never lowered herself by being on the grounds of a 7-Eleven store in her life, but today she just might have to break her own rule. That Volvo was too hot to drive to New

York, and besides, Poppy and her gang are surely on her trail already. She has to blend in. Oh, thank heaven. There's the perfect mark—a family getting back in their car, which must surely be refinanced within an inch of its axles. Dork-knob Dad with his baseball hat on backward. What difference could it possibly make what it said on the front? She knows how unremarkable the phrase he is trying to communicate must be, so she refuses to put the letters together to spell it out in her head. Mom is already all used up. You can tell having children has cursed her forever. Why isn't she striking out at her own mother for allowing this to happen like Marsha was about to do to hers? Must mothers raise their daughters only to be violated by men's fingers, tongues, and penises? This must stop. Now.

And those kids! Somebody in this whole wide world might think these identical white twins are cute but Marsha is not one of them. Dressed in some sort of matching Walmart tracksuits with the pants worn sliding down, these eight-year-old boys (the mother actually tells her their age later as if this is a fascinating fact) are already imitating the gangster look. Marsha does not appreciate the sight of their Dollar Tree boxer shorts much less their preteen plumbers' cracks.

"Bernie, help me with the bags!" she hears the mother shout to one of them in an accent that sounds part Philadelphian and part Baltimorean, if you can imagine such a thing. What could these people have possibly bought? Slim Jims? Fish sticks? One thing she knows for sure—there are none of the fancy crackers she's craving anywhere on the shelves of this goddamn place. "Barney, put the sodas in the truck," she hears Dad order. Barney! She heard it with her own ears. Bernie and Barney. Good God. And the delivering doctor didn't call child services to report this name abuse? And "so-das"?! Such an uncivilized word for soft drinks. The word they used to use for Coca-Cola in Dutch Village. Not only ugly but incorrect. Soda is carbonated water, not a sugary cola. Does anyone speak English around here?

"Excuse me," Marsha says in her best victim voice, "could you give me a ride to the bus station? I was just carjacked." "What?" blurts the mom in confusion and the usual fear Baltimoreans of a certain age always feel. "Have you called the police?" Dad asks with some suspicion. "Yes, of course," Marsha answers stoically, "they did the report, but they're so understaffed these days." "It's just what Baltimore is like now," explains Mom, her natural skepticism melting slightly. "Did they have a gun?" pipes in Barney without the slightest concern that she might have been traumatized. "Yes, they did," Marsha responds, careful not to sound too dramatic, "I have no idea what kind though. I just froze when I saw the one they pointed at me." "You're lucky they didn't shoot you," Dad announces. "If they had, you'd be dead!" cries out Bernie, obviously the less intelligent of the twins. "Bernie! What a terrible thing to say," scolds Mom in embarrassment. "That's fine, son," Marsha answers, "you're right. I'm lucky to be alive with you nice people."

"Seems like the police could have given you some kind of lift?" reasons Dad, still unsure. "Oh, I asked them," explains Marsha, "but they said regulations are much stricter these days and now they aren't allowed to give anybody a ride." "What bus station do you want to go to?" asks Mom, warming up to Marsha's lies. "The Bargain Budget Bus is the only one that takes cash," Marsha explains in faux panic, knowing they also don't even ask for ID.

"I know where it is," Dad snorts, "across the street from

the old Dundalk bus terminal." "The Bargain Budget buses don't even have a real station," Marsha sputters sadly. "No kidding," replies Mom, "they just pick you up in the parking lot across the street from the McDonald's like day laborers." "Hop in," says Dad, suddenly the Good Samaritan. "We'll take you," agrees Mom with that hon-like kindness many Baltimore women affect. "Sit up front," wails Bernie. "Yeah, keep your cooties to yourself," adds Barney with a smugness Marsha will make him regret. "Boys!" yells Mom as she climbs in the back seat with them. "Where are your manners?" In the trash can of breeding, thinks Marsha as she hops in the front passenger seat next to Dad. A position in a vehicle she is unused to from being chauffeured everywhere by Daryl. Daryl. Thank God he's gone. Him and his filthy boner. She hopes they're both sitting in jail somewhere.

Dad pulls off. Marsha buckles her seat belt as the two little heathens in the back seat squirm on either side of their overly protective mom. Imagine these two future hopheads as babies sucking greedily on this unremarkable woman's breasts! Marsha had never allowed her own daughter, Poppy, to put her germ-filled lips on her grotesquely swollen-by-nature nipples. Maybe that is why the child had sucked her thumb until she was fourteen years old. How should she know? She's not Dr. Phil, is she? Besides, sucking her thumb is better than sucking a dick, isn't it?

Just the thought of such oral invasion inspires Marsha's tongue to move in another lie. "Did you hear the awful news?" she suddenly asks, turning to the dullards in the back seat as Dad pulls off Exit 35A toward Golden Ring mall. "What?" asks the mother, suddenly scared. "The Jonas Brothers were all killed in a terrible tour bus accident last night!"

Bernie lets out a shriek of disbelief that sounds like it is coming from a wild animal. "No!" wails Barney before breaking into loud sobs of grief. "That's awful," cries Mom as she puts both her arms around her dim-witted sons in a futile act of comfort. "Is that true?" shouts Dad over the howling of his horrified children as he slows down at the fork of Boston and O'Donnell Streets. "Oh yes," answers Marsha, feigning sorrow, "I heard it on three different news reports. Joe Jonas was beheaded!" Barney lets out another deafening cry of anguish from deep inside his childhood soul as Bernie begins shaking in spasms of blubbering grief. "And the other one . . . what's his name?" Marsha asks nonchalantly. "Nick!" both boys shout in unison through a torrent of tears. "Yes, that's him," Marsha continues, "he was thrown from the car and run over by a tractor trailer." Both children are just speechless, but after the new details sink in, they let out a fresh howl of horror. "OK! OK! That's enough," orders Dad much too late. "They don't need to hear any more." "Kevin lived for a while after the accident," Marsha tries to explain in phony concern, "but he died later in a hospital from a massive brain hemorrhage." "Enough! Enough!" yells Mom as the boys dissolve into a quivering pile of blubbering boyhood bereavement.

"We're here," Dad announces loudly in relief, eager to get rid of this insensitive passenger at this O'Donnell Street bus pick-up stop. "There's another waiting passenger," Mom points out, hoping to get Marsha out of their car as quickly as possible. "Thank you very much," Marsha coos with deceit as she exits their vehicle, but, before Mom and Dad can sigh in relief, Marsha opens back up the front door and addresses the children in the rear. "You're too young to remember but lots of other stars died in car accidents, too. James Dean. Jayne Mansfield. Even Princess Di was beheaded." The entire family freezes in disbelief until Dad snatches the door shut and peels out. Marsha can hear the children start to wail again as the car fades in the distance.

7

◈

Daryl had to pull over this rust bucket of a car. What else can you do when your own dick is talking to you? Once his traumatized member was set free from his pants and let out of its splint, he heard a sigh of relief. Can a dick actually sigh? Is it a meaningless question once you hear it say the words "New York" out loud? That's right, his cock just enunciated the words "New York." Good God, has Daryl lost his mind? No! He can see the opening in the head of his penis, and it says the name of the city again. Plain as day! Some sort of infection must have spread through his reproductive organ, giving his penis supernatural powers. Is that really so bad? Was his dick like Kreskin? Could it actually see the future? Jesus! He could go on fucking *America's Got Talent* and actually win! "New York," it says for the third time. New York what? Was that where Marsha was going? Is his dick now like a payday pubic GPS? Daryl may have toxic cock syndrome but maybe that's a blessing in disguise. He's got a new friend down there. He'll call him Richard. Yes, Richard.

"There's only one place left for that witch to go—her mother's!" snarls Poppy through clenched teeth as she speeds by the Maryland House service area on her way north on I-95. She's too young to remember the details, but Marsha has told her countless times about her father, who supposedly abandoned both of them after being caught there in some sort of parking-lot sex orgy by the police and then ran off to Provincetown. Marsha lied so much, Poppy never believed it was true, but even if it were, she'd still like to see her father again. He'd accept her bouncing fanaticism and she, in turn, would try to understand his sexual experimenting. Tit for tat. That would be that.

"New York City, here we come!" sings out Twisted Billy as he successfully backbends and grabs his ankles from behind without losing his balance. "Your grandmother will help us this time!" wails Vaulta as she bounces both up and down and sideways from the hydraulic lifts. "Adora wants her gone, too!" adds Campolina, naming Marsha's mother out loud between attempts at applying her own mascara midair. "We'll land on your mother's head," seethes Leepa on her way down with a thud. "Crush her to death," screams Poppy in upward recovered rage. "Nobody steals from Bouncy-Bouncy," adds Springboard Sam in an aggressive, low-chested yodel as he hops from minitramp to minitramp with perfect musical timing. "Marsha Sprinkle must die," hollers Double Back Barbara in a rousing, jumping falsetto finale of echoed conspiracy.

Poppy sees the sign for the first tollbooth and springs into nonaction. "Land," she orders her followers, who begin reducing their motion obediently. "Descend," whispers Vaulta as she decreases her natural-born vault-iness. "Freeze," adds Leepa, proud to be so programmed. As Poppy pulls into the tollbooth, the Bouncy-Bouncers are all suddenly still. Fixed. Unmoving. Inert. And yes, miserable. When the toll-taker looks inside their vehicle, all appears normal.

Poppy accelerates away and so do her followers. Slowly yet fiercely, filled with adrenaline to spring again, they come alive, bouncing and vaulting and leaping their way in place toward the Delaware Memorial Bridge. Springboard Sam and Double Back Barbara aren't lowriding anywhere, they're joy-jumping and proud to be doing so! Just for the hell of it, Poppy goes full throttle on the hydraulic lift system and makes the whole van "hop" an astounding five feet in the air. Revenge will be even better now that they're bouncy-bouncing across state lines.

Marsha stands there waiting for the bus. There are only a few other travelers and they all seem to be complaining about the service. "It's an hour late already," gripes a huge white lady of undetermined age to Marsha even though she has not once looked in her direction. This woman is holding a very pasty baby in her arms, who looks dead, but whom Marsha presumes is sleeping. Her husband is just standing there but manages to be just as repellent although he comes in a much smaller size. "Another couple already left," he offers up as if anyone but these people would care. "Got sick of waiting," explains the big one. "The man had to go piss in the bushes,"

her mate continues to Marsha, who still doesn't answer but is relieved not to be recognized. These people have never watched the news. There's nothing current about the events in their lives and there never will be.

"There are no services here," complains a Native Hawaiian woman who obviously just had her hair done. Jesus Christ, she's got some scrawny cat in her purse she's gonna try and sneak on board. Before Marsha can point out the no-pets policy she hopes the Bargain Budget Bus Company adheres to, another waiting rider with acne who's dressed in some sort of work clothes with the name BRUD stitched on the front pocket asks the large one's husband, "Hey, how come you got your shirt on backwards?" "He just likes it that way," explains the wife as if she's used to sticking up for her husband's fashion sense. "That's why we call him 'Shirt Backwards.'" "I like the feel," he answers, as if all the bus riders were fascinated by his sartorial choices, "the pulling back of the material on my neck." "Makes him stand up straight," adds the corpulent wife before introducing herself as "Big Marge." Christ, they're a comedy team, Marsha marvels to herself before the baby wakes up and starts whimpering. "Oh now, Blanket," its mother coos, "it's all OK, we're going to go to New York and ride on the subway!" "'Blanket' is its name?" Marsha suddenly blurts out, unable to control her astonishment at such embarrassing parenting. "Yes, just like Michael Jackson's baby," the mother with glandular problems responds, unashamed. "Michael didn't do a damned thing," pipes in the Hawaiian lady. "He's a child himself!" "We sing 'Beat It' to him every na-na before he goes to sleepy-sleepy, don't we Blanky-Blanky?" Shirt Backwards asks in baby talk. Blanket gurgles back happily, and Marsha turns her back on the whole scene hoping it will magically disappear, but oh no, here comes another carload of Bargain Budget wannabe riders.

An elderly white-haired Italian American couple are dragged out of a car driven by what must be their daughter. They don't look too happy about their upcoming journey. "We don't want to go," pleads the old man in a heavy accent as his wife shakes her head negatively in agreement. "Nonsense," barks their offspring, "you're going to have a great time in Manhattan. I bought you theater tickets for *Wicked*." "We don't want to see *Wicked*!" blurts out the old lady in Italian. "We want to stay home," begs the father in English. "No!" admonishes the daughter, suddenly angry. "I got you these tickets and you're going! Do you know how much these tickets cost? You know how many other old people would kill to see *Wicked*?" "We wouldn't!" they both yell back in unison. "Help us," begs the older gentleman to all the awaiting bus riders. "We hate New York," sobs his wife in despair. "Please! Take us home." But suddenly nobody is listening because here comes the bus. Finally! It looks filthy and is traveling at much too fast a speed for this secondary road but at least it's here. "You get on that bus," the daughter threatens, "or I'll put you both in a home!"

Poppy and her jumpers had to stop at some point. Their digestive systems are in top form from their trampoline lifestyle but still, nature calls. They needed money, too. The James Fenimore Cooper service area seemed heterogeneous enough to try a little bouncing panhandling. What else could they do? Poppy remembered the Hare Krishnas who used to plague airports everywhere. Somebody must have given them money, or they couldn't have been there, right? Why not Poppy's gang?

The Bouncy-Bouncy fanatics split up. Vaulta seems like the best candidate for charity due to her supposed disability. She stands near the entrance with a sign she had earlier drawn on a piece of cardboard reading BOUNCING AND BROKE in shaky letters. You try writing with one arm and rebounding in a moving vehicle and see how neat your penmanship is! Vaulta has done her best and this sign will have to do.

"What's a bouncer?" Poppy hears a man ask his wife. Others look away. Only one nice Asian lady stops and puts a dollar in Vaulta's donation bucket, which is really just a Big Gulp cup she picked out of the trash can. Poppy starts hopping nearby, trying to show team spirit, but when another white lady with frizzy hair reaches for her wallet, her grubby daughter pulls her away and hisses, "Are you crazy?"

Leepa, the big-boned one, figures she'd better position herself at a different door to target the overweight families who might be rushing in from the gas station for their last minute to-go snacks. She places a dainty little tarp she uses as a traveling launching pad, decorated with cute spring-up cartoon figures she has drawn herself, right on the ground and starts chanting, "Hoppers are hungry, too!" But it's hard for the travelers, no matter what their weight, to feel too much sympathy for a gal this size's hunger, especially when she's bouncing in place like some kind of a lunatic. "Get a job, lard-bucket," some evil man with a DOVER, DELAWARE T-shirt yells smugly, before entering the service area with his contempt-before-investigation parents, who wouldn't know how to bounce properly if someone gave them lessons.

The rest of the gang splits up to use the facilities, bouncing at the lowest level possible to not attract attention. Springboard Sam would have chosen a stall in the men's room for more private up-and-down urination, but Twisted Billy takes the last one available and already all the pissers are reacting negatively to the sight of Billy's head popping up and down over the top of the stall, especially with his neck twisted in such an unnatural way.

When you gotta go, you gotta go. Springboard Sam also begins hopping in place at the urinal and no matter how subtle his movements, others react badly. Yes, there is a privacy shield between urinals, but the next-door pisser would still see you were bouncing, and let's be frank, aim was always an issue. "You got a problem?" snarls a trucker type as he glares at Sam. "No, all good," he answers as he hops in place rhythmically, his balance stimulated by his consistently vertical way of life.

When Campolina enters the ladies' room, hopping in the most feminine way she can pull off, she still doesn't really "pass" as a woman and all that drag queen leaping scares fellow female travelers even if they are fans of RuPaul's TV show. The honest truth that you can sit down and piss in a toilet while hopping in place is something Campolina wants to show the world by leaving the stall door open, but she realizes from the dirty looks she is getting that this is a concept most women, even liberal ones, are not ready to accept. Double Back Barbara is in such great urinary shape due to trampolining that she is on, up, down, and off the pot before the static pissers even noticed. Her kangaroo-like exit does, however, leave a few of the turnpike-women freshen-uppers speechless, and when one little girl urinator even blurts out,

"Why is that lady jumping?" her mom shushes her up with "She's just excited," because she can't think of any other reason to explain the bouncing to a child of her age.

Twisted Billy should have kept his talents to himself. As he exits the pit stop, a few uninitiated angry men follow him, shouting something about the movie *Matilda*. But no, Billy believes his contortion skills have gone beyond the beauty of dance into pure performance art. Feeling the muse, he suddenly twists his body and bends his limbs into a grotesque shape before crouching down, flipping his whole torso over, and crawling like a spider toward Poppy and Vaulta at the concession stand.

Many patrons start shouting, while others flee, but a small percentage are delighted and break into applause. Children especially love Billy and start twisting their own bodies into freakishly double-jointed poses. Poppy, seeing that Billy is the one who will bring in the cash, tells Vaulta to join her in line with the other bouncing followers for food at Burger King. Campolina grabs an empty BLT salad container off a table and starts passing the hat, while she, too, launches herself upward. Leepa rushes in from the parking lot and is amazed to see members of the nonjumping public actually throwing in dollar bills. A few of the more adventuresome fast-food customers start jumping in place along with the newly arrived Springboard Sam and Double Back Barbara. Twisted Billy, still in spider mode, starts walking with both his hands and feet upside down and right side up. Children squeal in delight while their parents' concerns melt away. A shower of money rains down over Poppy and the jumpers.

An irate manager who looks like a veteran of many bad fast-food jobs charges over and yells to the crowd, "Stop this bouncing!" "We have the right to jump in place!" challenges back Poppy. "And you!" the tin despot growls, ignoring Poppy completely and pointing his finger at Twisted Billy. "There are no street performers allowed on the New Jersey Turnpike." "We are paying customers," Campolina sasses back, emptying the "donations" into her purse between jumps of unashamed pride. "Yeah, 'tramps' are people, too, and we are hungry," scolds Vaulta, shaking the end of her residual limb at the man like a militant's fist and hurling herself upward from the carpet stained by a million spilled take-out meals.

"Stand still, you awful people!" the manager orders to all, but by now some of the defiant regular customers and even a few of the employees behind the counter are jumping in place with wide-eyed new enthusiasm. "No employee bouncing!" he screeches to the few mutinous servers who continue to leap while filling the food orders of Poppy and her hungry gymnasts, mostly cheesy tots because they are easy to pop in their mouths while springing upward. "You people have to leave or I'm calling the cops!" the bouncist bully says directly to Poppy, realizing she is the leader of this lunatic fringe group.

With many still-unresolved lawsuits against her coming up, not to mention her murderous plans, Poppy understands this could get ugly. The police have a history of intolerance toward jumpers and the people who support them. Besides, they must have taken in over a hundred dollars just here in this rest area, certainly enough for gas and tolls to New York City. She nods to Springboard Sam and Double Back Barbara, who immediately break into a cowboy version of "Rubber Ball" by Bobby Vee. "Bouncy! Bouncy!" the newly recruited jumpers in the crowd sing back as Poppy and her small army of dedicated fanatics leap toward the exit door with Twisted Billy bringing up the rear in full Itsy Bitsy Spider contortionist mode. United, they all yodel out beautifully, "Ahi-dee-oh-lay-ee-hoo, I'll come bouncing back to you." Fully fed, beaming at the crowd's approving cheers, Poppy and her gang are ready to strike. They're on a mission and one day the general public will remember them.

8

◈

This driver seems nuts, Marsha thinks as the Bargain Budget bus veers around the corner going what must be seventy-
five miles per hour and they're not even on I-95 yet. "Slow
down," one panicked rider yells from the back, but the His-
panic man at the wheel ignores him. It's hot as hell on board
and, even though there's a NO SMOKING sign prominently
displayed in the front, the air still smells like stale cigarette
smoke. Marsha has managed to get an aisle seat halfway
back, but she has to sit next to a white man who insists on
talking. He introduces himself as Mr. Conrad and goes
on to explain he's a "traveling trinket salesman." Marsha
nods her head politely but says nothing to further the conversation, but that doesn't stop his mouth. As the driver pulls
onto 95 without the slightest effort to merge safely, other
motorists blare their horns and the passengers on board let
out howls of protest, but Mr. Conrad is oblivious to their

panic and pulls out a little "show kit" of items that Marsha "may be interested in purchasing."

Shirt Backwards yells from the rear of the bus, "Hey, there's no toilet paper in the bathroom," but the driver just holds up a scrawled sign reading NO ENGLISH. Big Marge, still holding Blanket and a dirty diaper in one hand, bellows back, "So what do we wipe up our baby's poo-poo with?" but the driver disregards her too as he answers his cell phone and starts shouting angrily into it in Spanish.

"These little babies won't break the bank or nothing," explains Mr. Conrad as he shows Marsha a New Jersey Turnpike key ring—"only ninety-nine cents." "No thanks," says Marsha, attempting to get up to move but finding one of her feet actually stuck to the floor in what must have been a large soft drink spill that was never cleaned up properly. "How about a gimp bracelet?" he offers, undaunted. "I made it myself!" "I'm not shopping for anything," Marsha responds with what she hopes is off-putting contempt, but this guy goes for the hard sell. "Look," he says in a pushy voice, pulling out a baggie of plastic "collectible charms," "you don't even have to buy a gumball to get one—fifty prizes, fifty cents!" Marsha turns away in a fury. This is a test, she thinks. She escaped Dutch Village for this?!

The Italian senior citizen couple have managed to find two seats together across the aisle and one row back from Marsha, but one of their cushions is malfunctioning and the entire bottom of the chair keeps snapping up and pinning the tiny woman in its grips. The husband is panicked and keeps trying to help her but every time he pries the seat back down, the driver, who now appears to be texting, swerves around another vehicle and the seat snaps back up like a mousetrap. The wife starts yelling and her husband joins in, but the driver, now purple-faced in rage, is banging his cell phone angrily on the steering wheel and pays them no mind. Marsha decides she likes him. He's like her. He lives dangerously.

Across the aisle, through the window, Marsha sees cars and trucks being whizzed by, left behind by the bus's speed. Good! She'll get to New York in record time. The Native Hawaiian lady has managed to get a seat up front but next to her is a real slob of a white man who sits in his window seat with full manspread, his ham-hock thighs wide open, pushing the uncomplaining woman almost out of her seat into the aisle. Her cat starts hissing and clawing the wires of the cage and the big guy lets out a groan of overheated annoyance and rips off his T-shirt. He's now totally topless without the slightest trace of embarrassment. Still, the woman doesn't complain and tries to quiet her cat lovingly. "Shh, Banjo," she coos with little success. "Jesus Christ," the sweat hog yells, "she's got a rabid animal with her!" "It's just a little pussycat," she tries to reason back, but her cat lets out an ungodly shriek and goes into the coital-crouch position, which can only mean one thing—it's female and it's in heat. "Now the cat's trying to fuck me!" he cries out in full melt-down mode.

Little Blanket finally wakes up from all the hubbub and lets out a small cry, a whimper really. But suddenly Mr. Conrad loses it. "Shut that fucker up!" he yells with such hostility that even Marsha is shocked. "He's just a baby, mister," Big Marge hollers from the rear, shielding the infant protectively in her arms before softly crooning the "Beat It" song inside her agitated child's ears. "Hey, that's my son you're talking about," Shirt Backwards bellows, suddenly the macho one even though his backward T-shirt semistrangles the words in his throat as he speaks. "How am I supposed to make a sale with a rotten fucking baby shrieking?" shouts back Mr. Conrad. "I'm not interested in your wares, sir," Marsha hastily volunteers loudly, hoping to deflect attention away from her.

The driver, oblivious to the drama on board, is tailgating a car in the fast lane, which is already going ten miles or more over the speed limit. Other bus passengers are watching in alarm, braking in their own seats, as if that would telegraph the message to the crazy driver to slow down. Suddenly this madman veers into the slow lane to pass, but there's another car going the normal speed in front of him so, without putting on any turn signals, he careens onto the shoulder lane and narrowly misses a family whose dad is changing a flat tire. All the riders on the bus lurch forward and scream. Blanket finally lets out a real cry. "Muzzle that little cock-sucker," shouts Mr. Conrad, spittle flying from his mouth, arms waving in the air like a complete monster.

Marsha has had enough. She quickly kicks open the salesman's show kit on the floor, reaches down, and deftly pockets the velvet money pouch she spotted earlier when he was showboating his worthless junk. Chump change, but maybe this'll change this chump. She pries her other foot off the flypaper-like sticky floor and moves to another seat across the aisle a few rows back. On the way she sees that the elderly Italian American woman has given up and sits crushed in the V-shape of the faulty, out-of-order bus seat as her husband meekly holds her hand in emotional support.

The smoke alarm in the bathroom in the back of the bus goes off and Brud, the pimple-faced one who got on when Marsha did, comes flying out with a huge cloud of smoke following him. "It's like a chimley in there!" he announces with a laugh, hoping his bad word usage will excuse his triggering of the annoyingly loud, beeping fire alarm. The bus driver seems unfazed and, rather than dealing with it, lights up his own cigarette and accelerates, swerving past trucks, even an ambulance.

Just when Marsha is about ready to sit back and finally enjoy this terror-ride, she sees the cat lady inserting a Q-tip into the vagina of her still-howling in-heat pussycat and moving it rhythmically in and out. Even the topless oaf seated next to her is shocked into silence and watches, transfixed. Guess what? All that insertion works. The cat lets out one final orgasmic yowl and then shuts up. Marsha never knew there was such a thing as feline afterglow, but she sure does now. When she looks back up, all she sees through the bus's windshield is sudden, unexpected fog. Then the back of a stopped truck. She doesn't even have time to brace.

"Accident ahead," Daryl hears his own penis . . . excuse me, Richard, yell through the tight restraints of his underpants. Wow! His wiener is better than Google Maps. He lets him out with one frantic zip of his pants and even though any form of crotch movement still hurts, it's worth it. "Roger," yells back Daryl, getting used to the two-way communication with his damaged privates. And wouldn't you know it—there *is* a big accident ahead. Move over, Jeane Dixon. Hello, Edgar Cayce. Take a hike, Uri Geller. His name is Richard and he's psychic supreme!

A Bargain Budget bus lies on its side. Luggage is strewn all over the highway. There are still some bodies in all three lanes and fire trucks and ambulance workers are doing their best to rescue the survivors. "Three dead, many injured," announces Richard through the tiny lips of the pee-hole at the end of Daryl's in-recovery unit in a voice that is self-assured without being overbearing. "Take cover!" Daryl commands in a friendly voice as they are forced to slow down their Ford in this building traffic jam, fast-breaking news event. "Copy that," his eager appendage answers before stealthily shrinking back inside Daryl's pants to hide. They're not crazy. They're a team and they're both gonna do Marsha. Marsha Marsha bo-barsha. Banana fanna fo-farsha. Fee, fy, mo-arsha. Marsha! Hey! Richard can even sing!

She's banged up a little but as far as Marsha can tell she has no broken bones. She got off easy. It's hard to get your bearings when the vehicle you were riding in has overturned on its side, but she can still see out because there's a big hole on the other side of the aisle where the bus must have crashed into the guardrail and flipped over. It's getting dark out, but she can sense that the passengers sitting across from her fell on top of the fellow bus riders in her row. Luckily, nobody landed on her. Luggage that was thrown from the bus lay outside on the highway. Some of it was on fire.

As she crawls her way across the half-overturned seats toward the hole, she climbs over that idiot trinket salesman, who now looks in really bad shape, covered in blood with an ugly white bone sticking out of one of his arms. He's trying to retrieve his stupid baggie of prizes that must have flown from his hands and burst open when they crashed. His worthless little treasures litter other bodies, many unconscious, but this doesn't stop him from trying to gather them up. Marsha feels her knee go right in his open mouth just as he cries out in pain for the first time.

Big Marge's excess adipose tissue saved not only her but Shirt Backwards, too, by cushioning their bodies on impact. Stunned to be alive, they try to climb over the seats looking for their baby. "Blanket! Blanket!" they both yell, but Marsha doesn't see the infant anywhere. The Native Hawaiian woman is unconscious but still breathing. At least she can't worry about her horny cat. As Marsha drags herself over the lady's limp body, she's amazed to see up close that her hairdo that looked so freshly done is actually a wig. Marsha gives it a yank and, after a couple of tries, the bobby pins give way, and the hairpiece is hers. She slaps it on over her own short hair and accepts the fact that without a mirror it may be on crooked, but so what? She's already feeling a new identity washing over her and that's all that counts. She's a method actress through and through.

Brud the chain-smoker and the shirtless manspread guy are nowhere to be seen, so presumably they were thrown from the bus. Good. If Marsha had to pick, they'd be the dead ones. The elderly Italian couple are alive, but their journey has turned even more humiliating. Marsha can see both of them outside the bus, but the older lady is upside down in a tree still stuck in her malfunctioning seat as her husband tries to comfort her while a fireman is putting up a ladder for rescue.

Wouldn't you know it, the driver seems to be uninjured and, yup, he's back on his phone, still bitching to whomever he's been having a beef with the whole trip. Marsha picks through all the hand luggage and pocketbooks that had fallen from the overhead bins and rifles through a few wallets for cash. There are even some shitty saltine crackers in a lunch bag that must have been left uneaten by one of the riders. Beggars can't be choosers. She's hungry! Yay! There are a couple of plastic packages of ketchup inside, too, that will come in handy right now for special effects to make herself look more injured. The trinket salesman sees her in her ill-fitting wig, smearing the fake blood on her forehead, and clutches his plastic treasures to his chest as if they were gold. As if anybody would want them! Marsha swallows the cracker and then the next one. She's glad there's not a third. That could lead to a bowel movement larger than she'd be comfortable with. She hasn't had to wipe in over ten years and plans to keep it that way.

As she proceeds to the nearest exit, which is now the jagged hole in the side of the bus, she spots Blanket where he's landed, lying atop a pile of dirty laundry spilled out of a bag. The goddamn baby is cooing and laughing, uninjured except for a Bic pen stuck in the side of its head. Marsha does what any Good Samaritan would do and pulls it out in one quick yank. The infant starts howling but it's all a happy ending for Big Marge and Shirt Backwards. Blanket is alive! "Beat it," they sing in unglued parental domination, happy as can be under these very special conditions.

Marsha flinches when the two ambulance attendants, who must have succeeded in prying open the front door of the bus, grab her from behind. "You're in shock," one of them says to her. "We're taking you to the hospital," the other announces like he's some kind of knight in shining armor. That's just what Marsha wants to hear. She's sure there's an all-points bulletin out on her and now she can hide in plain sight in the emergency room. "What happened? Where am I?" she moans convincingly, holding her "bleeding" head as they begin to load her onto a stretcher. Here's the perfect moment to deftly pick the wallet out of the medic's back pants pocket. One would think a trained professional would know better than to carry his valuables while working an accident, but not this guy. And then she sees it. That darn cat! Banjo might have had nine lives, but this was definitely not her tenth.

9

◆

"Mayday! Mayday!" Richard the dick yells up to Daryl in full Marsha alarm, but Daryl *still* doesn't see her, even though his own crotch is feebly pulling him out of his car like a Saint Bernard rescue dog in an avalanche. He spins his own head to the left, to the right, frantically searching for even a glimpse of his erotic obsession as Richard, lurching forward with new urgency, suddenly begins to get semihard. As the blood swells in Daryl's healing penis, he lets out a shriek of agonizing pain and nearby families stuck in their cars begin rolling up their windows and locking their doors. When Richard unzips Daryl's pants from inside the jail of underpants and breaks out, Daryl realizes who the new master is and lets him lead the way. "Charge!" Daryl thinks he hears Richard holler, but maybe he's just having an erotic breakdown. Penises aren't people. They're *parts* of people.

Poppy couldn't believe it when that out-of-shape static bitch told her to "stand still" when she got out of her car to bounce while other motorists gawked at the carnage of the bus accident. You'd think these stalled drivers would be thrilled that Poppy and her extended family could jump up to see how far the backup was, but oooh-no! This crowd of possible bouncy-bashers seemed way more hostile than the more liberal ones they had won over back there at the service area. "Lay off her!" snarled Vaulta, butting in, protecting Poppy as she landed from her first full jump. "Resist gravity," shouted Leepa as she defiantly springboarded upward in renewed militancy, while other static supporters jumped from their cars to yell insults. "Jump" is actually a misnomer here because these fools were stepping out of their cars horizontally, not jumping up *or* down vertically. Language is important in defining today's bouncing politics.

"Stay down!" one old geezer, who couldn't jump if there was a stick of dynamite up his ass, hollers out from his crusty old Dodge Charger. "You're too fat to jump!" bellows a younger woman to Leepa through the wound-down windows of her expensive SUV. You'd think an in-shape girl like this one would be more accepting of alternative exercisers, but Poppy's cult seems to bring out the reactionary worst in all walks of the general public. It's always a shock when gay people show prejudice against other minorities, but one pissy middle-aged queen in a convertible he was much too old to be driving shouts out in an overly grand voice to Campolina, "Drag queens go *down*, not up!" "Yeah! Go back to the Walt Whitman service area where people like you belong," growls a jock-type homophobe to Campolina from his muscle car, proving that hatred of bouncers is crossing over at an alarming rate.

"Stay on the goddamn ground," another militant receder orders Twisted Billy from below as Billy purposely throws his joints out of whack midair just to torment his detractor. "Stop jumping! Stop jumping!" several motionless-agitators chant, forming a mob, red in the face in fury. Springboard Sam and Double Back Barbara do a full body twist in the air together, which further enrages trapped motorists who are now forced to feel squarely earthbound by a band of vertical freaks. This free-fall free-for-all is turning into a real rise-riot.

Richard screams, Daryl screams, they all scream for cream. It's her. Marsha Sprinkle being hauled off the bus on a stretcher. She still looks hot even wearing that ridiculous wig. Daryl can tell she's faking. She doesn't bleed. There's nothing human inside her veins, just ice. Richard realizes what a slave he is to this woman's muff, yet in a masochistic way he welcomes the arousal rearing its ugly head in his own broken, damaged self. But dammit, can Daryl feel his pain, his struggle, his low self-esteem?

Yes, he can, but what's Daryl supposed to do? He can't pounce on her yet. The accident scene is crawling with cops now and running toward a woman on a stretcher with your lizard out is not exactly the way to blend in. Marsha breaks character only once. Just as she leans off the stretcher to let her one arm dangle down to retrieve a wallet that has been somehow dropped in the mayhem, she sees him. Daryl Hotchkins. That dumb fuck followed her! Still horny. Still trying to collect his due when their nonbinding vaginal agreement, which would never hold up in a court of law, became null and void back there at the airport. And Jesus, he's got his peter out, but worse, he seems to be talking to it!

"That's my gal!" Daryl cries out to Richard as he sees Marsha rifle the wallet of bills with sleight of hand and quickly hide them under the blanket after the attendant loads her into an ambulance. Daryl can't let that vehicle pull off with her inside and Richard outside . . . of her. Both of them are ready now. They're a team! A two-headed transplant. Just call us repo-dicks. We're here and ready to collect.

"Jesus Christ, it's Poppy!" Daryl yells out in disbelief as he sees her getting knocked around by yet another bounce-phobic lunatic. He's had past issues with Poppy of course, but now that they were both in trouble maybe it was time to forget their differences and team up against Marsha Sprinkle together. "Save her!" hollers Richard, suddenly the leader. It's hard to run with a penis fracture. Your manhood is bent at an unnatural angle and bleeds from the head at irregular times without warning and dribbles embarrassing splatters of urine, but Daryl takes off anyway, beginning to understand just how brave Richard really is.

Poppy sees Daryl running toward her attacker, who is trying to force her to the ground, painfully choking her into an earthbound landing. Is that Daryl's penis out? My God, it is! She always hated Daryl and felt he was a fool to follow her evil mother's every whim, but she has to accept the fact that his avenging unit, as alarming as it is, is arriving in the nick of time. Daryl grabs the horizontal right-winger from behind and turns him around so Richard can slap his hateful face back and forth until he's so humiliated all he can do is run away in mortification.

Daryl turns to Vaulta, who has just been tackled by another high-altitude hater, and signals her to grab hold of Richard by the shaft with her one arm, and while she is somewhat apprehensive to be rescued by a penis, she has little choice. Richard swings her and yes, it hurts him, hurts so bad, but sometimes righteousness numbs all pain. The Richard-Daryl team, now a functioning combat unit, hurls Vaulta into the air and she's alive again in vertical victory. Free to bounce! Free to bounce!

Poppy sees the traffic is finally beginning to move again in one lane around the rescue vehicles. Daryl locks eyes with her, and when he sees the ambulance carrying Marsha begin to leave, he lets out a shriek of anguished penile need that startles even Richard. Suddenly the back door of the rescue vehicle flies open and both Poppy and her bouncers and Daryl and Richard witness an astonishing sight. Marsha Sprinkle, propped up on the stretcher, is pickpocketing the other paramedic, who is trying to give her oxygen through a resuscitation mask while the first attendant grabs frantically to close the flapping back entrance to the emergency vehicle.

Poppy and her frazzled followers boil with rage at the sight of Marsha Sprinkle stealing again, while Daryl and Richard's sexual adrenaline surges through their shared manhood like a tsunami wave ripping through a small Japanese village. As the mob of bouncer-bigots gets a load of Daryl and his talking appendage, now teamed up with this openly upward crew of arising radicals, they go ballistic. Poppy and the Bouncy-Bouncers race to their van and give chase to Marsha, but Daryl's vehicle's tires have been flat-tened by the downward deplorables. What are he and Rich-ard supposed to do? Poppy screeches the leaping van up to them and orders, "Get in!" unaware that Marsha had said those same words to Daryl the day they met. Twisted Billy leans out from the front passenger seat backward and up-side down and gives Daryl and Richard a lift inside with his feet.

My God, Marsha thinks, this driver is more insane than that one on the bus. Zigzagging lane to lane, even passing slow-pokes on the left doing seventy-five miles per hour by swerving around them on the wrong-side shoulder. Wheeee! This is fun! She breathes in the oxygen and gasps in theatri-cal recovery while the attendants take her vital signs, trying to steady themselves while the emergency first responder behind the wheel accelerates with an Evel Knievel–like recklessness.

Lo and behold, who does Marsha see through the back window being left behind? That ungrateful daughter of hers in hot pursuit in that ludicrous trampoline van she must have bought cheap from a shut-down circus. And look who's sit-ting right up front with her. Daryl and his talking woody. That's right, she saw it mouthing off back there like it had a moral right to be heard. Marsha's vaginal lips are sealed for-ever under a self-imposed gag order. There'll be no pussy talk from her, thank you very much.

The ambulance swerves off the highway to exit at the very last minute and even if Poppy's van *could* jump over cars, she'll never have the time to merge over to the exit in this traffic. Besides, it's almost completely dark out now. Marsha is sorry she doesn't get to see more clearly Poppy, Daryl, and the rest of those idiots' outraged faces when they lose her trail. Eat my dust!

10

◈

It's been a long day. Poppy and her gang have found one of the last remaining waterbed motels in the country. The Free Flow Motel, which boasted in the ads "H_2O mattresses that generate significant wave action." It wasn't *that* far away either—only about fifteen miles west of Newark on the nondescript Highway 1 in Arsenal, New Jersey. They probably *could* have made it all the way to New York City, but it would have been late and they need Marsha's mother, Adora, to be wide-awake if she's going to join them in the final attack on her daughter's lying, conniving, thieving way of life. Poppy's grandmother may think that the restraining order she has out against Marsha will protect her but Marsha obeys no judge's orders—local *or* federal.

Daryl, who seems to have been driven completely out of his mind from sexual frustration, keeps ranting about some kind of carnal deal he has with Poppy's mother, but anybody who has detailed conversations with his own penis can only be used, never trusted. Still, she owes Daryl. And Richard, too, she supposes. They saved her and the bouncers' lives and now they've reached a truce. Poppy and her family of tramps can kill Marsha after they get their money back, but Daryl and Richard get to fuck her first. Just not in front of the grandmother.

There were so many ambulances arriving from different towns at the St. Francis Medical Center emergency room in Trenton, New Jersey, that "bedlam" would be the only word you could use to describe it. Marsha had grabbed a soiled lab coat off a loading dock as soon as she fled the ambulance out front and even the shouts from the attendants were drowned out by the press clamoring for blood-and-gore details from the arriving crash victims. Marsha knew to keep moving and never look back.

Up in the elevator she goes and, bang, right into an emergency examination cubicle that had been set up to handle the overflow of patients. What little privacy these flimsy curtains offered is good enough for Marsha's hit-and-run thievery. She immediately begins rifling through a semiconscious survivor's purse. Hey! It's that lady who had the cat on the bus! When the dazed and confused victim spots her missing wig on Marsha's head, she clutches her bag tighter to her chest in fear.

How dare she resist? Marsha grabs a fresh hypodermic needle still in its package off the mini supply shelf, unwraps it, and eenie, meenie, miney, moe, picks at random a vial full of medicine—who knows what kind—fills it up, shoves the needle into the stubborn accident victim's arm, and injects it. Whatever was in there works. Oh, the lady is still alive, but her eyes pop open wide, she gives up her purse quickly, and Marsha helps herself to whatever cash is inside. She then removes her wig, which had miraculously stayed on all through the ambulance ride, and plops it down on the rightful owner's noggin. When Marsha yanks it down hard, it seems to fit the woman just fine. Pretty? Pretty? Trenton Makes. Marsha Takes.

The Free Flow Motel wasn't exaggerating in their advertising. This place *is* a horizontal hideaway of secret repose. A sloshing paradise island for bouncers to refresh their powers of vertical escalation. If you can't be in the air, at least you can go up and down on the water mattresses and, believe me, there's all kind of novelty ones here; bunk waterbeds, circular ones for "adult experimentation," even little water "cots" for pets.

The bouncers are crammed into the Esther Williams Suite, a large, reasonably priced two-bedroom showcase filled with custom-designed aqua mattresses of every shape. Even the kitchen has one. Poppy has set up a whole rippling buffet of bouncing treats—small apples, cherry tomatoes, grapes, any food that can spring up once it is thrown down. Hungry trampoliners pick up the circular hors d'oeuvres jumping from waterbed to waterbed like they're playing a game of human jacks and gobble them down hungrily.

Once their stomachs are filled, its par-tee time! Vaulta puts on a Big Freedia CD and the whole gang starts twerking to the New Orleans bounce sound while riding the ripples of the many pads of wave bedding. Campolina, ever the film buff, lets out a scream of glee after turning on the television and seeing the movie *Bounce* is available on pay TV. Sure, it's a lousy romantic comedy and they've all seen it a million times, but just the title alone makes them feel less anxious. Besides, it stars Gwyneth Paltrow, who has been known to be sympathetic to the bounce movement, yet so far has ignored their pleas for financial help. But they can hope, can't they?

Past the empty nurse's station Marsha flies into another patient's room. The middle-aged Mexican lady with long, gray roots in her henna-dyed hair is fully conscious but seems to have some sort of internal injuries. Marsha doesn't recognize her—she must have been sitting farther back on the bus. Figuring this injured traveler is now immobile, Marsha starts rummaging through the pockets of a coat hanging on the back of the door. "Hey, you," the woman manages to sputter out, shocked at the bold-face robbery attempt, "that's my coat!" Marsha pretends not to hear her as she empties the pockets, leaving the pesos and grabbing the few dollars inside. When the bruised woman attempts to get out of bed to stop Marsha, she forgets she is hooked up to an IV and trips over the connecting tubes, landing hard, maybe even breaking the arm she tried to cushion her fall with. Well, that's what you get.

Coast clear. Right into another hospital suite Marsha goes. This time it's an Amish family gathered around the mother whose bonneted head is bandaged and face badly cut. God, it's like that old film *Around the World in 80 Days* that Campolina was always raving about. Marsha's marks are *so* diverse, coming from every damn culture in the world!

"Did you hear?" Marsha asks with breathless sincerity as she grabs a surgical mask from a shelf and puts it on. "*What?*" the whole family yells in alarm. Marsha's voice is now muffled through the gauze, but they still hear her warn, "Legionnaires' disease has broken out in the hospital!" The family stampedes out of the room in panic. Now it's easy pickings. Serial lying is almost a transcendental high, Marsha realizes as she empties the frightened lady's change purse. Marsha hopes to never come down from this magical bliss.

Daryl sits in the corner of the motel suite, the only one in an actual chair, nursing Richard and feeding him, through the hole in his dick, fish food he swiped from under the lobby's tropical aquarium. Ironically, Richard, who always craved deep throat from Marsha, doesn't have one himself and can barely get down these much-needed vitamins without gagging. He's *trying* to participate in his fellow travelers' bouncing elation, but to be honest, watching them all cascading from waterbed to waterbed makes him feel seasick.

Daryl suddenly spots a Magic Fingers device on a shelf that must have been left over from the old days of regular motel beds. It's still attached to the little motor and seems like it's just begging to be used again. Daryl sloshes over on the undulating mattresses while Richard shouts out something about "having the whirlies," but Daryl ignores his cries of distress, knowing the "tingling relaxation" this little contraption promises might just be the alternative medication they both need. Luckily, he has a quarter and that's all it takes to turn on this vibrating little muvva. If you can attach it to a bed, why not your waist, Daryl surmises like the genius he knows he is. He takes the four nylon ties that are plugged into the side, attaches these to some batteries from a flashlight he finds in a closet, and tapes the whole makeshift power pack onto his belt.

Before he can insert the coin, Richard projectile vomits out of his hole some sort of penile urinary tract infection that just misses Twisted Billy, who doesn't even notice because he's trying to turn himself into the human slipknot he once learned in Boy Scouts but is having trouble getting traction on the lapping water mattress. Poppy and the bouncers are all running out of steam. When the last cut of Big Freedia's album is finished, so are they. Settling in for a cozy night of slosh sleeping that keeps their active constitution from shutting down completely, the trampoline fanatics create a human rug of movement and fall asleep bobbing up and down.

Daryl pops in the quarter and presto, Magic Fingers works! His whole body starts shaking and shuddering, spreading complete relaxation even down inside his pants. Richard seems suddenly relieved but at first is not sure if it's because he finally vomited or just that all that elevated vibrating gives him flashbacks to adolescent masturbation. Either way, his entire penile self feels at peace. Richard falls asleep and as soon as Daryl hears him snoring softly below, he cranks up the power level and dozes off himself in quivering pleasure, finally understanding the rewards of constant motion. Nighty night.

Marsha sees security guards are now patrolling the hospital corridors but, just as she begins to get paranoid, a whole new gang of medics comes flying out of the freight elevator with some patients on stretchers rescued from a new nighttime turnpike pileup. As they pass, Marsha steps into a nursing station and grabs a cell phone left behind on a desk. And what do you know, there are some crackers left on the counter, too, Carr's English Water ones, not too shabby. A little bland for Marsha's sophisticated palate but God knows a step above those common saltines she had to choke down earlier in the day. All this thievery can give a girl an appetite.

She ducks into a much larger examination room and sees a male patient, blue in the face, who appears to be having some sort of stroke. There's not a doctor or nurse in sight. Oh my God! It's that crazy bus driver! He's probably been so awful to the medical staff that they just said, "Fuck him," and moved on to more grateful patients. Marsha feels a certain kinship with this disagreeable man. Imagine how she would act if she had to get a real job! She understands his policy of the customer always being wrong and mentally salutes his distrust of the general public.

She's not sure but he seems to recognize her, too. He starts gasping and shaking in rage and she moves closer, feeling a warped tenderness for their curious bonding over their shared hatred of mankind. His eyes light up in anger at his own physical failings and the imperfections of the human body but what can you do midstroke? Marsha leans down over his bed and pinches his nostrils shut and then dives her lying mouth down to his for sealed resuscitation. Fifteen times she compresses his chest and with every pound, he sputters, chokes, and gurgles his way back to life. Of course he doesn't thank her, and Marsha understands, she wouldn't have either. Duty is its own reward. Instead, he farts, but Marsha doesn't take it personally. Matter of fact, she can feel a small slug of feces being formed inside her own rectum right this moment. He won't be mad if she uses his private bathroom. It will only take her a few seconds to fire it out. No, not a few. Two. Then she can catch up on her beauty sleep right outside in the waiting room. Nobody will notice her there. She can hide in plain sight. Maybe even have time to snag another wallet.

11

◈

It's a beautiful clear morning in New Jersey, and after a complimentary bouncing buffet in the breakfast room where Poppy and her followers, even Daryl and Richard, were treated with proper hospitality by the motel's other waterbed enthusiasts, it's now time to get back on the road. Marsha Sprinkle may have accidentally outfoxed them once with the tricky little ambulance maneuver but that will be the last time she escapes. The last time she steals. The last time she'll be a bad parent. The last time she doesn't respect her own mother. The last time she stiffs a stiffie of his rightful wage. Today will be Marsha Sprinkle's last day on earth, period.

Daryl has managed to swipe a couple more Magic Fingers devices from unoccupied rooms before they checked out and a few of Poppy's followers have taken his bait of hooking themselves up and experiencing a new trembling movement that suddenly seems more alternative than jumping. Poppy, a bouncer purist, has refused to experiment, and you can tell by her slightly sour expression that she disapproves of any wandering away from the original tramp dogma. But others, especially Springboard Sam and Double Back Barbara, are quivering sideways with newfound glee. Daryl has no desire to rock the boat by challenging Poppy's vertical politics, yet others can see that Richard, now resting softly and quietly and trying to heal, is soothed by the sideways shaking.

When they pile into the van en masse, some continue with shaking but the most loyal to Poppy, Vaulta and Leepa, only move upward in solidarity. Campolina, always looking for a new diversity to celebrate, takes Daryl up on his offer of a new Magic Fingers vibrating experience as they peel out of the parking lot in the van. Whoa, Richard thinks from the safety of Daryl's underpants after Campolina plugs herself in and he can feel her starting to vibrate like a human tuning fork. "Easy now!" Springboard Sam warbles out in a sideways version of "Whole Lotta Shakin' Goin' On." "You can shake it one time for me," Double Back Barbara joins in, yodeling like a cowgirl and taking his musical cue. "Shake it baby, shake," bellows out Campolina, ever the diva, shimmying faster than Joey Heatherton herself.

You can tell Twisted Billy is I-am-curious, too, and when Daryl, undulating laterally, offers him the device, he takes it like a pot-to-heroin gateway drug. Poppy floors it onto the highway and bounces so high inside the van that she hits her head on the roof. It hurts but so what? She must remain a strong example to all her cultists. Professional trampoline activists must not be tempted to wander sideways. Shaking is but a harmless fad. Bouncing is the only true path to salvation.

◈

Marsha hadn't really slept that well. Oh, she had dozed off for little power naps sitting up, but you could hardly call that sleep. No one had really bothered her last night except for that one nurse who asked who she was but Nurse Nosy went away quickly enough after Marsha patiently explained she was legal counsel for the Bargain Budget Bus Company. As if they had one!

All this family drama going on around Marsha is depressing. Relatives praying. Doctors running around with their heroic medicines. The saving of lives seems just plain tedious to her. Would the world be one bit different if all the others on the bus but her died? Admit it, every single one of them would be forgotten soon enough. Even if there really is a God, he couldn't be expected to remember each and every person, could he? She'd better get outta here just in case he is watching from above. She wouldn't want him to think she was one of them!

There's a car. She can see the door isn't locked and—voilà—the key is lying there right on the front seat. Don't bus-crash victims' families realize you can't rush inside an emergency room and just leave your car like you're some kind of celebrity at valet parking? You have to park it, lock it—and duh—take your keys with you!

Just as Marsha opens the front door to take possession, a large dog—who knows what kind, they all look alike—leaps up from the floor of the back seat where it had been lying in wait and bites Marsha on the left hand. Marsha is disciplined enough not to scream even though she sees the beast's fangs sink into her flesh, but she does attempt to pound the mongrel's face with her one good meat hook. Yet this dog takes its job seriously and continues to gnaw her hand. Marsha finally manages to disengage her paw from the dog's growling mouth, but she's bleeding, and that is a bore. At least that rather modest orange cocktail dress and brownish trench coat she stole from another patient's room right before she turned in last night didn't get stained. She still looks presentable.

Where do you run when there is a worldwide conspiracy against you? There's nowhere to hide when you are bitten by dogs, possibly infected with rabies, wanted by the police, on the news, and outside a hospital crawling with security teams, reporters, and lower-echelon accident victims' families. She'd believe in a higher power but only if she could control him. God, it would feel good to dominate God.

"Need a lift?" says a perfectly normal-looking white man driving a green SUV. Well, not perfectly normal. He's middle-aged, not yet balding, and dressed like many of Marsha's airport victims, but his nose hairs have obviously never been trimmed. They are clean, wiry, and show no trace of mucus yet remain erect. Could it be possible he thinks these nasal follicles are his fashion signature like Frida Kahlo's eyebrows?

"Yes," Marsha replies, pretending to be all needy as she climbs in. "A companion dog attacked me," she explains with a straight face, "and there's more of them back there at the hospital. I'm afraid to go back." "That's just terrible," he says in a loud, clear voice made possible by his healthy lungs that have been overprotected from germs, funguses, and spores by the extreme forest he's cultivated inside his snout. "I'd take 'em all to the farm," he adds with a wink and a conspiratorial chuckle before handing her his handkerchief to wrap around her dog bite. "The farm." That's a good one.

She realizes all men are certifiable. Filled with that hormonal urge to invade women, damaged from the weight of their natural-born gristle, humiliated by the downward gravity of their own testicles, and filled with the polluted fluid of life that surges from their eventually cancerous prostate glands. It's amazing they all don't just commit suicide!

"Hand me my sunglasses, will you?" he asks matter-of-factly as they pull back onto the New Jersey Turnpike going north. Marsha looks around but doesn't see them. "In the glove compartment?" he suggests, like this is some sort of "Hot Buttered Beans Come to Supper" children's game. She opens it up and freezes. There's a head shoved in there. A woman's head. The driver lets out a cackle. Is this some kind of practical joke? If so, Marsha better go along with it. It looks real. The dried blood could be fake but the clumsily sawed skin that was once connected to a neck seems fresh and ugly enough to not be special effects. "I wonder what your head would look like on a stick," old hairsnout asks with what seems like gallows humor or horrific curiosity. Either way, she had better act. Marsha looks back at the head. For what? Sympathy? Advice? It shows no reaction—how could it when the last look of terror is frozen onto its face for eternity?

But Marsha's not scared. Not intimidated. She grabs the head out of the glove compartment with both hands and maybe it's just her injured mitt, but it's heavier than she had imagined. Like the weight of a bowling ball. The big kind with three holes. Good! She slams it into the driver's skull. Once. Twice. Is it her imagination or does his nose hair shrivel up inside? He tries to fight back a little but how do you protect yourself when you've just received a concussion from another head?

She grabs the steering wheel and veers the vehicle toward

the slow lane, cutting off a FedEx truck and a U-Haul rent-a-van. She's surprised to be already alongside Newark Airport. As a large American Airlines 747 gracefully descends from the sky right over their barely controlled SUV to land on the nearby runway west of the Turnpike, she cracks the man's head one more time with his victim's cranium and it pops open like an overripe coconut. She hopes one of the airline passengers got a split-second glimpse from a window seat of her attack before the wheels touch down on the runway. Just think of the stories he or she could tell in baggage claim. Ah, baggage claim.

As Marsha steers the skidding car to a halt on the side of the highway, she suddenly realizes the head had been wearing a wig. Another one? What was this, A Night of 1000 Wigs? It's ash blond, too. She's been a regular little Clairol color chart all day! Marsha tries to pull off the fake hair but it's pinned on so tightly you'd have thought the woman was going skydiving. She yanks. She pulls. She hears the scalp ripping but the wig finally comes off. Marsha is surprised to see the woman was mostly bald-headed. Must have had ringworm. Oh well, she's not contagious now that she's dead, right, God?

Right, Marsha, must be the correct answer because as she slips on her new hairdo, a modified shag I guess you could call it, there it is—a miracle right in front of her. A whole family just a few hundred yards up in the breakdown lane outside their vehicle. She can see Dad is taking a piss in the small area of greenery he might think of as "the woods." The few trees are reedy, and the weeds and half-dried grass are but a landing ground for plastic bags, discarded take-out food containers, and cigarette butts blown by the winds of auto pollution. Can't the long-suffering dumpy wife stop him from pulling a root-out in front of his boneheaded children, who Marsha's surprised don't wander out onto the highway absentmindedly looking for a four-leaf clover or a lucky penny or some such nonsense?

Marsha wants their car, and she wants it now. A Ford Explorer. One of the top selling automobiles in America. Perfect. Invisible almost. But Dad's still pissing. That means he's a drunk. Beer probably. She's not worried about this family seeing her knocked-out traveling companion still behind the wheel of their vehicle. He's propped up with his wounded head turned away. It looks like he's taking a nap. But the other head is a whole different story. She needs to get rid of it but the only dumping ground is that same damn thicket of underbrush this dad's standing in, now shaking his shriveled up penis of the last dribble of dark brown urine. Marsha tightens her own urinary muscles and hurls the severed head toward the lowest patch of this eyesore of a landscape. She hears it hit the hollow trunk of a dead tree. *Bonk!* Two points!

The mother, who Marsha now sees has buckteeth that should have been put in braces when she was a child, is looking up from a Save A Lot bag about to hand a Zero candy bar to her daughter, who Marsha imagines has allowed boys to snap her bra straps at local swap meets almost every weekend. Marsha breaks into a gallop toward them both, even though her hand injury impedes her gait, knowing she must take the family by surprise. Mom and her daughter freeze in confusion as Marsha charges past them to grab open their car door. "Hey, you!" yells the new-wave-skate-turd of a son as he careens over on his board and falls down trying to block her. Marsha ignores his total uncoolness and hops in, knowing the key fob she sees dumbbell Dad left on the middle console is enough to start the car. "Call Triple A," the

dad yells, stumbling up the hill beside the highway, still trying to blot the wet spot on the front of his trousers that no
amount of shaking could prevent.

When the mother runs toward Marsha to try and join her
idiot children in attack, Marsha strikes blindly in mortal
kombat. Yes, with the injured hand. *Pow!* Right in the kisser.
But who would want to kiss Mom now? She's too scary with
her front teeth knocked out. The Zero-gobbling daughter
grabs Marsha by the hair to try and stop her from getting in
the car, but it's a wig, bonehead, and it comes off easily, and
the girl falls backward and lands on the sharp gravel of the
highway. Dad comes charging toward the car like Captain
America yelling something about "Geico." The son ignores
his heroics and tries to pull Marsha out of their vehicle from
the passenger window, but it's too late. It's Marsha's car now!
Up goes the electric window, crushing his grimy little fingers at the top. He lets out a long, piercing cry of pain. So
does the whole family. And then they do it again.

Marsha looks up and wants to do the same. There right
in front of her, outside their van, running toward her in the
breakdown lane is Poppy and her brain-dead bouncers teamed
up with Daryl, Richard, and their shaking converts. Look at
them! As serious as suicide bombers yet as ridiculous as a
Road Runner cartoon. Convulsing sideways, and leaping upward, they're the ricocheting Rockettes run amok. The hijacked car's family cannot believe their eyes. Fuck their
vehicle! These springing, trembling human vibrators can have
it! What's happened to the New Jersey Turnpike? It used to
be a nice place!

Marsha has had enough of this bullshit. She floors the
accelerator and aims straight for Poppy and her cronies, but
the vertical and horizontal acrobats know how to judge

distance, speed, and the rhythm of horsepower. She can see her daughter's defiant face but all the shakers, including that bozo Daryl and his dim-witted dick, start zigzagging back and forth aggressively and moaning eerily, agitated by their power pads of Magic Fingers. It's downright spooky.

Poppy lands from above right in the pathway of Marsha's car, snarls, "Give us back our money," and in the nick of time hurls herself back upward before impact. "Goddamn it!" Marsha howls as she gives the car more gas. Vaulta lands with a thump on the roof of the speeding Ford, and while it startles Marsha, she continues roaring ahead, seeing Vaulta in the rearview mirror landing squarely on her own two feet and then springing right on up again all on her own.

Worse yet, Marsha can see Daryl and his lust-driven penis ahead, shaking like a leaf, trembling happily, and grinning like Siamese twins on laughing gas as Springboard Sam and Double Back Barbara lead the others in some sort of quivering, quaking Electric Slide line dance. Let them have their hollow victory, Marsha thinks as she puts pedal to the metal and imagines them trying to land long enough to pile into their van and give chase. Good luck, you motion morons! Marsha zooms straight ahead. Not up. Not down. Not sideways. Right through them, straight to the Holland Tunnel. And you douchebag losers will never catch me!

12

Adora Sprinkle never really felt safe knowing her daughter, Marsha, was still circulating in society. That's why she had a "stay-away" warrant out against her. An "ex parte," as it was referred to down at the House of Ruth shelter for abused women. And you couldn't call Marsha's relationship with Adora anything but abuse. Yes, her granddaughter, Poppy, had called this morning, all worked up, babbling about killing her mother for stealing from her again and warning she might be on her way, but Adora was ready if Marsha darkened her doorstep. Number one on her speed dial was the cops. She'd call them in a New York second.

Otherwise, Adora was feeling fairly carefree this chilly autumn afternoon on the Upper East Side, awaiting her first customer in her office at Sit Happens. Mrs. Winstead had been pleased with the brow-lift procedure Adora had done on her pet Shih Tzu, Weezie, and was considering some

Botox injections and a possible chemical peel to refresh her dog's "fa-chay," as she cleverly pronounced "face." Weezie had handled the anesthetic well and the bruises were fading as expected so Adora knew it would be an easy sell. Dog lovers get quickly addicted to pet plastic surgery and Adora was one of the first to recognize this need. She's unlicensed, unashamed, and never claimed to be a veterinarian. No, she's a sculptress, an artist, some have even called her a magician. Like her granddaughter, she is working "outside the system." Unlike her daughter, who also defies local ordinances but is nothing more than a common criminal.

Has anyone ever complained about Adora's services? Hell no, the Upper East Side—well, almost Upper, she's located on Second Avenue between 62nd and 63rd on the third floor—is a national destination neighborhood for lovers of dog cheek implants and canine chin augmentations. Sure, there've been some silly articles in the papers saying the Upper East Side is no longer fashionable and cool people don't want to live there anymore. Fine, let them stay in Brooklyn. Her clients may be old in age and political choices but they're decidedly radical when it comes to their dogs' reconstructed beauty. Here on Second Avenue is where the extreme pet-lift explosion began!

Adora's pet owners felt "rich" and wanted the world to know that. Some even chose face-lift scars on the front of their dogs' ears just to prove they could afford this luxury. If Adora ever made a mistake, they were willing to look the other way, as long as it was farther uptown. Like the time she accidentally punctured the internal organ of a pampered English toy spaniel when she injected dog fat into the animal's muscles to smooth out an especially unflattering wrinkle. Who said beauty was easy or painless? Not Adora. True, she may have overdone the buttocks augmentation on Dragon, the Pekingese owned by the late Madame Chiang Kai-shek, but what dog wants to sit down once it's gotten a booty lift?

Adora's real bread and butter is helping owners of newly neutered male dogs regain their masculine confidence by implanting "Neuticles," purely cosmetic testicles that pass for the real thing. Once she advised an animal-rights-type pet owner to add back only one ball and claim it was cancer, not birth control, that caused the initial mutation. You know what? The story worked. Nobody suspected castration.

But what she's really known for is going beyond and over the top of what could be called "creative." That entropion surgery she did on Cindy Adams's Yorkshire terrier, Jazzy, was a showstopper, and many Park Avenue matrons wanted the same eyelift done on their own lapdogs. And while PETA may have targeted her in the past, calling her cruel and greedy, who wouldn't spread a good word about the discreet work she did on "Catwoman" Jocelyn Wildenstein's dog, Simba? She was no four-legged Tara Reid, I promise you. Adora could be the classiest plastic surgeon this side of Switzerland if the situation demanded.

A pup's panting mouth often needs surgical help to remain lovable and not distract from the master's own human vitality. Nobody wants to see disappointment or sadness on their dog's face. Bulldogs don't really smile naturally but after Adora pulls up the edges of their mouths, one could almost call the expression a grin. Cutting small wedges into the back part of a dachshund's nose makes the nasal opening wider, giving the animal a classical look, and combining this fine chiseling with modest leg extensions turns this much-mocked breed into a bloodline with a high pedigree. Lucky dogs!

Adora herself has had almost no "work" done. Long ago she realized her own facial bags and wrinkles and the natural sagging of her body parts were about average for a woman her age (late sixties) and if she tried to fool Mother Nature herself, her customers would have been confused and distracted from the plastic surgery plans for their own pampered pets. Adora's practice was about projecting the human fear of aging onto four-legged animals who could reflect back up and make their masters feel younger themselves.

Adora did have a secret, one that none of her plastic surgery enthusiasts knew about. Adora *had* had a procedure herself. One where only she could see the results. Umbilectomy. A belly-button operation. In her case, turning an "innie" into an "outie," a rarity indeed. Most belly button patients wanted it the other way around. But not Adora. This was her personal decision on a very personal part of her body. Hardly was she worried about appearing in public in a two-piece bathing suit—those days were thankfully long gone. No, having an "innie" made her hate her own body. An "innie" was nature's trash can for belly lint. The first time she saw this disgusting ball of filth she felt paralyzed. Sickened. Soiled. Aghast at her situation. Adora Sprinkle. A dignified woman yet she had a hole, a receptacle, a pit, a trash can to attract, protect, hide, and house this appalling refuse made from dead skin cells, body hair, and fibers from her own clothes that she falsely assumed were better made. This was unacceptable, she could not walk the earth with an attached Venus flytrap cavity for one second longer.

It was a simple procedure. The plastic surgeon numbed her innie with a local anesthetic, created an incision to get to the hernia that creates the belly button position, and poked it out. Presto. No more landing pads for sweat and oil residue, no more squatters' rights for corporeal debris. This garbage pit for the imperfections of the human body was now officially closed! The entire procedure took only thirty minutes and healed in just four weeks. Total cost? Thirty-five hundred dollars. A deal. Adora finally felt good about herself. Worthy of her career.

Some of her clients want their dogs to look like Barbie. Others mention Tiffany Trump, Priscilla Presley, even Michael Jackson at his most lifted, but Adora never encourages these pet celebrity doppelgänger makeovers because she saves these for her own dog; a cocker spaniel named Surprize with a Z that looks exactly like Joan Rivers. Adora has spent years sculpting, tucking, pulling, and lasering her dog's skin into that "wind tunnel" look that Joan made her signature. Even if you use dog years, Surprize is no spring chicken, but does she look old? Hell no. She looks like an alien. Just like Joan.

Long ago Adora realized she couldn't allow Surprize to be seen in public. Some people screamed, others laughed, and children sobbed. Even a militant ASPCA member Adora remembered seeing in the news protesting puppy mills had hollered, "Put her down," when he saw this radically altered but finely tuned animal. Surprize had had a neck lift, a chin augmentation, hundreds of laser peels, bow-wow Botox, and at least two stomach stapling procedures. Some may have called Surprize a freak, or worse yet, the new Flub-a-Dub, but Adora doesn't care. She knows a dog can suffer from body dysmorphic disorder, or BDD, as it's commonly called. The inability to see oneself as others do leaves Surprize clueless about her appearance. She doesn't realize Adora has triple-processed the original color of her coat so it now shimmers on top in a blond-on-blond helmet she wears like a crown. Surprize is Adora's real baby. And that awful daughter of hers knows it. Marsha ain't no dog in the looks department, but even Surprize knows what a bitch she is.

Long ago, Adora had given up trying to figure out what had caused her daughter to go bad. Marsha never really went bad; she just always was. Like that movie Adora loved, *The Bad Seed*. That was Marsha. Dogs knew instinctively that Marsha was evil. Why else would Adora's first dog, Intruder, have bitten her baby the first day she brought her home from the hospital? Because she was Beelzebub, that's why!

But who has time to dwell? The doorbell's ringing and she has a practice to oversee. Good. Mrs. Winstead is on time. Adora buzzes her in and looks forward to seeing the progress of little Weezie's brow-lift that went off without a stitch . . . well actually, a lot of stitches, ha ha! If Joan Crawford had been a dog, she would have been proud of those brows: arched, stenciled, doggie-dearest to the max.

Adora knows that other pet owners might not fully understand Surprize's avant-garde look, so rather than veil her, which Adora had first considered, she's trained Surprize to scurry under the slipcover of the waiting room couch when any possibly closed-minded clients visit. Another dog has never actually seen Surprize in the flesh and Adora isn't sure but that may be the best way to keep it. Her dog is so unnaturally gorgeous that Adora feels only she, her creator, should be allowed to behold the beauty.

Mrs. Winstead, a Nancy Reagan look-alike like so many of Adora's customers, rushes in, seemingly upset. Weezie is whimpering, which isn't all that easy with the stitches still in. "There was some incredibly pushy woman downstairs trying to come up with me," she announces, rattled. "What do you mean?" asks Adora, suddenly paranoid and rushing to pick

119

up the receiver of her landline. "I don't know who she was, but she just kept saying she was a customer, but she didn't have a dog with her and something about her was fishy."

Adora begins calling the police and Weezie starts barking wildly, which pops open several stitches underneath the dog's newly heightened brows. Before Adora can grab some cotton balls to blot up the pus oozing from Weezie's past incisions, the door swings open and there's Marsha! "Mother! It's so good to see you!" she cries as she grabs the phone cord and rips it from the wall.

"Weezie, sic her!" yells Adora in real fear as Mrs. Winstead's dog leaps to the rescue like some sort of mutated Benji meets Mickey Rourke in drag. Marsha, now dressed in a blue cotton-blend patio dress with a pink fitted down jacket to match, both liberated from that buck-toothed lady's suitcase back on the highway, reaches for the hand mirror lying next to the operating table. She holds it up to Weezie's face and for the first time the dog sees the results of her makeover. She freezes for a second, blinks painfully, and then lets out a twisted bark of despair that forces her entire brow-lift to quiver, pop open, and collapse. Mrs. Winstead tries to pick up Weezie to comfort her, but the crazed dog bites off a large chunk of her nose in revenge. Blood shoots out like a geyser and Mrs. Winstead screams louder than Janet Leigh in *Psycho*. Weezie rushes to the nearest window and starts banging her head on the glass in despair as Mrs. Winstead struggles to plug the new hole in her face with hunks of wet paper towels. "Do it," yells Marsha to the humiliated dog, "do it!" "No! No!" sobs Mrs. Winstead in disbelief at Weezie's frenzy of self-destruction. Adora rushes to grab her cell phone to call the authorities but Marsha quickly sticks out her foot to trip her, and her mother goes flying, as does her phone, which Marsha quickly picks up and confiscates. The constant, rhythmic pounding of Weezie's head finally breaks through the glass and the shards rip open the few unlifted patches of skin on the canine's face. Weezie doesn't even look back before she hurls herself out the window to certain death.

"Charge!" yells Adora to Surprize in a smoldering rage that has been building since the day Marsha was born. Hearing the secret "panic" word she's been taught for emergency situations, Surprize runs from under the bed with newfound exhibitionism and does her best to look ferocious. Unlike Weezie, she has seen her newly sculpted face and, hey, she thinks she looks pretty damn snazzy! This is her big chance. But when you have been altered to such a state of surreal distortion, it's hard to be taken seriously. Marsha lets out a howl of laughter before grabbing a scalpel off the operating table and throwing it directly at Surprize's freakish head. Surprize's eyes may be lifted, but she's learned how to see and stay out of harm's way. She painfully swivels her head to narrowly miss the blade, hunches up her bruised and stitched back like a vengeful four-legged Donatella Versace, and gurgles a tortured yelp through her permanently stained-red, swollen lips, but because of the retainers Adora has placed on her teeth to correct her "unflattering" tooth alignment, her bark is high-pitched, almost nelly. How can Surprize explain that a tracheal collapse due to repeated nasal experimentation is the real culprit here, she wasn't born with this woof-impediment? She can't. All she can do is pounce toward Marsha's lying mouth.

But Marsha is quick, too, don't forget. She grabs Surprize by her altered hind legs before she can even bite, swings her around like a lasso, and hurls the whole lifted body through the air, past a screaming, bleeding Mrs. Winstead rushing out the door. *Bang!* Right into Adora's noggin Surprize lands, knocking the older lady backward into a chair that topples over and sends her slamming into a wall where a framed photo of Deputy Dawg comes loose and crashes right down on her head.

Marsha picks up a chisel from Adora's surgical equipment and aims it at Surprize, who has been knocked silly but still hasn't given up. "Not my dog," sputters Adora, still seeing stars as she struggles to get up, "she's my baby!" "I'm your baby and I'll kill your fucking dog," Marsha hisses, pulling back her arm to throw the projectile blade at Surprize. But before she can hurl it, someone grabs her other arm from behind. The injured one. It's fucking Daryl, bouncing up and down with Richard fully out yet not properly hard. How dare they?

Suddenly the whole room starts shaking and in bounces Poppy, springing through the door, sideswiping the walls, trying to land on Marsha but her movements are so out of control that all she does is knock over furniture. "Kill her, Grandma!" she shouts as Vaulta and Leepa shake their way in the front door behind her, jiggling intensely toward Marsha as Daryl desperately fondles Richard to get him erect. Poppy lands right in front of Marsha, snarls, "Happy Mother's Day!" and begins to strangle her as Adora roots her on with cries of "Die! Die! My Darling!" one of her favorite old horror films, starring Tallulah Bankhead. Campolina, Springboard Sam, and Double Back Barbara, followed by Twisted Billy walking on his hands, shake their way inside, causing the very floorboards of Adora's office to rattle. The ever-moving cult members surround Marsha, hopping and pulsating as she turns blue from Poppy's choking, red in distaste at Richard's pubic exposure, and finally purple in rage from Daryl's pathetic manipulation of his own member. Gasping for air and flailing her arms she forms a fist of fury and strikes Daryl right in his vibrating mouth, leaving Richard whimpering below like a little girl dick.

Marsha headbutts her daughter, which makes her bounce off the walls clumsily, and then karate kicks both Springboard Sam and Double Back Barbara, whose own rodeo responses are no match for Marsha's expert ground-level martial arts. Vaulta leaps upward in such a rage that she misjudges the ceiling, hits her head painfully, and lands sideways in a chair, which takes the wind right out of her. Leepa bounds upward in anguish but her weight throws her off balance, and instead of landing on Marsha, she splinters a coffee table below. Before Adora can grab Surprize, this bewildered animal is snatched away by her vengeful daughter, who finally can complete her mission—the murder of her mother's favorite dog. Marsha grabs Surprize by the ears and hurls her through the air with all her might. Adora tries to catch "her baby," but let's face it, she's up there in years and, come on, it's been a really stressful afternoon. She misses. Surprize crashes into the wall and yet . . . yet . . . she's OK. Not only OK—she's a new animal. She looks up at Marsha . . . and screeches like a cat. This onetime cosmetically made-over dog has now, because of sudden neurological injuries, become trapped inside the mind of an angry pussy. In one single bound, Surprize leaps toward Marsha with her imagined claws drawn and lands directly on top of her head, pawing and ripping her natural brown hair. Marsha struggles to pull off this species-confused animal like Tippi Hedren in *The Birds*. "Bite her! Bite her!" they all shout to Surprize, but she's no match for Marsha, who, filled with evil adrenaline, dislodges this angry transitioning animal from her head and throws "them" like a speedball. Adora, bless her heart, actually catches her pan-species pet this time. She smiles and begins petting Surprize, who shudders, twitches, and then relaxes in her arms, purring happily. Poppy and gang cheer while Daryl and Richard move forward, bumping and grinding with a revitalized potency. Marsha may be outnumbered by these freaks, but she's not outfoxed. Just you wait. They'll pay the piper! She turns and flees faster than a speeding bullet. But Poppy knows where her mother's going. The same place as she is. To her father in Provincetown, the only family member left.

13

Marsha wishes that nurse's phone she swiped back at the hospital had the Lyft app, but no, she had to have Uber, which almost rhymes with loser, while Lyft definitely rhymes with grift, but who cares? Either way Marsha won't be paying out of her own pocket. Oh, the days when she had her own chauffeur! Before his dick took over and turned him into more of a prick than he already was. But who's in the figurative driver's seat now? Certainly not Daryl or his blue balls. They're riding inside a crowded, sweaty, BO-drenched, unsafe van with a bunch of deranged fitness fanatics who couldn't even kill her when there were nine of them (plus a fucked-up dog and a blabbermouth dick) and only one of her. Even the scab from the bite on her hand is still intact.

Yep, Marsha's the one in control here, about to be dropped off by a glorified hack at LaGuardia Airport, but what the hell, rideshare drivers keep their mouths shut because they usually have a shady past. If they had a real job, they wouldn't be doing this, right? The male ones, like the guy she has today, probably spend too much time watching sports highlights on TV and beating off. He obviously has no navigation skills either. What New York driver needs to use a GPS to get to the airport? He doesn't know where LaGuardia is? Don't they have to take tests or something?

Uninterrupted moments of truth bore Marsha so why not have a little fun? "Excuse me," she says with exaggerated politeness, "what do you think of the news?" "What news?" he asked with mild alarm. "Dolly Parton revealed today that she's a man," she explains with a straight face. "*What?*" he howls. "I know," she says with a nod, "drag queens are everywhere these days, aren't they?" "She has a dick?!" he howls in disbelief. "Apparently," she announces. "What kind of dick?" he demands in utter confusion. "An uncircumcised one," she continues, "*if* you believe the leaked reports from this Sunday's upcoming *60 Minutes*!" "You're kidding me!" he shouts over the traffic noises as he pulls up to drop her off at the departure door to JetBlue Airways. What fun is it to lie when they believe you right away? Convincing them is the thrilling part.

Marsha rates the Uber-goober zero stars on the app, clicks off "no tip," and hits the "send" button. "Officer," she says to the power-hungry airport traffic cop on the curb who is needlessly harassing noncommercial vehicle drivers pulling over to drop off family members for flights, "that car over there has been circling repeatedly." "Thank you, ma'am," he says with a macho load of law and order pounding through his veins. Marsha has no particular beef with the random innocent driver of the vehicle she had just fingered, but that was the point. The poor schmo was lucky to be part of Marsha's random acts of meanness. He's in this book, isn't he?

She spots a small carry-on suitcase behind a female passenger who has obviously just arrived but is in the wrong place for Uber or Lyft. She's practically auditioning to be a victim, so Marsha obliges and deftly grabs the handle of the rube's roller bag and heads inside the terminal. But instead of going directly to the check-in counter where she's eventually headed, she goes downstairs to the baggage level. The girl can't help it.

Marsha's got plenty of stolen cash and a new disguise, so now's not the time to steal a bag, but she can't let the smug little airlines get complacent, can she? She moves quickly, as always. First she puts the freshly swiped bag back on a carousel of moving luggage arriving from Chicago, Flight 5371, she notes. Why? Because she can, that's why. She can't wait to see the red-faced security spokesman try to explain her move here once they get a load of the surveillance tape. She then grabs an empty cart from an unsuspecting skycap who is scanning the conveyor belt and, without breaking stride, wheels it to the far side of the carousel and picks up two new bags that haven't been retrieved, swivels around to the next-door baggage claim, and places them on that. Wheeee! Baggage anarchy. Catch me if you can!

But she's not through yet. She's got over an hour before the flight and she needs a new fake ID to check in. She barges right into the first airline baggage office she sees: American. There are women working but one is Black and the white one weighs at least thirty pounds more than Marsha. Alaska Airlines. Jesus, a woman her age but Puerto Rican. And a goddamn man. Not one of them looks one thing like her but there's a lot of airlines serving LaGuardia and she's not giving up yet. United. Yes! A white woman with brown eyes like hers, roughly her age and weight. Not as pretty of course, but same color hair as Marsha's current shade yet worn in a different style. Oh well, what woman her age doesn't change her hairstyle? Women in Baltimore, that's who, but we're not there, are we? No, we're here in New York and this lady will do just fine.

The stage is set perfectly. Unclaimed bags litter the floor as always and the sort-of-look-alike handler is checking tags and praying no more irate customers come in. "This has never happened," Marsha says with phony concern, "but I think my bags have been lost." "What flight were you on?" the clerk asks, her heart sinking, hating this job ever since she was transferred to this department. "Chicago, Flight 5371," Marsha answers, all business, without being rude, as she imagines most customers are. "Can I see your luggage claims, please," the woman asks routinely. "That's just it!" Marsha says, breaking into sobs. "I lost mine. I'm such an idiot! It was stuck to the boarding pass but the paper you use now is so flimsy that it gets all bunched up in my pocket and must have fallen out." Well, that's a new one, the attendant thinks, suddenly a little suspicious. This couldn't be that lady suitcase thief security has been warning us about, could it? As she turns to sneakily look at the "wanted" flier on her desk, partially covered with other paperwork, Marsha sees the purse. The one this fool stupidly left hanging right on the back of the door on a hook. "Nope, not her," thinks the lost-baggage lady, looking at the surveillance photos, "not as mean looking, almost looks like me except I'm better looking, of course. Besides, this woman lost her luggage, she didn't steal somebody else's."

Lightning. That's how quickly Marsha strikes. Fingers in. Fingers out. Wallet gone. "Oh God," Marsha wails as if a comic-strip lightbulb went off in her brain, "my husband has my boarding pass! I forgot. Let me go get it. He's waiting outside with my children and our carry-on luggage." Before the United Airlines worker can respond, Marsha is gone. Good riddance, moron, the clerk thinks, you deserve to lose your luggage.

How oblivious can one employee be? There Marsha was, Public Enemy Number One baggage thief and she's not recognized? It will be hours before she realizes her wallet is gone, too. OK, let's take a look inside. What? No credit cards?! All maxed out and canceled? She's more of a loser than Marsha imagined. Here's the ID at least. She ducks behind a crowd of passengers struggling to exit with their luggage and sits on a bench next to a bachelorette party in full regalia. Nobody will look at her here. Now she'd better memorize all the information on the license. Her mind is like a camera. Visualize. *Click!* Your life depends on these details, remember them. Address, date of birth, especially the zip code. A steel trap. That's what Marsha's mind is and you know what? She could pass as this dim-witted airline worker if the TSA security officer is distracted long enough, and Marsha knows how to do that. She's a better actress than Meryl Streep. It's time to win the Liar Oscar!

What's this ahead? A whole gang of greeters are waiting for arriving passengers with signs. THANKS FOR YOUR SER-VICE, WELCOME HOME SOLDIER, PROUD TO BE AN AMERI-CAN are just a few. Marsha hates patriotism. She has nothing against armed-service members really, at least they got out of Dodge, but why do their relatives have to be so gung ho

American in public? She'll give 'em something to be zealous about. "I'm sorry for your loss," she whispers to a younger man who could be a flag-waving relative. "I didn't lose anything!" he cries out in sudden concern. "There's been an accident," she says under her breath to another woman, possibly a tag-chaser, right before she scurries away. "What do you mean?" the panicked military spouse asks as she chases after Marsha. "Look at the arrival board," Marsha stops and says with concern. 'See chaplain,' that's all it says. You know what that means, don't you?" The lady cries out in horror, and Marsha pulls up her trench coat's collar and heads to the ticketing counter.

She takes the elevator up because she knows travelers who use them are in worse physical shape, more cowardly, less sure of their own destiny, and plan poorly on luggage restrictions. In other words, they can't chase you. There're two sets of passengers inside, a single man dressed in full Yankees swag even though it's football season with a cart loaded with a large suitcase to check and a carry-on bag probably too big for the overhead bins. The other two, who look like they've never left home, have poor posture. Has no one told them that standing up straight is the key to success? They must be married because they're arguing over the price of long-term parking lots. Both are pulling carry-on bags that will definitely be taken away from them if they are seated in Zone 4 or 5, which Marsha is sure they are. "Have you heard the new airline policies?" Marsha asks, suddenly the do-gooder. "No, what?" asks Mr. Sports-Fanatic, suddenly paranoid. "You're only allowed one small bag that will fit under your seat, no overhead bins available due to new safety regulations," Marsha offers. "That couldn't be true," huffs the married lady, envisioning the hell she and her husband have before them if that policy is indeed in place. "I know, it's insane," Marsha sympathizes, "but it's every airline. And wait, it gets worse. Now you aren't allowed to wear your shoes anywhere on board!" "The floors are filthy on a plane," the wife sputters, suddenly feeling too hot and breaking into a sweat under her arms. "I'm not going in that germ-filled lavatory in my socks!" howls her husband. "No man can aim with turbulence!" agrees the Yankees groupie in a loud voice that forces the married lady to turn red with embarrassment over any public mention of a penis.

The elevator door opens and Marsha gets off first and whispers to a couple politely waiting to get on, "They're closing JFK Airport because of a deadly new virus!" The lady gasps and Marsha chuckles to herself. Some people will believe even the most ridiculous lies! She rushes off, the sound of fear spreading behind her.

OK, here goes, she's about to buy an airline ticket with cash backed up with a look-alike-ish ID that's not her own. It's the final exam in fraud graduate school. Will she pass or be expelled? That is the question. Last minute airfare prices are such a rip-off! They know you have to go; someone died, someone was born, and they've got you by the balls even if you have a vagina. You end up paying way more when the ticket should have been the cheapest. The seat is unsold and would have remained so if you hadn't shown up to buy it. That mother of yours is the one who should be paying. The one whose disgusting birth canal you fought your way out of the day you didn't ask to be born. Same with that womb-ravager, Poppy. Marsha didn't steal her daughter's moola; she took what was rightfully owed in cash money for ripping open her own personal oven and popping out uninvited. And filthy men! They are the ones who should shower her with gold for what they've done. Whoremongers! Sex addicts! Molesters! Worse yet, fathers! And next up, the most terrible man of them all . . . her ex-husband.

14

◈

The Cross Bronx Expressway isn't as bad as it used to be but still: Poppy saw that Pam Grier movie *Fort Apache, the Bronx* and she had no desire to pull her van over and meet the locals before arriving in Provincetown. "Only my father can help us now," she announces to her followers, and they give her a rousing cheer back. Yes, technically she knows he was a "mother-fucker," but if he hadn't had sex with Marsha, Poppy wouldn't have been born. Never would she have become the chosen leader of this joyous jumping lifestyle. She hasn't seen him in decades but maybe it's time for a reunion. Maybe her father wants Marsha dead, too?

Yet her gang is in trouble, she can see that. Poppy's just fine, she continues to bounce in her seat at a steady rate that causes no attention from other motorists passing by yet produces that special rhythm she needs to enhance her mind-body-spirit connection, but how about her grandmother?

Adora knows she's a little old to bounce, but should she pretend shake to show affirmation to this new gang of Marsha-hating . . . what? Militants? Outsiders? Yes, that's the word young people use today, isn't it? Ejecting "outsiders." Just saying this term mentally makes Adora feel younger. Her dog, and she knows the word "dog" is now considered judgmental and somewhat imprisoning, seems accepting of her master's first attempt at sideways quivering, so why not give this whole new lifestyle the old college try?

Is that Surprize purring? Yes, she's purring like the proud cat she's decided to become. Can a dog even be cross-species, Adora ponders. Why not? Anything is possible in this eccentrically utopian lifestyle she's been catapulted into. But does Daryl *really* need to still have his penis out? Richard seems nice enough and his shaking isn't in actual fact sexual and she won't take it personally, but for a woman of her generation, admit it, it still takes a little time to get used to.

Just when Daryl and Richard are perfecting shaking together rather than bouncing, they start to lose power in their Magic Fingers. Campolina is already out of juice but has found one lone quarter in the bottom of her handbag to load in and buy a little more shaking time. "We need change," pleads Twisted Billy, contorting himself to look under the front and the back of a row of seats for any spare quarters that may have fallen under. Double Back Barbara tries to jerry-rig her phone charger to the Magic Fingers motor to no avail, and Springboard Sam, practically motionless as the spasm of his device sputters to a stop, is frantically trying to hook up the relaxation system to the E-ZPass transponder attached to the front windshield, but no dice. "How about the car battery?" Poppy shouts, proud of herself that she's not pointing out the practical limitations of shaking versus bouncing. "That won't work!" yells a panicked and suddenly sideways-deprived Daryl as he defaults to vertical movement while his inert penis, Richard, panics and begins to soften. "We need a power source," the suddenly limp one yells, trying to shake on his own without the help of Magic Fingers but only succeeding in wobbling. Poppy knew this would happen. Splinter groups like shakers need time to assimilate into a movement, yet bi-bouncing may be the future and she has to accept that fact. "They need coins," yells Leepa, her toned excess body tissue still aflappin' as she stubbornly bounces, a traditionalist to the end, "but your goddamn mother even took the nickels!"

"Pull over!" shouts Richard through the rubbery hole at the end of his defeated shaft, and while Poppy doesn't like taking orders from anybody, especially a weakened penis, she knows her gang of movers and shakers are on their last legs so to speak. Her vehicle doesn't need gas yet, but her followers sure do. Here's an exit. Third Avenue. Sounds innocent enough, but this is the Bronx, don't forget. *Last Exit to Brooklyn* might be nothing compared to this.

As Poppy veers down the off-ramp, her original bouncers try to be understanding and give moral support to the newly shaken, who've panicked at having no choice but to sit still. Twisted Billy and Campolina try to get back to bouncing but after they've tasted "the shakes," it's just not the same anymore. "There's a laundromat!" shouts Campolina in excitement, her head hitting the roof of the van painfully once again because of her militant body self-projection. "And they'll have a change machine!" hollers Daryl, getting her drift as he half-heartedly tries to go back to bouncing, but his quivering muscles go slack and he quickly begins building back up the tension shaking had released so remarkably.

Richard tries to cheer along with the rest of the special-needs movers but is so flaccid they don't even hear his muffled cries of support. Surprize lets out a yowl of territorial concern that could pass muster in any clowder of cats, no matter how skeptical some of them might be. Dat? Cog? What's the right term? It doesn't matter anymore. Surprize is now part of the gang.

When they rush inside, Poppy in the lead of course, they are surprised to see the laundromat, which is so generic it doesn't appear to have a name, is actually crowded. Good. They need funds. A war chest. Quarters to feed the addictions of their guerrilla movement that needs movement. The nonbouncers, doing their laundry, look up in dumbfounded awe from their wet clothes, towels, and bedding as the desperate motion-maniacs bound past them, some hopping, others still trying to shake. "Quarters now!" Poppy demands in an authoritarian voice as she snatches a roll of coins from a white, mule-faced girl with a gray ponytail who was about to feed the washer's slots. "Hey, lay off!" she sputters in confusion, but Poppy has already bounced up so high, she is out of reach. Vaulta leaps up on top of a washer, hops to another, and lands right in front of the change machine just as it spits out eighty quarters from a twenty-dollar bill. "Sorry," she snaps to the tough-looking dame with rollers in her hair as she scoops out the lady's coins with her one good hand into an empty coffee cup she had grabbed on the last hop down. "That's for my dryer!" the fleshpot growls as she lunges at Vaulta before she can spring back up. As they battle for laundromat change, Campolina grabs a wet towel out of a Jamaican lady's hamper and snaps it like a whip, hitting her middle-aged ass. "That fuckin' hurt!!" she yells in post-rinse-cycle rage. "We're on a-move-hoo-hoo!" Springboard Sam and

Double Back Barbara weakly yodel in unison, so disabled by going shaking cold turkey that they don't bother explaining to the clueless launderers their political reference to John Africa's Philadelphia back-to-nature activist group, MOVE.

A would-be hero, some Puerto Rican tough guy with dandruff and a poorly inked neck tattoo that reads R-E-V-O-L-T, tries to grab Daryl, who is feebly attempting to go back to jumping until he can recharge his worn-out battery of shakiness. Richard comes to Daryl's rescue by shooting a surprisingly strong stream of urine right in the attacker's face, which turns Mr. R-E-V-O-L-T into Mr. R-E-V-O-L-T-I-N-G faster than the ballpoint ink dries on the page of this book I'm writing here today.

Pandemonium breaks out. The mule-faced girl tries to throw the contents of her small box of Tide into Poppy's face, but an environmentalist-type male college student grabs the box of "toxic" crystals from her hands and smugly pours them in the trash. An old homeless guy who is sadly trying to erase the stains from his underwear with Clorox bleach puts the cap back on and throws the whole bottle to an old strumpet who catches it, uncorks it, and splashes out the liquid toward Campolina, who does what any self-respecting drag queen under duress would do given the circumstances and lowers her scalp so the whitener hits her dark roots she hasn't had a free minute to touch up. Yeah, it stings but so what? Who has time for beauty parlors when you're a revolutionary?

Our tattooed tough guy gets the bright idea he can jump, too, but when he leaps up on a dryer that is overloaded, the machine starts making scary knocking and thumping sounds and then lurches side to side. As Tattoo-Neck struggles to balance, Twisted Billy is so furious to see a nonmovement civilian parroting their exciting new gymnastics that a fresh wave of shaking pride sweeps over him and, using his last ounce of adrenaline combined with extreme flexibility, he bends backward all the way until his fingers touch the floor, raises one leg up, does a full split, and elegantly quivers over on his elbows to the enemy pseudoshaker without once losing his balance. One kick of his split legs does the trick. The failed would-be-human-hand-buzzer falls off the dryer to the linoleum floor where he belongs.

The shakers begin shoving quarters into their attached Magic Fingers devices and immediately start vibrating sideways in ecstasy. Poppy and the tramps run interference, bouncing and hopping spasmodically to frighten and block the attacking irate laundromat customers who feel their wash day has been unfairly interrupted. Suddenly the roar of an engine is heard and all eyes turn toward the front window, where they see in the distance a shaking Adora behind the wheel, speeding the hopping lowrider van straight toward them. The customers dive for cover and Poppy and her gang hop and vibrate with new fanaticism. Adora crashes the van right through the front windows, breaking and splintering the wood and smashing the vehicle directly into the change machine, which knocks over but still doesn't split open. Not to be stopped, she turns her old age into rage, backs up the van, takes aim, and floors it again, ramming the stubborn little piece of metal for the second time. The customers run outside, a few of them attempting to drag their still-wet laundry with them while Poppy and crew cheer Adora on. One more time she peels rubber and rams the change machine, and this time it works.

Coins scatter everywhere. It's a gold mine of Magic Fingers power. Daryl is stuffing quarters in his device so fast that

Richard panics and warns him of shaking overdose possibilities, but Daryl is such an addict he throws caution to the wind and turns up the speed to beyond "high." Springboard Sam and Double Back Barbara are already quavering full force, harmonizing nonsense western-swing lyrics that only sound more bluegrass when they are sung out with vibrating vocal cords. Twisted Billy is flipping coins dramatically with his hands, feet, and even his tongue, and unbelievably the quarters always land dead center in everybody's Magic Fingers accepter slots. Campolina is stuffing the excess twenty-five-cent pieces up inside her fake pubic hair "cheater" wig like a crazed squirrel hides nuts for a winter day. It's not easy being a drag warrior, but when you're a shaker, it's even harder.

Poppy, Vaulta, and Leepa, the old guard of bouncers, help Adora out of the van, and the newly agitated shakers join them in cheering her courage. Adora beams in acceptance as Surprize, finally feeling welcome, jumps into her arms as the fully evolved creature she has become and convulses in fluidity. Adora smothers her with kisses and joins in the animal's vibration with newfound enthused aggression. Even Richard echoes the others' ovation, erect again from the surge of quarter-driven energy. Surprize begins barking and purring as she shakes, no longer attempting to "pass" as any kind of pet, yet proud to finally be herself even with all the complications. A siren is heard in the distance. Will the world ever understand?

15

God, Marsha wishes you could book and pay for a flight at one of those airport kiosks, but with cash you can't. She gets in line knowing her takeoff time is near but figures her rushing to buy and board can only help. There are two actual humans working behind the check-in booths, one African American lady with a great hairdo that must have hurt to have done and a white man who'd never understand. They're both free. Marsha chooses him.

"One-way to Boston, please, on United Flight 78 connecting to Cape Air Flight 2116 to Provincetown," she announces with confidence and politeness as she arrives at his counter with ID ready. "You have confirmation numbers?" he asks routinely. Marsha breaks into crocodile tears. "I don't," she sobs, "my mother died this morning suddenly in a freak dog-mauling accident, and I just found out. I have to get to the funeral home in Wellfleet to make arrangements."

She purposely lets the clerk know she won't be actually *staying* in Provincetown, just landing there, in case he might mistake her for a lesbian and treat her accordingly. "Please," she begs, "these are the only flights left available today."

The clerk is actually moved. His own mother recently was in a dog-related accident herself and he's happy to share the details with someone who will understand. "Tripped over the leash of that damn collie of hers when she was out walking him." "Happens all the time," comforts Marsha, reeling him in. "Such a dumb dog," he continues. "Guess what he bolted away for?" "What?" answers Marsha as if she gives a fuck. "To eat a pile of crap that was left behind by a police horse patrolling the park!" he hollers in much too loud a voice. "Disgusting," grumbles Marsha in agreement, trying not to tap her foot in impatience. "Mom didn't die but she broke both of her legs," he wails, "and who do you think has to take care of her now?" "You?" answers Marsha like a ventriloquist dummy. "That's right!" he announces for the entire check-in line to hear. "I do! That's who!"

"You're lucky," he says, suddenly calming down after looking back up from his computer. At first, she thinks he means "lucky" because her mother supposedly died but soon realizes that he means the flights. "Both planes, seats available," he announces happily. "Aisle or window?" "Aisle," Marsha wails, "the same as my mother always chose." She cries harder, rubbing her eyes, willing mucus to pour from her nose, knowing he's about to look at her ID. He glances away, embarrassed by the spasms of sorrow, then right back to her picture and then up to her phlegm-filled face. Who could tell *who* this was through the blubbering? Besides, he knows her flight has already started boarding. Get this poor woman to Provincetown. "Here you go," he says benevolently, taking

141

her cash (thank you, Poppy!) and handing her the boarding pass. "But hurry," he advises, "your flight is about to leave." "Thank you," Marsha bawls, a glob of overacted snot falling from her nose and landing directly on the portion of the card that announced her departure gate, smudging the numbers. "Thank you for flying United," adds the helpful clerk just like he's been brainwashed to do. "Thank *you!*" Marsha chirps back before swiping his pen off the counter and hurrying toward the security checkpoint.

Good! The queue is long enough that she'll be able to get an airline employee to rush her up in front of the other passengers who have planned properly and butt in line. Look at those fools over there who pay for CLEAR, Marsha thinks. Giving the authorities your DNA, fingerprints, and facial recognition info just for cutting-in-line rights. But how about later? When they use that private information to convict you of any old crime the police department needs to wipe from its unsolved case list? They'll CLEAR you all right. Straight to jail! No thanks! All you need is a bullshit story about heavy traffic or a sick child at home and a gullible airline employee will get you to the front of the line. And it's free!

Marsha ignores the furious look from the grumpy woman she's ushered in front of by that nice employee from United. "What's better than margarine?" the lady in line asks her angrily. "I beg your pardon?" answers Marsha confused. "*Butter!*" shouts out the senior citizen accusingly like a child in kindergarten, but there's not much she can do about it, is there?

Marsha's heart *does* skip a beat when she sees another old surveillance photo of her, taken from a different angle, lying right on the desk of the guy checking IDs as she approaches.

Marsha goes into full performance mode, sobbing convincingly, "My mom died unexpectedly this morning!" "ID?" he snarls, cutting her off with a shocking lack of empathy. Uh-oh. This guy's no pushover. Thinking fast, she takes the boarding pass—luckily it's the old-fashioned sturdier kind—and slices off the scab of her dog bite with it. "Damn it," she cries, "a paper cut." "Jesus Christ," the security guy barks as she hands him her license that now has a splattering of blood across the picture. "Address?" he quizzes her as he reaches for his handkerchief to wipe off the clot leavings, but not offering her even as much as a Kleenex for her own coagulating injury. She rattles off the same address he's looking at while trying to blot her cut with the airline envelope, which distracts him even further from looking at the surveillance photo. Men never notice the details of a woman's face anyway, Marsha thinks, all they are looking for are entry holes into their bodies.

It works. He circles the number on her boarding pass with some kind of code that makes him think he is superior to others and waves her through, shaking his head in disdain. Marsha likes the panic most travelers feel when they approach the luggage-scanner belt; take off your shoes, put stuff in bins, remove belts, take out medications, toiletries in special-size baggies, computers in different bins from their cases. It gives her time to plot her crimes. There are two separate lines she can join, but first she has to do a little scanning of her own. Let's see. Who's the most amateur flyer in the queue? Not that guy, he's too European, nope, not her either, she's too well dressed. Yes! There she is! An elderly woman from good stock who Marsha can see hardly ever flies. She has a water bottle sticking right out of her purse and doesn't even know it will get taken away from her. Perfect.

Marsha rushes over to her, goes into the full act of bereavement and begs the woman to let her go in front of her to make her flight before the boarding doors are shut. Of course, the woman sympathizes and lets her proceed. "Just a tip," Marsha volunteers kindly as she puts her own bag on the scanner belt first, "that water bottle should go in your pocket for the body scan, not your purse. They'll take it away from you." "Really?" the woman says, relieved, obediently putting the small bottle of Deer Park water in the pocket of her culottes. "I haven't been on a plane since 9/11 and it's all new to me." "Oh, they change the rules every day," says Marsha with a sigh, sensing that the lady is no different from any other and will *always* put her purse before her roller bag on the security belt so she can grab it first on the other side.

Marsha stealthily removes her real ID from inside her bra, places it in the pocket of the coat she removes, and easily passes the body scan, firmly convinced that the male TSA employee has just ogled her underpants, but what are you gonna do? It's a sick world out there. She grabs her coat and looks back. Yep! They've pulled her mark out of the line and discovered the water bottle. As the victim sputters and tries to explain, Marsha spots the lady's pocketbook coming through the scanner. The sign says some bullshit like don't reach in blah blah blah, but Marsha grabs it out anyway and walks off with the bag slung over her shoulder at a brisk speed while she checks her boarding pass. The blood had blocked the flight numbers, but the snot has dried enough that she can read the gate. Let's see. Gate 24. What a snore.

OK, here we are. ON TIME says the board. There's the crew getting on. She sits illegally in the seat reserved for the disabled and slips her Marsha Sprinkle ID back inside her bra next to the breasts a man will never fondle. Let's see what's in that pocketbook. Chiclets. How old-school. Band-Aids! This must be her lucky day! She takes a small one and quickly puts it over her agitated dog-bite scab. Here it is finally, the wallet. So many wallets, so little time. Two hundred and some bucks. Not bad. She rips out the bills and stuffs them in her bra, too. What do you know? There's a rain hat in here, too. One of those old-fashioned plastic kind that fold up like an accordion and used to advertise Wonder Bread. God, she hasn't seen one of them since Dutch Village. She puts it on. The Marsha Sprinkle of the surveillance photos would never be caught dead wearing one item of clothing she now has on. She'll keep the bag, too—it's a good prop for what's next. Ahem! She's ready to board now. Hurry the fuck up!

16

◆

The U-Haul truck they had carjacked right out front of the laundromat hasn't been customized for movers or shakers, of course, but the inside of the ten-foot storage area is perfect for hiding and shakes enough to keep all Poppy's cult unsteady on their feet just the way they like it, all the way to Massachusetts. That siren they hear wailing in the distance doesn't scare a one of them. Hell no, those two student truck-renters, who must have flunked out of Bronx Community College midterm and decided to do their own laundry before heading home to tell their parents, were easily overpowered and ran like the lightweights they were as soon as Poppy pulled a bottle of fabric softener under a towel on them like a gun. One even dropped the agricultural studies textbook she was clutching before she took off. Who would study agriculture in the Bronx but a moron? She wouldn't even know *how* to call the police. Maybe a farm animal will help her!

Poppy and Adora are up front in the bucket seats with Surprize hissing and acting like a crazy cat in a moving vehicle, hiding wherever she can wedge herself. Daryl tried to get the better seating on the argument that he and Richard are a team that needs only one seat, but so are Adora and Surprize and they're family so that's that. Poppy is thrilled to feel the shocks in this truck are shot so she bounces enough not to feel any withdrawal symptoms. To keep Adora in shaking practice, Poppy swerves the U-Haul whenever she can, but it's a fine line between movement maintenance and attracting police attention.

In the back, the gang lurch from side to side in no-seat-belt bliss or bounce up and down every time Poppy purposely hits a pothole to help project them upward. Communicating from front to back is almost impossible, but if you really yell, the others can hear *some* of the words being shouted. "I'm gonna . . . something . . . something . . . myself," Twisted Billy hears Poppy yell from the other side of the wall, but it's Richard, whose penile sense of hearing must be superior to his master Daryl's, who fills in the words "kill her" at the top of his . . . lungs? Urinary meatus? Springboard Sam and Double Back Barbara reinterpret shaking as they purposely bang their bodies into the truck's divider to show their support for Poppy's shouts of revenge. Campolina, over the top as always, goes into a spasm of theatrical shaking to upstage her fellow coconspirators but loses her balance and slams into the sidewall instead. Poppy can still hear the thud and floors the accelerator as a sign she's acknowledged the physical impacts of their commitment.

Up front, Adora strains to hear the threats Vaulta and Leepa shout as their heads just clear the interior roof of the truck, and even though she can make out only the words "bounce . . ." and "flatten her to . . ." she gets the gist. "On her" and "death" fill in as easily as the phrases she used to solve every night on *Wheel of Fortune*. Not to be outdone, Richard and Daryl join in the shouted verbal abuse, but the truck backfires at precisely the same time and, luckily for Adora, covers up one of their words, which she's pretty sure began with an "f." OK, she's all in on the eradication of her daughter, but is all this sex talk really necessary? Yes, Marsha owes Daryl her vagina for a onetime payment. Richard, too, she supposes. So, call unemployment! But please! An elderly woman's in the van with you, so try, at least try, to respect the limits of her newfound liberalism. Surprize is way too confused to take a stand on what constitutes a living wage these days so instead leaps up from under Adora's seat, lands on the dashboard, and hisses like the woke pussy she has become. Awwwwwww!

Just as Poppy looks back over from Surprize, wondering if she should now pronounce the "z" in her name with a soft "s" whenever she's in cat mode, she sees it in the road. A large animal. Running. Trying to escape from a tattoo-faced man wearing a zookeeper-type jumpsuit and heavy gloves and carrying a catch pole and animal net. "It's a hedgehog!" hollers Adora with authority, but Poppy doesn't care what this spiky quill-covered beast is—she just swerves to miss this panicked animal whose grunts are surprisingly loud. The gang in the back cheers in excitement, thinking it's just more stunt driving by their leader to enhance the frenzy of their self-movement, but no, this is real. A pileup accident just waiting to happen. Adora screams, "Look out!" and in the nick of time Poppy swerves across the rumble strips of the highway, narrowly missing a Breyers ice-cream truck whose driver has slammed on the brakes to avoid rear-ending a pulled horse trailer full of possible Kentucky Derby winners who now may end up in a glue factory. Poppy grabs the wheel with both hands and goes into a full donut maneuver, skidding circularly, burning rubber, and miraculously coming to rest with two tires blown out and the engine smoking in the breakdown lane facing the wrong way on 95 North.

She and her grandmother, with the frantically meowing Surprize in her arms, leap from the cab of the truck to help free the followers from the back. They are shaken up, shaken down, shaken over, and bounce-ready-to-pounce. Suddenly Surprize sees the hedgehog, who has darted its way to safety alongside the interstate and rolled itself into a ball the way those animals do when alarmed. Forgetting she is now a cat, Surprize starts barking and charges this unnatural-to-the-area freak mammal. But before she can sink her still-capped dog teeth into this circle of quills, an earsplitting cacophony of car horns distracts the cross-species pet from its prey, and the sinewy trainer, completely winded from dodging speeding, out-of-control vehicles, saves the day. "He's mine," he says, picking up the spiky, hissing creature, who immediately relaxes and uncurls. "I'm Poacher Bob," he announces, "and *this* is the biggest hedgehog in captivity. His name's Rooter and he's from New Zealand."

"It's illegal to import such an animal in this country," Adora immediately challenges this rogue zookeeper, noticing the words "critter" and "caged" inked under each eye vertically like a falling tear.

"It's only illegal in *some* states," the trainer sassily counters, "and besides, this hedgehog tops the scale at twenty-three pounds, and in the exotic pet trade, that makes him worth his weight in gold!" "Look, we don't care about the law," Poppy butts in before Adora can continue her possibly pointless debate. "We are outlaw trampoline radicals on the run," Vaulta announces. "And we need a ride," demands Leepa like the leaping leader of the left she's become. "All of you?" Poacher Bob asks as he surveys the bouncers and shakers who are struggling to maintain their movement so as not to alarm this potential rescuer. He can see their vibrating, though. Feel their urge to rise upward. And God, that look in their eyes! Who *are* these people?

Surprize reverts back to she-cat behavior and purrs in full softness to the animal keeper's face. Christ, even their pets are nuts! And what the fuck? One of the males has his member out and seems to be having a conversation with it! Who knows? Maybe he can sell these space cadets a de-scented skunk or that penguin he can't unload because the warm climate gives it body odor. "Where to?" he asks. "The train station," Poppy commands. We'll see about that, Poacher Bob thinks as he runs to his van, hops in, and jackrabbits it over to them. Who's the boss now?

Crammed inside the broken-down, stifling-hot, stinking-to-high-heaven animal-trainer vehicle that was obviously ground zero of Poacher Bob's illegal pet-smuggling business, Poppy and the rest of her gang try concentrating on their eccentric gymnastics just so their stomachs won't turn from the odor of the onboard imprisoned animals' waste. Adora was allowed to sit up front once Poacher Bob's menagerie got one look at Surprize and threw themselves against the bars of their cages in horrified disapproval. An imprisoned psychotic monkey in the back lurches toward Campolina and she lets out a drag queen scream, but this jailed Frances

Farmer–meets-Cheeta primate tops her with a jungle howl that could shut up even Tarzan.

The trapper turns off Route 91 West like he knows where he's going and blithely explains that this ape had somehow caught parvo, a disease that was thought to infect only canines, but was it his fault that the country where the monkey was born was so backward that the virus was confused? "You can take this animal with you for just twenty dollars," Poacher Bob offers, but nobody on board seems the slightest bit tempted.

Turning to Adora and ignoring her still-beginning attempts at shaking—who knows, maybe this old broad's got Saint Vitus's dance—he tries to barter. "OK, I'm slashing prices," he announces like a cheap air-conditioner salesman in September. "Fifteen dollars and Ding Dong Kong is all yours. Maybe this little freak of a dog of yours wants to mate? Think of the litter! You could open a punk-rock puppy mill!" Before Adora can even react to this unspeakable idea, this crazy chimp takes a ferocious piss right in front of company and all the passengers thank their lucky stars that the vehicle's built-in cage drains are still operable.

Kool, the penguin—presumably named after that menthol cigarette's vintage ad campaign—well, her deodorant has definitely failed. Vaulta and Leepa try to bounce as far away from her side of the van as possible but the rancid-cheese-meets-fruity-onion odor of this overheated bird makes even the perspiration-drenched bouncers and shakers themselves yearn for an industrial power washing that will never come. "That stench is just guano," Poacher Bob explains. "That's penguin poop. It don't smell bad to them, why should it smell bad to you? Tell you what. Take this dirty bird off my hands and I'll get you to Amtrak."

When nobody responds, he tries another sales pitch. "Look, penguins bounce, you know." Poppy looks over in astonishment at Kool, who seemingly on cue holds both her feet together and yes . . . bounces. "Penguins don't fly, they bounce," he continues. "She's one of you!" Kool bounces again and Poppy's heart feels a tug. That is until she gets another fresh whiff. "We can't," Poppy begs off, "hygiene issues sometimes outweigh inclusion." Kool stares directly at her with fresh hostility, erects her chest, and growls. Yes, growls like a dog. "That's what penguins do when they're pissed," explains Poacher Bob. Surprize hisses like a rabid cat and both animals make eye contact. There it is—nature's standoff. They retreat to their sides of the van, frustrated at their perverted place in domesticated wildlife. But what can they do? Nothing.

"OK, your loss," Poacher Bob shouts as he veers off 95 North into the Branford service plaza and parks in the rest area. "Ralph's hungry and the badger don't care what you call him as long as you don't call him late for dinner." Springboard Sam and Double Back Barbara think they've seen everything but when Poacher Bob expertly grabs a live rattlesnake from a cloth zoo bag and throws it into the badger's cage, they don't need quarters to shake, they do it all on their own. Old Ralph is fearless! He barrels over, lunges at the rattling reptile, biting and swiping and clawing. Even after the diamondback sinks its venomous teeth deep into Ralph's tough skin. He passes out for a few seconds but he's playing possum. Badgers are one of the few animals immune to snake venom. Fuck you, rattlesnake! Ralph gobbles the whole snake down, rattlers and all. Poppy gags. Vaulta blacks out. Leepa for the first time ever loses her appetite. Campolina shoves old rags she used to sniff Carbona off of inside her ears to block the awful noises of badger digestion, but all they do is muffle these terrible sounds. With Daryl's obvious help, Richard shoots out a penile discharge to show his displeasure, but a feverish parrot, who has somehow clawed the tape from around its beak, intercepts the leakage and gobbles it up greedily. "Last call for alcohol," the bird yells in a perfect imitation of Poacher Bob's voice.

"Tell ya what," says the reluctant chauffeur as he swerves the van out of the parking lot back to I-95, "one of youse give me a hand job and I'll take you where you want." Poppy and her whole gang choke in revulsion at this new aural assault. "Woo-wooh!" Bob cries out lewdly, pretending he's a horny train. "I think I can! I think I can!" he taunts, but nobody's going for this little engine who couldn't. "Lalalalala!" chants Adora as loudly as possible, hoping to drown out his obscene words in her head. All the animals, including Surprize, try to cover their eyes, unaware of what sexual harassment actually is but knowing instinctively that this male is . . . well, an animal.

Only Richard, the trouser snake, has the nerve to rise to the occasion. They have to get to the train station, don't they? Sneakily, he inches Daryl toward the front of the van with a penile pull that is programmed for pussy yet can be willed to a fellow penis in times of emergency. Could Richard touch one? Is it rubbery? Does it smell like musk? Suppose he gets ticks? Not an unreasonable fear around an animal kidnapper's private parts. Yes, he will be a war hero, curling his way forward and executing the hand job to advance the troops onward like a proudly shaking Douglas MacArthur. Conquering Connecticut, Rhode Island into Massachusetts, and all the way up to Provincetown, where the real Battle of the Bulge will begin.

But how? How does a penis give a hand job? Richard slithers his way up behind Poacher Bob's seat before Daryl can even figure out what's going on. "My way or the highway," Poacher Bob announces, unzipping and whipping out a medium-size uncircumcised wang. "Not in front of the animals!" yells Adora in a panic. Daryl pulls back but he's no match for Richard, who thrusts himself between the front seats before Adora can swat him away or Surprize can take a big bite. He touches the much older and weathered staff of Poacher Bob's unit with his head and guess what? It feels good! How can that be? Richard is a heterosexual penis, and the full-blown stallion of another man is not something he has ever chosen to rub. Yet now? What the hell, he's aroused! Poacher Bob likes the male-to-male contact, too, it seems. He doesn't care what's touching his dick as long as it's doing its job. "Eyes on the road," orders Adora, realizing that in times of emergency a man's gotta do what a man's gotta do. Surprize lies back provocatively, spreading her legs in sexual confusion.

Daryl tries to yank Richard back to the safety of their shared heterosexual underpants, but Richard likes this new frication and obviously so does his partner. "We're straight," yells Daryl in male panic to his own penis, but Richard just moans back in genital reawakening, building to his first gay climax. "Save it for Marsha," cries the horrified Daryl, but it's too late. "New Haven train station here we come," bellows Poacher Bob as he enacts this same verb all over Richard's shared shaft, who then explodes in the bliss of male-on-male frotting. Daryl lets out a cry of shame. Richard looks up at Daryl's fearful face and whispers tenderly, "Accept me."

Daryl sputters in confusion but tries to help Richard

clean up with an animal wipe. Poppy, Adora, the whole gang, even Surprize, are so grateful that their murderous journey can continue they ignore the debauchery around them and resume bouncing in place and shaking sideways as they take Exit 46 for Sargent Drive. Even Poacher Bob gives it a try as he peels up to the train station on Union Avenue, zigzagging the truck so his own animals can taste this possible new sensation from inside their cages. "All . . . all . . . a . . . board," he yells, his voice quivering in a newfound awareness that calms his natural-born belligerence.

Twisted Billy is so exhausted he contorts himself into the letter "A" for Amtrak and it gives him a brand-new thrill. Poppy is the first to pick up on this breakthrough form of literacy and soon the others notice, too. Being a letter brings power, Twisted Billy realizes, so why not try the next one, "B"? It's harder, but with a little shaking to further oil his joints, he does it. Bent in the middle with his left hand over his ninety-degree extended head and his right leg curled around to meet the same, he's a "B." "B" as in beautiful! There's no letter he can't be. Last to exit the animal van, he curls his body into a "C"—an easy one—and comes out sideways following the others. He's the human alphabet now and nobody can stop him.

17

◈

All that talk about "boarding" and now the goddamn flight is delayed? For what? They never tell you right away, do they? No, they just put the dreaded D-word up there on the announcement board and expect you to guess why. Let's see, Marsha fumes, what could it be this time? The arriving crew who dillydallies around just to exceed their union turn-around times from last night's flight? Pothead mechanics imagining all sorts of nonexistent issues so they can be heroes when they "fix" the problem? Caterers with hepatitis C forgetting to put in those hard, cold, unspreadable packets of butter? "Weather," as they so irritatingly put it? Don't they mean "bad weather"? There's always weather, isn't there, ignoramuses? Fog? So what? Pilots can see in the pitch blackness of night, can't they? What's a little gray? Wind? We're about to *fly* on the wind, aren't we? Drunk air traffic controllers? *There's* a real problem that's never brought up. And suicidal pilots? Remember that flight from Barcelona to Düsseldorf? It could happen to any of us!

Yet what do they give us as we wait, terrified to board, imagining the thousands of things that could go wrong on every flight due to subhuman error? Not a friggin' thing. Don't they have any crackers for Chrissake? Marsha's starving. Oh, what she'd do for even a Triscuit!

Finally, it's a go. With no explanation for the delay. Not a peep. Just the usual boarding order, which always drives Marsha insane. First "customers with disabilities" (fakers), "active members of the military" (post-traumatic stress time bombs), "United Global Services" (jet-lagged travelers with air-rage issues), "families with children under two" (nutcase Catholics), "Premier 1K Members" (frequent-flier scammers), "first class" (freeloaders who never actually pay for their own ticket), "Premier Platinum Members" (heroin dealers), "Premier Gold Members" (their drug "mules"), "Premier Silver" (uppity coach impersonating business class), "United Explorer Card Members" (suckers who fell for that onboard credit card pitch on past flights), and then finally, *finally* Marsha Sprinkle.

She darts over to the nearby next gate on the way to the Jetway and switches her pink down coat for a black leather jacket lying on a seat some hag isn't watching as she blabs on her phone. It fits. Good. A new outfit is always necessary when boarding. And yes, once again she will suffer the indignity of coach due to the number of passengers and theft possibilities. Marsha smiles after exiting the Jetway onto the plane, but the flight attendant's rosy expression fades as soon as she sees a "Group 3" on her boarding pass. She'll regret that.

Pretending to trip over another passenger's bag in the aisle, Marsha purposely creates a commotion in the front of the plane, dropping the old lady's stolen purse unzipped so the hankies, mints, and other crap spill out in the aisle. "Oh, I'm so sorry," Marsha sputters as the flight attendant gets down on her knees to help retrieve the items and other Group 3 boarders behind her join in the rescue effort. Marsha reaches above and swipes the . . . what else can you call a woman this easily fooled . . . the *stewardess's* pocketbook right out of that first little overhead bin where you get on the plane. The same place where they *always* keep their valuables. Marsha thanks all her helpers profusely and continues to walk through first class back to her seat in Siberia, ditching the first stolen bag in another compartment.

Look at these privileged bastards calmly scrolling through their overpriced phones, not even realizing they're being spied on this very moment and their porno searches and credit card information are being forwarded to Russian hackers for blackmail or identity theft. What's that fucker looking at? That guy wearing some sort of dogcatcher uniform with a patch sewn on his top right pocket showing a muzzle in a circle with a line drawn through it like a "no smoking" warning. To top off her confusion, he's daring to make eye contact without permission. Worse yet, he's smiling! And good Lord, he's missing one of his front teeth. Is there no end to the humiliation of today's air travel?

Suddenly, she's paranoid. Did he see her steal the cabin attendant's pocketbook? As she passes his aisle seat, refusing to acknowledge his . . . grin . . . yes, that's the only way to describe his lewd look, she waits for him to blink. A blink is all the time she needs to grab his little bag overhead in the bin he purposely left open to kindly signal other first-class passengers that there's still room. That's what he gets for being a luggage liberal!

OK, Row 17, Seat F. Aisle of course. First out if you have to tackle some lunatic passenger who tries to open the emergency-exit door midflight, or smack the traveler in front of you who reclines the seat without warning right in the middle of that bad, edited-for-airlines Hollywood movie you'd never see at home even if it was playing down the street and they let you in free. Of course, there are two people already in her row. Roly-poly types. Marsha saw them get on board with other passengers claiming they needed "extra help" in boarding. Wouldn't you know it? The woman, the stouter of the two, is in the middle seat. And you can tell she wants to talk.

"Oh, I know," she bellows, "I'd hate to sit next to me, too. I'm a biggun! I'm Myrtle and this is my husband, Gus-Gus, better known where we live as 'Lord of the Onion Rings'!" "Hello," Marsha manages to respond, her voice dripping icicles, hoping they get the hint that chatter is not an option in Row 17. "I could eat a horse," Gus-Gus shouts out, completely unaware of Marsha's need for aural space. She ignores his outburst as she cranes her neck to see if that arrogant dogcatcher is still spying on her. He is! Standing in the aisle, peering back her way with the same audacious gap-tooth come-hither grin. Ha! Wait till he goes to get his dog-bite serum or whatever he keeps in that now-missing kit of his. That'll show him.

"You'd think we'd get food on this flight like they used to serve," Myrtle gripes to anybody who will listen. "But no, now if it's under a two-hour flight we gotta fast," her husband complains. "I'm starving to death!" Myrtle bellows out to Marsha, who ignores her outburst. "They could give you a sandwich at least," Gus-Gus yells. "Or one stinking bag of pretzels to tide us over," Myrtle reasons to Marsha, who still has shown no signs of even hearing the conversation.

Marsha is trapped. The flight is now full and there's no-where to move to, even if that were allowed. "We gotta bring our own food from home on board," Myrtle whispers to Marsha, who is shoving both of her newly stolen bags under her seat. But Myrtle doesn't even notice because she is strug-gling herself to retrieve a small plastic container of macaroni from underneath her skirt. "Airport food is just too expen-sive," volunteers Gus-Gus. "Does United Airlines think we're made of money?" "Those security cretins always try to seize our onboard snacks, but who's gonna wanna search up here?" asks Myrtle as she retrieves another container, this one packed with egg salad, from up inside her nether regions. "Want some?" she blithely asks Marsha as she opens the Tupperware container. "No," sputters Marsha, instantly regretting joining in the conversation no matter how minimally.

Uh-oh. That dogcatcher, or whatever he is, is now stand-ing up searching the overhead bin for his bag. Please God or whatever lower power can hear me, make this plane take off. Presto—the announcement comes on that the airplane doors are now closed, and you must take your seat and fasten your seat belt. See? Nobody can ever accuse Marsha of not being spiritual.

Do these people next to her ever shut up, Marsha won-ders. No! Even as the plane taxis down the runway, Myrtle is still yacking, only louder to be heard over the roaring jet en-gines. "We love cheese the best," she pontificates as they rise in the air through a few bumps of turbulence. Once they reach cruising altitude Myrtle takes a large cheddar wheel out of her hand luggage. "The airport X-ray scanners always think it's my hat," she whispers conspiratorially to Marsha as if she's revealing state secrets. The circular round is covered in lint and parts show mold but that doesn't seem to bother these two. Myrtle whips out a baggie filled with crackers from inside her industrial-strength bra, and she and Gus-Gus start making hors d'oeuvres.

Marsha's eyes light up. Crackers. Now we're talkin' the same language. Not her brand but at least they're not Cheez-Its! "We love Keebler's best," bellows Gus-Gus, sounding like anything other than Cinderella's mouse friend. "No, I love Ritz better," argues Myrtle, "they're more highly processed." "Give me one!" blurts Marsha, grabbing the bag out of Myrtle's hand. "Sure . . . help yourself," she stammers, delighted to find common food ground with a fellow passenger.

Chewing slowly, Marsha feels the grams of fiber mixing with a hint of grain. Mmmmmm. A smidgen of sodium. All going down the conveyor belt of her digestive system with the speed of nourishment, the joy of gastronomical simplicity. A cracker is not a snack, it's the ultimate meal that energizes her psyche, a nutrition that produces very little waste. The only solid that Marsha's highly selective anus rejects is organic. Some call it the truth.

18

◈

On board the Northeast Regional train to Boston, they've had to split up, but at least they're in the same car. Poppy had accidentally led them first to the Quiet Car but, once the train pulled off, she instantly noted the other overreserved passengers on board who greeted their arrival with annoyance, then alarm, and finally outrage. This wasn't a goddamn library, was it, she wondered. No, it was a train. Bouncing didn't make that much noise and, unless you were wearing jewelry, shaking was a relatively quiet activity. But this was no time for debate. None of them had tickets, so unless they could hide in the bathrooms, which was unlikely, the conductor would find them and throw them off at the next station, which was Mystic, Connecticut. Who wants to introduce radical kinesis in that town? They sure don't.

The regular coach car's passengers seemed more accepting. Springboard Sam and Double Back Barbara were the first of the shakers to realize they didn't need the Magic Fingers apparatus any longer. They could shake on their own and the trauma-releasing side effects were just as beautiful as they were with the cumbersome devices left behind. Shaking had now broken the chains of capitalism and become a proactive practice for superior individuals like themselves who are forever unable to sit still. The Amtrak basin and antiquated tracks made all the other passengers on board lurch from side to side, too, yet these clueless shakers never even noticed the transcendental bliss that came free of charge with this onboard quivering.

Poppy was lucky enough to find two seats together toward the back so she could sit with Adora, who hid Surprize in a EZ Dollar plastic bag she got out of a trash can in the train station. "If you see something, say something" was Amtrack's slogan, and Surprize was definitely something! A couple across the aisle gave them a possibly high-and-mighty look, unsure if Poppy was unnaturally buoyant from the train movement or purposely bouncing for reasons they couldn't begin to comprehend. And the other one? Who knows? She was shaking like a leaf. Maybe she was from Philadelphia and had been a passenger in that terrible train derailment that happened there back in 2015. Was she having flashbacks? Your guess is as good as theirs.

Vaulta and Leepa keep changing seats so as to disguise their bouncing, but Vaulta's height makes all upward movement on a train problematic, plus, even if she had a paid ticket, the "air rights" over each seat are ill-defined in the fine print of Amtrak's policy. Leepa's well-fed but in-condition body makes a thundering sound when she lands on a seat. Maybe in business class the padding would be more forgiving, but here in coach it's brutal. As a friendly gesture to the other passengers, Springboard Sam and Double Back Barbara break into their version of "The Lion Sleeps Tonight," one of the few popular oldies that includes yodeling, but they don't get much of a response. Richard, now out of the closet with an assertiveness that would give even Larry Kramer pause, is craning his . . . his . . . head to see if there are any cute guys nearby, but Daryl is covering him up with an Amtrak *National* onboard magazine he hastily grabbed from the pocket of an empty seat back and making eye contact with any woman he sees just so other passengers don't get the wrong idea about the dominating sexual preference of this now bi-curious, bi-furious penis combo.

Twisted Billy is up to the letter "H" now and it's a hard one to do on the train, especially with all the disapproving eyes on him from the other rail-riders. He's a capital "H" of course, can't they see that? No small letters like they are. Balancing on one leg with the other extended vertically and his whole torso sticking straight out horizontally with one hand reaching up and the other down, he is the letter "H."

"Tickets please," calls out the good-looking middle-aged conductor, who's proudly featuring beard stubble as he enters the car from the front end. Poppy begins to freak seeing all her followers before her spread out in their seats, heads bobbing up and down or shaking side to side while other passengers remain relatively motionless. Is it just Poppy or do the others notice that the conductor seems to be bouncing on the balls of his feet as he scans tickets with his little machine? Leepa and Vaulta see it too, and he catches their eyes and gives them an approving wink. Could he be one of them? Springboard Sam and Double Back Barbara wonder the same thing. Hallelujah the hills!

As the conductor walks up the aisle, he sees Poppy's people moving in place, and as the train goes around a corner at what seems like an excessive speed, he shakes with it while still retaining the bounce in his walk. When they tell him they lost their tickets and he just chuckles, they begin to be sure he's on their team. Campolina, ever the showstopper, starts shimmying in place like one of those *Hullabaloo* go-go dancers she saw on YouTube. The conductor bursts out laughing and bounces up quite deliberately, ignoring the quizzical looks of the normal passengers and showing approval of drag bouncing. He doesn't even ask for her ticket.

Richard's gaydar suddenly goes off full tilt and he pokes his head right through an article on "The Charms of New London" in the Amtrak magazine to get a better look at this African American hunk. Daryl is horrified to be connected to anything this obviously gay and tries to drag Richard back into the down-low of his pants to cover up this blatant cruising, but the conductor notices Richard right away and, rather than being offended, aims his scanner at his penile head and zaps it in foreplay. Oh God, the conductor is a bouncer-flouncer, Daryl thinks. How will Richard ever be able to fuck Marsha now that his own guided missile has turned queer?

By now Poppy is convinced they're safe here on board, bouncing and shaking naturally from the diesel electrical power of a General Electric locomotive engine. And hopefully that onetime freeloader Richard can continue pulling his own weight and help the movement by doing something more than just hanging from the crotch of that fanatical employee of her mother's, who at last may be able to see the light at the other end of Marsha's tunnel.

"You two lovely ladies comfortable back here?" the conductor asks with a conspiratorial bounce as Poppy does the same in her seat out of mutual respect. "We certainly are," Poppy answers with amazement, stunned to realize there are other bouncers, unknown to her cult, who are bouncing freely on their own out in polite society without harassment from others. Adora recognizes she is among the converted and opens the plastic bag and lets . . . Al . . . that's the name he volunteered, isn't it? Yes, Al, such a simple name for a possibly complicated man, she thinks, allowing him to get a glimpse of Surprize inside. "Wow! That's a look," says the kindly conductor approvingly as the cat-trapped-in-a-dog's-body purrs back in thankful acceptance. Adora dares to shake sideways, "dropping her beads" so to speak, letting a fellow outsider know that she, too, marches to a different drummer. "You and your friends are too special for coach class," Al whispers in the voice of a Black savior, "come on back to the business-class car where you belong."

Poppy bounds upward from her seat with sudden optimism and gives a two-finger whistle to her followers. The whole gang leaps up, including Twisted Billy, who luckily is forming the letter "L," which even normal individuals impersonate daily without ever knowing it. They shake and bounce out of their seats and down the aisle, much to the anger and confusion of the other coach riders. There goes Richard, following the conductor the way a hound dog would a polecat, eager for the first taste of receptive male-to-male oral sex, but Daryl resists, pulling back, holding on to the rear of other passengers' seats as they pass, digging his heels in to avoid the sensation of male lips around his only-females-allowed private parts.

Al the conductor ushers the whole tribe into the business-class car, but a couple of the shakers, Campolina and Double Back Barbara, pause on the gangway connecting the cars just to shake violently while risking getting their daredevil feet mangled in the jaws. Once inside the almost-empty, more exclusive cabin, the others bounce and shake joyously to their seats together while a few of the riders, a prissy matron who is a dead ringer for the diet doctor murderess Jean Harris and some kind of reverend who is obviously turning his nose up at the vow of poverty by paying to be in this all-seats-reserved section, move away, remembering to take their free beverage vouchers with them.

Outside the lavatory, located right in front of the car, Al turns to a red-faced Daryl, who is still holding Richard back, and smiles seductively. Daryl sputters. Al lowers his hooded eyes down below. Richard blushes. God, the newly liberated penis thinks, this conductor is as sexy as the Brawny Paper Towel man, hotter than the Liquid-Plumr model. "Looking for a little action?" Al flirts in the best straight-acting gay voice since Jeff Stryker's as he puts one foot inside the bathroom door. Richard jiggles in erotic excitement and Al bounces back his cruising commitment. Daryl, for once, does neither. "No, no, no," he protests, "I'm one hundred percent hetero! A zero on the Kinsey scale." "How about that tickler guy?" Richard challenges from below the equator of the sexual divide in a loud voice with a sideways shake to punctuate his "gotcha!" moment. "He never touched my penis!" Daryl argues back, embarrassed to be reminded of this freak from his recent past in earshot of Poppy, her grandmother for Chrissake, and the rest of his new friends, much less civilian passengers who know nothing of his struggle. "A bro-job is a terrible thing to waste," Al says with a chuckle as he bounces up and lands back down, grabbing Richard by the neck of his member in a firm but loving way. Think one of those children's bamboo Chinese finger traps and you'll know just how tight this bond felt.

Twisted Billy is so preoccupied with being the human "Elemeno-P" of the alphabet that he barely pays any attention to the tawdry melodrama unfolding ahead of him. This aforementioned "L" is basic, the "M" and the "N" aren't that difficult, the "O" is a breeze, and the "P" even an amateur could do, but dissolving visually into each one and actually becoming this commonly used shortcut of these five letters takes a little practice. Poppy looks back at Twisted Billy and at first is confused but then suddenly gets it. She does a pretty good impersonation of an "O," but Billy's done that, she knows. It's a process! She sticks out her tongue and becomes the next letter, "Q," in their shared secret alphabet. Poppy! Poppy! Poppy! Why is she the one who always understands first?

Daryl jams one of his feet against the lavatory doorframe but Richard is already halfway inside with Al. And then Daryl feels it. A man's mouth encircling his own unit. The chaffing of whisker stubble comes next. The rough lips. And finally, the salty testosterone-filled saliva that lacks the estrogen he so craves. Can a gay bouncer give a homo-shaker with a hetero-bouncing top a blow job? No one would dare call it a threesome with this much confused consent. Daryl looks back and sees the whole carful of passengers, the bouncers, the shakers, and the motion-impaired, watching this sexual tug of war. Now everybody will have to answer the million-dollar question. Does "no" mean "no" when only half the person protests?

19

◆

Marsha sits on the toilet, rifling through her plunder. This is not a women's room, a men's room, or a gender-neutral room. Even the most exhausted traveler could never call it a restroom, either. It's an outhouse in the sky for every human orifice on board that needs evacuation. But at least she can hide here. First things first. Off comes that ridiculous rain hat. Next up, the flight attendant's pocketbook. She stuffs the bills in her bra and throws the bag and the rest of its contents down the trash receptacle with the contaminated paper towels. OK, let's see what that impudent dogcatcher carries in his little Dopp kit.

Bang! Bang! Bang! Who the fuck would dare interrupt her private time? "I'm in here!" she hollers out with indignation, accidentally telling the truth for the first time that day. "I want my bag back!" she hears in a voice that sounds much too authoritarian and male for her liking. "I don't have your goddamn bag!" she shouts back as she stares right at it sitting in plain sight on the sink.

Marsha hears a click in the lock on the bathroom door. What is this guy doing? You can't pick a lock on an airplane! *Click. Click. Click.* "I'm coming in," he teases in a comically threatening voice. "Halt!" she commands in her most high and mighty tone as she clamps shut her natural-born fissures in a righteous moment of self-protection.

But he refuses to retreat. *Click! Click! Click!* She can see the bolt on the door jiggling. The indoor light blinks on and off. She tries to hide his bag, but where? It's too big to fit in the trash chute and there are no other secret places inside an airplane lavatory. Just as she leans up against the door to protect herself, the lock flies back and he pushes his way inside and pins her against the right-hand wall. She struggles out of his grasp, accidentally ripping off the Band-Aid on her dog-bite cut while trying to balance herself, first on the toilet, and then on the other wall but she keeps hitting the flush button again and again, and even though the *woosh–woosh–woosh* suction sound of the toilet is loud it still doesn't drown out his snarl, "That *is* my bag!"

"I'm sorry, I must have picked up the wrong one," she feebly argues, checking out her exposed cut that has scabbed much more quickly than she had hoped. He pulls her by the wrist away from the sink and shoves her down to a seated position on the toilet in front of him. "Liar," he says with a smirk. She likes the way he says that word. Liar. Yes, she is, and she wishes she could shout that fact from the rooftops of every nation in this whole wide world.

The name LESTER is rather clumsily stitched on his jacket below the "no-muzzle" patch she noticed earlier. His olive-green work pants are worn and thick, and fit snugly. They

give off the oddly pleasing smell of gasoline, vintage Nauga-
hyde, and the challenged fresh air of a beach resort after a
restaurant fire. OK, it's a look. She'll give him that. One that
Daryl could never pull off no matter how hard he tried. She's
now directly facing his pelvic area, which showcases through
the rugged material a package that is both self-assured and,
well, respectful, even courteous. She is not used to being
confronted by a male organ that seems both domineering and
friendly, possibly aroused but willing to listen, ready to spring
to action yet not easily intimidated by her feminine wiles.

"Liar!" he says again in a slower drawl, making direct eye
contact before opening his stolen bag to reveal dog whistles,
bite sticks, and pepper spray. "That's my stuff," she brazenly
states, knowing he won't believe her but praying he will call
her that word again. "Liarmouth," he says with a missing-
tooth grin. Liarmouth? That's even better! Say it again, she
begs him inside her head. He does. Only this time he pauses
teasingly between syllables. "Liar . . . mouth," he whispers,
daring her dishonesty to rise up from her throat again. How
can one word, even one made up from two separate words
put together, melt away her lifetime of carnal caution, she
wonders silently. Who cares?! "Say it again," she pleads, this
time out loud. "Liarmouth," he growls more aggressively and
with no pause. "I swear to God it's not your bag," she per-
jures herself, proud to be daring to risk eternal damnation
yet shocked to sound seductive while doing so. "Liarmouth,"
he says again, and then again and again and again, building
in intensity and volume until the whole coach section on the
other side of the door must overhear that magic word. Knowing her next oath must be the ultimate lulu, she shouts, "I
swear on my mother's grave." But this time he doesn't say it.
"Tell the truth," he suddenly orders in a roughly sexual voice

171

unlike any she's ever heard. She freezes. "Just one time, tell me the truth," he demands as he rips off his dogcatcher baseball hat and slips it on her head. It fits. Before she can refuse this unfathomable command, he bends down and kisses her on the mouth. Hard.

Marsha can feel it inside their mouths. His tongue of truth serum mixing with her dental decay of deception. Finally, the oral lubrication of an abrupt change in sexual desire flows through her. His flexing pink tissue asking what's never been asked of her, triggering her own pink tissue down below to sense the new stirrings of sexual curiosity. The only thing she doesn't feel is him stealing her ID and cash right out of her bra with the nontouch of a complete pro. Well, not *her* cash exactly. First it was Marsha's victims', and then it was Marsha's, and now it's not.

20

Daryl is definitely not AC/DC, not a switch-hitter, not a closet queen, yet how does he rise above . . . well, technically he *is* above, the homosexual action that is going on full tilt "below 14th Street," as he once heard oral sex described by a seasoned jazz musician? Thank God, Poppy and his fellow travelers do not see firsthand his "fall." They don't have to hear the happy gagging of Al the conductor or the sloppy suction of another man's mouth around Daryl's certain width. He dare not shake sideways for fear it will be perceived as sexual encouragement. How can Richard, as a penis, thrust all on his own while Daryl stands like a cold fish inside the train's comfort station (yeah, right) willing flaccidity, praying for one of those chemical castration pills like Depo-Provera that they give sex criminals to ensure impotency? He thinks of Marsha's moist melting pot at the same time Richard throbs with the joy of getting his knob polished by a male stranger. Their sexual fantasies don't mix. The nerve endings connecting the penis to the brain are short-circuiting. Richard is hard but Daryl is mentally soft and, as always, a man ultimately thinks with his dick. It blows Daryl's mind!

This business-class car is a step up, Poppy thinks, as she rallies her troops by bouncing unashamedly in front of the few supposedly upper-echelon passengers who are already keeping a watchful eye on Twisted Billy, who is now up to the letter "T" and is a little sweaty from doing "R" and "S," which he pulled off flawlessly. Leepa may be a little loud when she springs to action and lands back down on a seat, but she has rights, too, don't forget. Obviously, Conductor Al will protect her crew, so who is Poppy to judge if he likes to chow down on Richard between tending to other passengers' needs? And Daryl, she thinks, protests too much. "It's practically Freudian," whispers Campolina as she shake-quakes her way to the row behind where her leader just landed. If Daryl expects them to understand his sexual payday with her mother, Poppy thinks, he should be more open to new ideas of erotic expression.

The prissy matron on board is fidgeting nervously with the pearls around her neck. Just the sight of Vaulta and Leepa landing nearby is enough to get on her business-class nerves, much less this circus freak who has somehow contorted his body into the letter "W," which must stand for "Wacko." But worse, she saw two homosexual men go into the bathroom together and she can hear, above the clackety-clack of the tracks below, the muffled sounds of a skull-fuck. Who's she gonna complain to? The conductor? He's the one doing the hoovering! And Father Buttplug or whatever his name is? He doesn't seem one bit perturbed. Even when a shaking Adora takes a trembling Surprize for a leashed walk up the aisle. No, he just sits there. You'd think the sight of Spring-board Sam and Double Back Barbara quivering like in an earthquake right in the aisle across from him would give him pause, but zero response. He can hear the pants and grunts of acts against nature being performed in the bathroom right ahead, yet he's not even praying. Not offering to hear any-body's confession. He's just watching. Jeepers creepers, this guy's a peeper!

Al is in full "talking to the mic" mode, kneeling in the train "tearoom" as Richard, the newly unchained headhunter, plunges himself down the throat of a willing man. Daryl oversees the suck-a-thon below with stunned revulsion. He's not "French" active *or* passive with anybody but a natural-born female. He's not deep throat, shallow throat, or any throat at all. A hum-job? He's not even sure what it is, but he knows he'll never sing that tune even if he finds out. Cupping another man's balls is a sport that will always have him crying "Foul!" And swallowing a load of jism? He's already thrown up in his own mouth visualizing it.

But that's just what's happening down below. Richard explodes in the stunt-mouth conductor's gullet and there's nothing Daryl can do about it. Filled with self-hatred and sudden gay panic, he starts beating himself in the face and calling himself the f-word. Al spits out Richard from the oven of his mouth and with a throat full of "life" gurgles, "What the fuck?" "No! No!" shouts Richard up to Daryl, "you're still straight and I'm gay, we're bisexual brothers!" Daryl looks down in disgust at his now-homo appendage and spits on Richard like the dick he is. Al burps a sperm bubble and giggles.

21

◈

"The truth feels good, don't it?" Lester pants temptingly as he lifts Marsha up bodily from the toilet and plops her down firmly on the lavatory sink. "I . . . I . . . don't know what you're talking about," she lies without the usual verve, nerve, or audacity. "Come clean," he directs before plunging his muscular tongue inside her lying lips again, only this time Marsha opens wider in full welcome of the cold hard fact that he may be her new Prince Harming. As he sucks the untruths from her falsified face, she can feel the molecular explosion of lies becoming honesty inside her soul and, for the first time, her altar of love sends signals of pleasurable high alerts.

"Hey! Other people need to use the bathroom!" an outraged male voice yells from the other side of the lavatory door. "Go away!" yells Lester, taking over the control Marsha was used to. "My mother only loved her pets, never me," she blurts out, startled to hear honest words tumble from her mouth to a complete stranger almost involuntarily. "There's two people in there!" the man outside yells in shock. *Bang! Bang!* "I have to go number two!" some woman with a Boston accent yells. Lester ignores the voices outside and murmurs, "The truth . . . the truth . . . ," before darting his oral intruder back inside Marsha's luscious lips, which now yearn to tell just that.

"Two people are not allowed together in the lavatory," the angry female flight attendant yells through the door, pounding her tiny little fist. "I have a first-class ticket," Lester answers indignantly before turning back to Marsha, who sobs for the first time in real emotion. "Let it out," he implores her sexily. "My father died because of my evil mother," she exclaims almost automatically. "I hear a woman in there," some other busybody lady yells. "They're having sex," the first guy smugly announces to anyone who will listen. "First class and coach are not allowed together in this area of the plane," the attendant pontificates with a little more respect now that the class difference in their seats has become apparent.

Marsha ignores the outside complaints and, overcome with a passion to bare her soul, continues her confession. "'Get the dog! Get the dog!' my mother yelled as my awful father, the one whose testicles I had to start out from, chased him into the street." "There are children out here wetting their pants," the same attendant pleads in a furious voice through the door, as the pilot announces the "beginning of the descent" and "all passengers must return to their seats." "A truck hit my dad and killed him!" Marsha wails in a trance, speaking as if she's on automatic pilot herself. Lester rewards her honesty by grabbing her hand and sucking the scab right off her dog-bite injury. He chews up the crunchy clot, grins, swallows it down, and then abruptly stands up, opens the lavatory door, and poof—he's gone. One thing Marsha knows for sure. He's not a poof. And that's the god-honest truth.

"Whore," the stewardess says directly into her face as soon as she steps out. "Wait . . . wait . . . there's more," Marsha vainly cries out in confusion, ignoring her, but the dogcatcher is already halfway up the aisle. "Do you mind?!" the man says as he pushes past her and lowers his pants to sit on the toilet right in back of her. "Close the door, lady," he yells before shoving her out with his foot.

Marsha is confronted by an angry mother with a toddler standing in a puddle of urine. "Happy now?" she asks as her child breaks into tears. Marsha wants to tell everybody on board the truth now even if they'd never understand. Didn't the most romantic thing in the world just happen to her right inside a plane's bathroom? Why not share it with the world?

Gus-Gus gives Marsha's new dogcatcher hat a wary look when she retakes her seat and fastens the seat belt, but Myrtle is more friendly. "Can I have your cookies?" she asks immediately, pointing to the unexpected free snack that was left at Marsha's seat earlier during the flight. "Of course you can," Marsha answers truthfully, "I'm hungry too—for a man!" As Myrtle and Gus-Gus sputter to respond, Marsha strains her neck to see if the dogcatcher is looking back from the first-class section to see if she's all right. But he's not. Uh-oh, she thinks, missing the feeling of the truth, I'd better give the money back I swiped from the flight attendant. Wait. Where is it? She definitely had the cash in her bra. Her real ID, too. It's gone. Who could have taken them? He did. That's who.

22

◈

"What the hell's going on here?" shouts the middle-aged no-nonsense female train conductor after she's stepped into the business-class section to take tickets and noticed the unusual movement from some of the passengers. "Stop bouncing," she yells to Poppy, flipping back her crochet braid attached to her own freshly relaxed hair. "We are exercising in place as allowed by the law," Poppy counters back, unafraid of small-time bureaucrats. "You!" she hollers to Campolina. "You handicapped or something?" "I am a shaker, ma'am," she answers back, ignoring the woman's rudeness. "Well. Stop it!" snaps back Ilsa, the She-Wolf of the Northeast Corridor. "What the hell's that thing?" she continues grousing after getting a load of Surprize being shoved into a bag by Adora. "She's a rare breed of dog," answers Adora haughtily, quivering as hard as she can to give herself courage, "and she's got Shaker's Syndrome. It's a disease that confused pets get from being trapped in the body of another species." "Amtrak does not allow diseased animals on board, ma'am," the Amtrak enforcer answers without an ounce of sympathy before turning to Billy, who was just finishing up the alphabet. "Hey, you, Mr. Zorro! Stop that shit!" she orders like a crass copy editor. Billy ignores her and relaxes from the "Z" he just owned, I mean *owned*, and morphs into a small letter "a" for "asshole," hoping she can "read" his next level of lowercase alphabetic sign language.

But she's spiritually illiterate, just as he expected. "You two! Sit down!" she orders when she sees more passenger movement. "Bouncing is freedom," bellows Leepa defiantly on the way down for a cannon-ball landing. "Blasting off is beautiful," shouts Vaulta on the way up, not even sticking out her only arm for balance. "Stop that!" shrieks the ticket taker to Springboard Sam and Double Back Barbara, who sing back, "Oh-dah-lay-hee-hee," sampling a verse of Gene Autry's "The Yodeling Cowboy" while shaking sideways in self-choreographed impudence.

"Hey, buster, no pocket-pool!" the conductor suddenly calls out to the voyeuristic "watch-queen" reverend who may be pleasuring himself through his pants without the slightest concern for her authority. "Well how about the male-to-male fellatio going on right now inside the bathroom?" he answers, not one bit repentant. "I'm trying to read," adds the persnickety matron in exasperation, looking up from a trashy Princess Grace of Monaco biography, "but no, I have to lose my place because of the unnatural sounds of homosexual suction. In business class yet!" The conductor's eyes light up in fury and she turns toward the restroom door. "Al," she bellows, "is that you?!"

Al wipes his mouth with a scratchy paper towel as Richard shrinks back inside Daryl's fly. Al and Daryl are now face-to-face in panicked embarrassment yet connected by sexual intimacy. No matter what just happened, Daryl doesn't feel like explaining his or Richard's complicated backstory to any closed-minded railroad employee. Suddenly the bathroom door flies open and there she is—the outraged conductor. She has used her emergency key to get in and Daryl can tell this is personal. "I told you, Al," she scolds in a fury, "no blow jobs on duty! Suck all the cock you want at home in New London but not here! Not on Amtrak's time!"

"But Edwina, I did all my work," he pleads as Daryl, red in the face, retucks his shirt and Richard hides in fear. "Trash emptied, tickets checked, paperwork filled out," he further argues, but she's not hearing any of it. "Nosirree," Edwina snaps, "no more wannabe Acela fellas for you, Mr. Mighty Mouth. You were on penis probation—which is now revoked. Get off! And I mean at the next stop, not in your pants. All of you freaks," she announces, turning to the other passengers and pulling rank. "Next stop, Providence, Rhode Island. End of the line!"

23

◈

Marsha hurries off the Jetway into the terminal at Logan Airport but Lester is nowhere to be seen. Sure, he was in first class, but couldn't he have waited for her? Especially after their kiss of truth! Panicked, she breaks into a run, looking in newsstands, craning her neck over lines of waiting restaurant customers, and pushing ahead of slowpokes on the moving stairways. Where is he? The men's room? She knows it's not a good idea to stand out when the authorities are looking for you but wearing this black leather jacket and a dogcatcher hat, these men will just think she's a crazy lady, not a luggage thief. Besides, she's a changed woman now and the truth will protect her just the way her lies did in the past.

She barges in and sees a whole line of males standing in front of urinals, but the one she is looking for is not among them. "Lady, this is the men's room!" shouts an elderly gentleman, trying to cover himself. "Lester!" she yells out, ignoring the old guy, banging on the stall doors, and accepting the cold hard truth that a he-man like Lester might have to unburden himself with a bowel movement bigger, more significant, even more powerful than her own miniature torpedoes. She cries his name out again and keeps pounding, but all she hears is "I'm busy in here" or "Go away!" until one door actually opens. Accidentally. The guy inside who forgot to lock obviously has spare time between connecting flights. He looks up in horror from reading a copy of *Golf Digest* on the toilet and shouts, "Jesus fuck! There's a woman in here!"

Damn right there is! And Marsha feels even stronger now that she's opened the can of worms known as human sexuality. Lester is not any man. No, he's the one man who made her tell the truth. So what if he stole her money? Her mother stole her emotions, her husband stole her libido, her daughter stole her dignity, and Daryl stole her right to sexual refusal. But this guy stole her damaged psychological baggage and good riddance to it. He can have her old ID card, too—she's not that person anymore anyway! Marsha Sprinkle will never tell a lie again.

"You have big feet," Marsha comments to the lady security guard sitting on a chair by the exit. It takes a second, she's never heard *that* one before, but the TSA agent laughs out loud. "I do," she calls good-naturedly after Marsha, who's already on the down escalator. At the bottom, Marsha has a pang of nostalgia at seeing the usual chauffeurs with signs waiting for arriving clients, but not for long. There he is! Or at least she thinks it's him. She's pretty sure she caught a glimpse out the window of that dogcatcher jacket on the crosswalk headed toward the parking garage. The expensive one, like the lot she and Daryl used to park in. She breaks into a full run. It *is* him! ANIMAL CONTROL, it says in big scary letters on the back of his uniform. Lester is getting into his vehicle now, a rusty but extremely sturdy hotrod dog-catcher truck that looks like it's straight out of a 1950s cartoon. The confusing slogan UNLEASH IT OR LOSE IT is sloppily but aggressively painted on the side. As she gets nearer, she sees in smaller but neater print the name of a village that is miraculous to her eyes. PROVINCETOWN, MASSACHUSETTS. Of course, this mysterious dogcatcher would live in the same small resort town as her hated ex-husband! It's divine intervention. Thank you, Apollo. Thank you, glamorous God of the Truth.

"Hey!" she yells. "It's me from the plane and there's lots more to tell!" He guns the engine and peels out just as Marsha grabs onto the door handle and runs along the side of the truck. If she wants an erotic life away from lies, she's gonna have to work for it. "The whole truth, nothing but the truth," he orders lustily with a whistle through the space between his dentally challenged front teeth. "I stole your bag first," she wails in honesty, much to the bewilderment of a family they pass, loading their bags into the back of a station wagon. "The naked truth," he hisses through the moving truck's side window. "I want my husband dead," she hollers over the backfiring of his truck's souped-up chassis. Lester slams on the brakes. Whoa! Maybe he's met his match. A woman with a secret as morally perverse as his own that eventually must be shared. Can two damaged people become one? And if so, does that equal three? The time has come to find out. "Get in!" he barks in a dominant growl that melts the last icicle of Marsha's carnal denial. "Get in!" Those same words she said to Daryl, now finally someone is saying to her! She climbs right up, ready for her first adventure out of sexual isolation. "Marsha Sprinkle," she introduces herself, sliding into the shotgun seat with new unchaste courage. "Lester Barnhill," he answers, swerving his vehicle through the exit by the suicide knob on the steering wheel and pulling over in a no-stop zone. "I bite," he pants with burning urgency. They kiss like cobras. They're a team now. Look out, world, look out!

24

❖

On board the Peter Pan bus, Poppy and gang are lucky enough to have the whole back to themselves. Having been thrown off the train, especially on morals charges, was a definite detour on their mother-murder, family-reunion mission to Provincetown, but they dealt with it like the bouncy guerrillas they are. Two extremely tall gentlemen in the train station who identified themselves as members of the Boston Celtics had taken pity on the stranded upward-moving travelers, explaining the only way to get to Provincetown is on this low-rent bus they are now taking. Had Poppy been seeing things or did they both bounce a little when they mentioned that it was just a nine-minute walk to the station at One Peter Pan Way? Could they, too, be part of the movement? Daryl had been too afraid to ask for directions for fear Richard would pop out of his pants and proposition these nice men, but Campolina thought the address "was a hoot" and said so as she mini bounced in place. You know what? The basketballers hadn't shown the slightest homophobia. They just dribbled their bodies in place to match her movements and shouted out, "We are everywhere!" in full camaraderie.

And now Poppy's posse is on the way to Hyannis. No such thing as a direct bus, you have to change there to get to Provincetown, but at least this time they have tickets. Thanks again to another subculture of rebounders: punk rockers. Bouncing their way to the bus station, the tramps had been trying to be as inconspicuous as possible in a city not known for being that accepting of exercise extremists. And there they were, six new-wave weirdos in a crummy alley, Dead Boys music blaring from a taped-together boom box, celebrating the hatred of everybody in the world but themselves.

The obvious leader, whose name, Lupos, was tattooed over and over everywhere on his body that you could see, including his forehead, was pogo dancing with his girlfriend, who they later learned was called Stickerbush. She still clung to a blowsy Nancy Spungen slum goddess look yet she pulled it off and even managed to make it look contemporary. Maybe it was the scabs around her nose from huffing spray-paint fumes from the cans, which were now empty and littering the alley. Another one of them, who introduced himself as Jonesey, looked exactly like Stiv Bators if he had lived and aged poorly. He still had those Sex Pistols skinny legs, but his potbelly made it impossible to button the top of his Ramones-type jeans. No mosh pit for this guy. He's too fat to catch!

The other three, and God knows what their names were, looked over from actually burning a pile of money and grinned at the skyward movements of Poppy and her followers. Kindred spirits indeed. The Latino one, who kind of looked like a more butch version of Darby Crash, explained that they had stolen the cash from a gay bar that played techno music that got on their safety-pin nerves. Poppy, a lifelong pogo dancer without realizing it until now, started upward dancing with Vaulta and Leepa to show their musical adaptability. Being from a different generation, Adora hardly enjoyed this type of hit parade. She thought bands played in nightclubs, not garages, believed all pop songs should be at least three minutes in length, and assumed noise was something you complained about, not bought. Yet when in Providence, do as the Providencetonians do. She grabbed Surprize out of the bag, crouched down, and shook her senior-citizen ass just to show her support. Surprize gave an uncannily accurate Sid Vicious sneer and joined in the sideways shimmying. The other punk girl, the one sporting a Rite Aid–dyed blue mohawk badly in need of a trim, leapt up after setting another wad of bills on fire. Springboard Sam and Double Back Barbara cheered her on as she broke into a slam dancing, pogo-sideways move and rammed herself right into her hardcore buddies, giving them a preview of an anarchistic choreography that didn't even have a name yet. Surprize barked bitchily and hissed her approval like the true punk-rock pussy she has always been.

Mohawk's girlfriend, whose tongue featured so many piercings that not one word out of her mouth was comprehensible to the human ear, joined in and the hybrid punk-twerk dance party began to build to a frenzy. Campolina, Springboard Sam, and Double Back Barbara proved their whole-lot-of-shaking politics could translate to this freakazoid shindig and started gyrating, too, but not Daryl. No shaking for him when he saw that Latino one squatting and thrusting right in front of him, about to burn the last big bundle of "filthy capitalistic cash." Nosirree, not when Richard might start shaking back in his pants, falsely signaling some sort of secret homosexual mating call to this punk-rock radical who certainly didn't *look* gay, but these days who can tell, right? It's the United Nation of Cocksuckers out there and there's not much you can do about it.

Twisted Billy was so proud of himself. After two body tours of the alphabet, both upper- and lowercase, he had finally managed to hold himself in the human position of the dancing dollar sign but none of these punks seemed to understand. Did they think he was an "S"? Couldn't they see his one arm twisted vertically to complete the symbol of what they needed? Duh! Cold hard cash! He can shake sideways and still think at the same time, why couldn't they?

But guess who came to the rescue? As the leaping, twitching, shaking, grinding, hopping dance disturbance reached a finale, Richard burst out of Daryl's pants and snatched with the hole in the top of his head the last bundle of wrapped cash before it could be incinerated. Never mind the bollocks indeed.

And now they're on a bus, with nine paid-for one-way tickets costing them $270 total, right in Poppy's pocket. Richard can still be a hidden package and Surprise, well, she has learned to stow away with stealth and cunning. As the almost-empty bus speeds up I-95 North through Fall River, the birthplace of Lizzie Borden, Poppy feels a spiritual bond with what she did and would like to give her *own* mother the same forty whacks and her father forty hugs. She yearns for the rewards of revenge, the closure she knows the embracement of her father and the murder of her mother will provide. But sometimes the pain, the damage, the dysfunction of maternal mayhem that mutates inside her is just more than she can bear.

"Thieving hussy!" yells Vaulta, seeing her leader's pain on her way up in a tricky leap that leaves room for her to turn her head sideways and avoid contact with this outdated bus's ceiling. "Motion bigot!" chimes in Leepa, landing with a loud boom as they cross the Bourne Bridge onto Cape Cod. "Let's keep it down in here," yells the white bus driver, surprised at any onboard trouble in these off-season months. Twisted Billy is poetry in motion as he repeatedly dances up and down the aisle through the letters L-I-A-R in sinuous left-to-right contortions that momentarily appease the venom pulsating in Poppy's vibrating victim-veins. But as the bus nears the Hyannis exit, the fellow travelers don't seem one bit impressed by his antics. "What's your problem?" calls out a smartass hipster dude with an I-just-kidnapped-Elizabeth-Smart-type beard. "Yeah, sit down, fool," grumbles a grouchy-looking woman wearing an I GOT ISSUES sweatshirt before moving to a seat farther in the front. But when Poppy lets out a sudden new howl of mom-ophobic fury, these two idiots freeze in place and dare not open their fucking mouths again.

25

❖

Inside the dogcatcher truck, Marsha continues her rant, unable to lie, gushing out the truth like a polluted river that now runs over the top of a dam after years of debris being trapped and stagnating. "I met my husband in college," she confesses as they cross over to Cape Cod's Route 6. "More personal," growls Lester as he pulls his truck ahead past a car with a dog hanging its head out the window in the breeze. Lester's very presence in the next lane drives this animal crazy. It starts howling, trying to climb out the window of its owner's car to leap onto Lester's truck like a prisoner hoping to be saved by the very man who would be his captor. The panicked family lunges to hold their dog inside their vehicle as Lester speeds ahead, hearing the dog's wail of sorrow fading in the rush of traffic over Marsha's orgy of truth telling.

"He seemed like a decent guy," Marsha confides, feeling a new warmth spreading between her thighs. "But then? But then?" Lester barks out with a sexy aggression as he speeds ahead, and then howls in the wind to show Marsha his excitement at her rebirth. "He never tried to paw my breasts or invade my vagina," Marsha admits as her breathing speeds up and her heart rate soars. "Let it out," Lester orders as he bangs the steering wheel in erotic rhythm. "On my wedding night I learned his secret," Marsha unburdens herself with a truth that could pass any lie detector test. Lester yowls like a hound dog in encouragement but then looks over and sees that damn car again with the family still holding their dog in by its hind legs as it attempts to jump from their vehicle to his. He understands. But not now. Marsha doesn't get it yet. Let her become a sexual being for the first time and then maybe he'll tell her *his* truth . . . the canine secret.

He reaches into his bag and grabs the special electric dog whistle he went all the way to New York to buy that emits an ultrasonic vibration only chosen dogs can hear. Good. It works. One blow and the cur instantly is neutralized, convulsing and twitching in helplessness. It's OK. It only hurts for a little while. Lester will be back for that dog. He'll show it the way.

The dog's owners freak. Their swerving vehicle merging erratically onto Route 6A at the Hyannis rotary gives Marsha the nerve to continue her tale of marital trauma, the erotic courage to let it all hang out. Lester is breathing heavily himself now, lusting for more of Marsha's inner secrets. She turns to him and shows her hand. "I married a rimmer," she announces unashamedly, finally free of the humiliation, sorrow, and pain that keeping this covert information brought her through the years. "A what?" Lester asks, trying to still keep his eyes on the road, yet feeling a prurient jolt at this new confession. "An anal-oral fanatic," Marsha explains as clinically as possible, still holding her head high. Now he knows. Finally, one person can understand the full horror of what it was like to be part of this so-called "holy matrimony."

"Use that pain," snarls Lester gently, daring to lead this onetime sex-hating liar, now erotically recharged truth-teller, to the next level of reborn ardor. "That's all he wanted to do," she cries, "day in and day out!" "Own the disgust, take charge of the damage," Lester yelps, leaning closer, scratching her face just right with his untrimmed stubble, letting her smell his breath that had a hint of Good and Plenty licorice mixed with the chemical fragrance of novocaine, yet could still work as an aphrodisiac. "No interest in my natural gateway ever!" she laments, the naked truth making her feel like a functional woman for the first time.

Lester licks his right index finger while he steers with his left hand and gently inserts the tip into Marsha's ear canal. Even noticing the little bit of grime under his nail, she doesn't mind one bit. In fact, it's the first penetration of a body part other than her mouth she's ever welcomed. "What did I know?" she sobs. "I thought anilingus was what was *supposed* to happen on your wedding night. I just lay there facedown, confused, and filled with disgust while he licked and slurped. This was love? This was what inspired all those romance novels I refused to read as a teenager?" she wails in anguish.

Lester floors the accelerator and starts whimpering like a puppy, twirling his finger inside her ear in auricular stimulation, pushing her to reveal more. "My hymen was untouched," she cries through the confusion of aural arousal, "but I got pregnant anyway!" Lester lets out a wolf howl as he passes by the ENTERING DENNIS sign on Route 6A to Provincetown. He knows that Dennis is a town, not a person, but he hopes

Marsha didn't since she is being entered for the first time herself. He continues plunging his digit deeper into her ear canal in a sensorial erotic probe and no questions about Cape Cod geography are brought up. Marsha doesn't care *where* she is, she just has to tell the truth.

"While mouth-to-anus sex was taking place on me, my so-called husband manipulated himself and his filthy sperm was ejaculated," she remembers traumatically, and in more detail than any sex therapist would need to know, yet somehow her psychological pain is lessened by Lester increasing and decreasing the vibrations of her vagus nerve receptor toward her brain. "No more stress," he snarls soothingly before yapping like a cuddly little pup. Is he now a dog or a person, Marsha wonders. "Dog Star Man," he whispers abstractly in a half-human, half-canine sounding voice, and even though she has no idea what he means, it sounds like a love poem to her, which gives her the courage to proceed.

"One little drop of his seed accidentally came into contact with my labia and snuck its way into my reproductive organs," Marsha whispers, torn between the pleasures of ear eroticism and the horrors of her marital past. "Bow, wow, wow," whispers Lester sexually in a human-type voice as he plunges his finger deeper and deeper into her ear-well of loneliness. "I got knocked up by swimmer semen," she moans in newfound intimacy. "Grrrr," growls Lester as he reaches over to bite Marsha's lobe, running off the highway for a split second before using his other hand, still on the wheel, to skid back in the lane. Plunging as deeply as he dares on a virgin-ear deflowering does the trick. Marsha goes into full eargasm as Lester deftly deposits his own identification card into her bra without her even feeling it. They are now one and the same. He should call her "Lesta." She could call him "Marsher."

They're each other forever now. "I had never had sex," she shouts out truthfully with the sudden power of two people mixed, revealing the roots of her erotic disorders in one final explosion of sexual anger. "Yet a rimmer child was growing inside me," she continues courageously, "and her name? Yes, her name was Poppy."

26

◈

Poppy and her bi-movement, bi-generational grandmother have entered Massachusetts like the real Pilgrim family they are. "Final stop, Hyannis," the driver calls out before opening the hissing front door that announces the arrival of this oddball gang of nervous, can't-sit-still travelers and the other few passengers, who now hate them. First off, the tree-hugger dude and the Valerie Solanas wannabe who seem to have suddenly hooked up, which surprises Poppy, who thought their possibly conflicting unforgiving politics might mute any sexual attraction between the two.

Next off, Daryl, shaking as little as possible to avoid the male gaze and ignoring Richard's unconvincing plea from down below to use the restroom. "You'll have to hold it," Daryl responds firmly, feeling a pit stop is just a ruse from Richard for more gay-on-gay cruising. Vaulta and Leepa bounce their way down the bus steps and spring across the asphalt lot toward the terminal. Campolina injures herself slightly shaking her way through the narrow bus door flamboyantly but recovers quickly, her tendency to bruise long conquered. Springboard Sam and Double Back Barbara hop and shake their way into the station, harmonizing a real barn-burner remake of Peggy Lee's "Old Cape Cod," which even the bus driver, still on board, can hear and finds entertaining. Twisted Billy brings up the rear, but as he attempts to exit, bolstering local pride in the human form of the letter "H" for "Hyannis" (which is almost impossible, go ahead and try it!), he trips and falls down the steps. You'd think this would stop him, but it doesn't. He hits the ground and starts rolling. And rolling. Oh my God, it's better than bouncing. More energy than shaking. Billy's rolling as fast as he can now, and he may never rise to his feet again.

Inside the terminal, it's drab no matter what time of year it is. They don't call it "Hi-Anus" for nothing. Only one employee actually works behind the counter, and he greets his customers with a weary superiority. "All passengers should proceed to Bay B to board for Provincetown," he announces over the loudspeaker in a thick New England accent even though no words he's saying end in an "r" for him to drop. Why on earth, Poppy wonders, would there be thirty or forty other people going to the tip of Cape Cod in the middle of fall? Springboard Sam and Double Back Barbara see a few other African Americans getting up to board, but they don't even make eye contact in return. Campolina notices gay men boarding, and though there's no surprise they're going to Provincetown, even the one in drag wearing some tacky tiara with the letter "R" on it turns up her nose when Campolina shakes amiably and waves. What's the "R" stand for—"rude"?

"It's like we don't even exist," Vaulta whispers to Poppy as they eye these mysterious fellow travelers and hop to the end of the boarding line to absolutely no notice. "See? Nada!" Poppy marvels, jumping higher just to prove her point. Leepa sees no other heavy people and can't imagine why, it's a gay town. No "bears"? No hairy big men growling in good-natured lust? And why are so many of them wearing that dreary shade of meatball brown?

Daryl gets in line with Richard but none of these new passengers could give two hoots about the constant quivering they must keep up to maintain their spiritual energy. What's the matter with these idiots? Outsiders usually support one another. Do they think they're somehow *better* than bouncers and shakers? All they do is flick their tongues to each other in some sort of coded greeting. What's that bullshit? Freaks! That's what they are, Richard and Daryl decide. Finally, they agree on something.

Even as Twisted Billy, in full contortion mode, comes rolling through the terminal door and across the floor, this covert sect doesn't react. Poppy is at first surprised but then amazed at seeing Billy's new blissful motor skill. Every difficult rotation brings fresh enchantment to Billy's face, and Leepa and Vaulta understand. Billy had now surpassed all of them in forward-thinking energy and, while rolling may not be for all of Poppy's followers, they can respect his new mobile coordination that, while hardly subtle, could possibly open the doors of perception to a revolutionary circular inner peace in others.

OK, they're boarding. The driver doesn't even bat an eye as Poppy and gang hop and shake their way on board. Once in her seat, Adora is relieved she doesn't have to hide her quivering now that she's harnessed its power, but why don't these new idiots rise to the bait of Surprize's catlike behavior? She's grown used to the controversy of her companion animal's extreme makeover. It's kind of fun to witness the public shock. Can't they see Surprize is the only pet who could win both the cat *and* the dog show? And why did that goddamn woman just flick her tongue at her? Speak up if you have a message!

The Peter Pan driver even puts down the mechanical ramp so Billy can get a start from the terminal and roll up and onto the bus. Most passengers could never get down the aisle of a commercial motor coach while rotating, but Billy's spiral skills allow him to curl his body and reach the empty seat saved for him by Springboard Sam. He picks Billy up and plops him right down next to one of these enigmatic fellow travelers who doesn't seem one bit perplexed at Billy's nontraditional entrance. Nope, not a word.

Once back on the road, nobody on the bus is singing "One Hundred Bottles of Beer on the Wall" either. These other cultists are moving their tongues even faster, up and down, side to side, just the way Poppy and her posse are doing with their bodies. Poppy tries not to judge. Live and let live. Suddenly these mysterious crusaders start rubbing their lips downward while eerily mumbling to produce an obscene sound that is part gibberish, part mating call and totally incomprehensible to outsiders' ears. Campolina has heard of speaking in tongues but this goes beyond that. Is there some hidden message she's missing out on? Even Twisted Billy is stumped on what letter they sound like, but that doesn't stop him from twisting his body into an abstract shape that he hopes shows affinity to their cause, whatever that could possibly be. If he expects the outside world to understand his new "rolling" obsession, he should certainly be open to the peculiarities of other self-help movements. But is their oral-bubbling lip-smacking sexual or spiritual in nature?

"Four on the floor," someone from the back starts chanting. Poppy turns around, and hey, isn't that the same white Earth First–type guy from the other bus? It is! And that same dreary gal is with him yelling it, too! *They're* part of this cult with no name? Now they're *all* yelling "Four on the floor." Why? Why? Can't she just bounce her way to Provincetown to kill her mother in peace?

27

In the luster of sexual awakening, Marsha is calmer, so filled with the mental benefits of training-wheel penetration that she doesn't even notice the Pilgrim Monument in the distance as they round the corner of Route 6 in Truro and see beautiful Provincetown laid out before them. "I wanted to get an abortion," she explains in a strong, confident, no-longer-ashamed voice, "but where? Where? The only back-alley quack I had heard about in our shabby apartment complex had been busted for charging a fifteen-year-old unwed mother one hundred dollars and telling her to swallow gunpowder." Lester lets out a low-pitched puppy moan and pulls out a can of Halt! dog repellent from under his seat. "I had read in the local library," Marsha continues, "that in the olden days Egyptian woman ate crocodile feces to cause miscarriages, but where was I supposed to get crocodile feces in Dutch Village?" Lester huffs a few blasts of the animal repellent and offers her some. She politely declines his magic vapors and resumes her pro-choice tale of woe as he turns off the highway at Stotts Crossing, the fumes invading his libido with hot canine deterrent.

"Sure, there was the Reptile House at the Baltimore Zoo," she reasons, daring to caress Lester's chiseled chin softly for the first time, "but you couldn't just reach into a pit and grab a gator turd, could you?" Lester may be buzzed from the scorching extracts of pepper fumes tearing through his clean, trimmed nostrils, but he spots the dog first. The very same dog they saw earlier on the highway that practically leapt from its owner's moving vehicle into Lester's truck. Right there, still leashed, struggling to escape its masters, who are moving their bags and beach supplies into one of those Monopoly-style cottages that are all in a row on Route 6A before you get into Provincetown.

Lester swerves his truck over and just as his blood vessels peak in dilation, giving him the ultimate canine-human head rush, he shoots a liquid stream of Halt! right into the dad's eyes. The mother goes crazy, shouting something about cruelty to animals, and the children try to restrain the dog, who's again in a frenzy. Dad is staggering blindly, rubbing his eyes, and almost gets hit by a passing car. Now's the dog's chance. It charges with all its might, jumps up on a picnic table, and propels itself through the air into the open passenger-side window of Lester's truck, landing in Marsha's lap, then freezes. "Some of them just know," Lester explains. Marsha is so stunned to have an actual dog in her lap that all she can do is mumble, "Good boy." She's not sure who she means. Lester? The dog? Both of them?

Lester peels out and speeds by what used to be the old

Holiday Inn. Then he spots an unleashed cocker spaniel wearing some kind of "pussyhat," barking its head off at its female owners, who think their pet's rage is political like theirs. Lester takes out an animal tranquilizer gun and fires the dart right into the dog's supposedly empowered ass. The couple shouts Gays Against Guns slogans before breaking down in sobs over this attempted "pet murder" in what has been called the "dog-friendliest town in America." Lester pulls over, ignores their theatrics, scoops up the dog's unconscious body like the professional he is, gently tosses it in the back of the truck, gets back in, and pulls off. "Some of the other dogs can't comprehend yet," he explains to Marsha. "I have to show them the proper way." Marsha looks down at the "rescued" dog in her lap and identifies. She, too, must learn Lester's truth.

As he turns a hard right onto a dirt road next to a two-car garage with a misguided imitation of Warhol's *Marilyn* painted on its double doors, Marsha continues her saga of labor lunacy. "I gave birth to the mutant daughter of a cum-rag rimmer," she announces for all nature to hear. Instantaneously the other angry dogs, who have seemingly converted to the pack mentality of alpha Lester, run out of the woods, howling a welcome to their arriving Pied Piper. "It was a humiliating, repulsive event," Marsha bellows as the crazed canines begin running alongside the truck, and even her new lapdog joins in the chorus of hellhounds. It feels like the dogs are actually on Marsha's side. For the first time ever.

Lester lets out his own low-pitched dog moan that can only mean her storytelling must continue. "Poppy ripped me open when I was still technically a virgin and no man, except you today, has ever been allowed back inside," she admits with a sexual honesty that drives Lester crazy with unneutered lust. The winds of her truth combined with the fresh breeze of Lester's acceptance howl through the nearby dunes and form tiny tornadoes of rebellion, which alert other angry dogs that it is safe to rise up and join their cause. Marsha looks up and sees Lester's "doghouse." His compound of K9 retribution. The castle-kennel of mongrel behavioral modification. Lester Barnhill is king and she, Marsha Sprinkle, will become his rightful queen.

Lester swerves his dogcatching truck to a screeching stop and immediately, awaiting irate tourists jump out of their vehicles yelling accusations of petnapping and illegal confinement, but he pays them no mind. Who're they gonna call? He *is* the authority when it comes to animal control in this town, and many of the townies fear the power Lester has over their own onetime obedient pets and have learned to keep their traps shut. Besides, Provincetown has always been a radical place. Revolutionary ideas breed here.

He flips a remote and the formidable razor-wire gate to the villa of dog-deprogramming swings open. It is a ramshackle château-reformatory made of rotting lumber, discarded carpeting, corroded steel caging, and torn-down roofing rescued from the town dump before it got all highfalutin. The dogs inside start howling in born-again revolt, but their owners misunderstand and believe they are crying out to be rescued. "You stole my dog, cocksucker!" a furious man yells in front of his crybaby children. "Max *was* on a leash!" a woman begs with a tear-streamed face. "I want my puppy back," shouts a teenager in a Dolphin Fleet Whale Watch sweatshirt as he shoots a rock from a slingshot toward Lester, just missing him. The dog in Marsha's lap has heard the cries of insurrection inside and is eager to join the uprising. He springs to action through the open truck window, charges the idiot who dared to fire the missile, and bites him hard on the hand.

"Oh, you'll get your dogs back all right," shouts Lester as the pussyhat couple speed up in their truck, jump out, and start yelling something about "male aggression" and "animal sensitivity." The now-coming-to cocker spaniel must hear its owners' female rants because just as Lester opens the truck's door to grab Marsha's hand and lead her inside, the suddenly vengeful dog leaps from the back, jumps to the ground, struggles instantly to rip off its pussyhat, and charges its owners with a ferocity they've never witnessed. How dare these women force her to wear millinery? The two so-called animal lovers jump back in their vehicle and lock their doors in fear as their dog jumps up on the hood and snaps off the windshield wipers with her newly empowered paws.

Once inside his dog reeducation camp, Lester gives Marsha a tour. "Here you go," he whispers to an especially angry basset hound inside a cage in the front hall as he holds up a photo of the pet's owners outside and activates the electric shock transmitter around its neck. The dog howls in masochistic pleasure and lunges toward the picture of his so-called guardians, practicing his future attack.

Marsha looks around in awe at the wall-to-wall animal holding cells lining the living room, made from invisible fencing that zaps these former pets, now soldiers in training, every time they try to run toward photographs of their previous homes, which Lester had printed out from Google Maps. She's impressed. These dogs are learning. Lester has harnessed their natural pack mentality and turned their past obedience into righteous revenge. She likes these angry creatures. Maybe one of them will bite off her ex's tool of penetration!

"I was raised as a dog," Lester suddenly blurts out to Marsha, telling *his* truth now and begging with hound-dog eyes for her to understand. "Why? Why?" he shouts to the heavens above. "I'll tell you why! My parents thought animals were cheaper to raise than babies," he remembers in never-ending resentment, somehow maintaining his masculine composure while still showing a sexy vulnerability.

Marsha gapes at a mongrel in another cage angrily shredding its own collar while strobing lights program him and disorienting sounds of distorted "pet" talk babbled by his supposed human "mommy and daddy" pound in his ear drums. Teaching an animal to view its owner as its enemy is the way Mother Nature intended, Marsha realizes, more enlightened as each second with Lester passes. Yes. Control must be recaptured by the canines and used for human retribution. Maybe life *is* fair?

"I had to eat dog food as a child," Lester bitterly confesses as he opens a minifridge, takes out a juicy bone, and gnaws off a hunk of raw beef gristle. "What did I know? Purina tasted good to me," he wails before politely offering Marsha a bite. For the first time she feels an urge for more solid food. She knows a dog biscuit would be the closest thing to a cracker he might have on hand, but it's no longer enough. She grabs the bone from his hand and bravely nibbles off a hunk of marrow. It tastes hearty and vigorous, and chewing it up is suddenly sexual. The beginning of a new kind of digestion energizes her body. Had she missed out on the most primal thrill of all? One that both dogs and humans have experienced forever? The breaking down of food into smaller and smaller components and then releasing it? Can Marsha actually defecate now without shame? No more pellets. It's time to fire off a fudge dragon. Maybe she and Lester can do it together?

"I was crated," Lester howls to Marsha like the top dog he is here today. "Crated!" he repeats in a lower-pitched growl that again makes Marsha stir in her happy hunting ground. "And I still am!" he snarls as he leads her into his bedroom. Marsha is at first terrified of the ferocious three dogs that await Lester in his crate-like sleeping quarters. Their eyes are afire with contempt, the only dogs left allowed to have a master. The supreme one. Lester himself. Dare she pet one? "Go ahead," he growls, reading her mind, "the Labrador retriever's name is Baxter." Marsha reaches her hand out and the dog doesn't flinch. She touches his fur. It feels rough but somehow right. And a certain moisture begins flowing through her private parts.

"My father claimed he could speak in a special dialect that was part baby talk, part growling that dogs could actually understand," he explains in an odd new accent, taking off his jacket to reveal strong arms and a *Doberman Gang* movie promotional T-shirt. "I can speak that language today," he boasts as he whispers in her ear nonsensical syllables mixed with guttural yelps. The three guard dogs bark back. "That means they agree," he sensually murmurs in a human voice as he slips off her blouse, and she melts into what's next—bra-removal-arousal. What's this falling to the floor? His driver's license? His very being being smuggled into hers? Dare she allow this fusion? Yes! Second base! Hot diggity dog diggity. Her nipples sassily twitch all on their own, signaling she's finally willing to become one with Lester without fear.

He turns to the large boxer named Travis and speaks another guttural sentence mixed with gurgling and yelping. The dog's eyes light up like that one in *Village of the Damned* and he howls back what sounds like a terrifying reply. "I asked him if he is ready to take my final orders," Lester translates as Marsha slips out of her skirt. "He answered 'grr-woof, grr-woof'—that means 'onward' in Dogese," he explains as his breathing, both human and canine, rapidly becomes a pant. Turning to Draco, the white bull terrier who waits for Lester's deadliest commands, he asks in both languages, "Will you bring us revenge?" The volume of the snarl, the ferocity of the animal's growl is so staggering that Marsha doesn't need further translation. It's the final battle!

"I learned to be a bad dog," Lester growls in half dog, half human English as he strips off his uniform pants to reveal a slender waist, surprisingly muscular thighs, and a bulge inside his worn but seemingly freshly laundered plain white boxer shorts. Marsha is in the presence of a penis and, for the first time, she welcomes such a member. Finally a man faces her from the front like she's a real woman, not from behind like that ex-husband of hers, who was a bad dog, too, but the wrong kind. "Woof-yip-yep, ruff-ruff," she hesitantly answers Lester, hoping he will translate for the dogs if they can't understand her first attempts at this crossover language. But they *do* understand. So does Lester. "Heel!" in either language is no longer a dog command; it is a secret word that signals sexual consent, and they all howl it out with a bilingual savagery.

"First I chewed up my father's slipper," Lester bow-wows in a heavily accented canine voice as he boldly thrusts his rather wide human appendage up and down her panty-covered pudendum, exploring new territories of anti-doggy-style sexual positioning. "Yes, up front," Marsha moans, mentally erasing her ex-husband's rear-entry. "I bit the hand that fed me," he growls in full Dogese, and yes, Marsha, now humanly aroused, can translate into English all by herself, thank you very much. "Down boy," she continues in their secret language, and Lester obeys, pulling off her panties with sharp nibbling teeth as the three guard dogs begin howling and panting, proud their kennel-commander can enter a bitch—and they mean this term in a respectful animal-world way—with a hard penis, unlike themselves, who must wait for theirs to expand once inside the female. "Mount me," Marsha says twice, once in each tongue, happy to be in control again. But this time it's different. She's a power bottom now and it feels fucking great!

Caressing, probing, and aiming properly, Lester pushes his bad-dog penis between her legs and it's not the home invasion she always feared. He's in the doghouse now! In front of her so she can see what's going on! Not behind her in a place so dirty it required cleaning up to three times a day. "We were both abused," Lester whispers, still inside her, staying in lane, accelerating and braking at a steady speed. In. Out. Not like that burger place in L.A., but like a souped-up piston that grinds to perfection. She's the master. He's the johnson. And together they redefine human sexual response.

Marsha lets out a dog yowl so authentic that Lester joins in and so do the three guard dogs. Thrashing in pleasure, Lester continues to thrust and bark like the animal she's now glad he's become. The other dogs in the house start howling, too, in savage celebration, building along with Marsha and Lester as they pant their way to sexual unity. Just before Lester is ready to detonate inside her, he reaches up and pushes a nearby button and all the cages in the rest of his doghouse electronically fly open. Baxter, Travis, and Draco stampede out, wildly excited that the time has finally come for them to be leaders of the pack! The other reeducated dogs bound from their cages, baring their fangs, eager for the blood of their onetime masters. There are no safe words to halt what is about to come. Dog Armageddon.

As Marsha hears the first screams outside, she explodes in dogasmic spasms of euphoria. So, this is what it feels like to be alive! The warrior goddess of hate has finally found love. Part dog, part human, they are now united in truth.

28

As the bus crosses Standish Street at the corner of Province-town's main drag, Commercial Street, Poppy looks out the window amazed to see the town is quite crowded. Packed, considering it is off-season. Tourists up and down the side-walks like it's summer despite the nip in the air. The other passengers on board seem excited, jumping up to look out both sides of the bus's windows, some even calling out the names of people they recognize. Then Poppy sees it, the banner stretched all the way across the street announcing ANILINGUS FESTIVAL NOV. 20–22. She gulps and starts bounc-ing in her seat instinctively, the way she always does when she feels stress. Adora looks over to her granddaughter in confusion when she sees a placard reading I'M A RIMMER. Before Poppy can think of a polite way to explain, Daryl pipes in, "It means licking assholes!" Richard pokes his head out, intrigued, but Daryl shoves him back into his pants with a protection that's almost paternal.

There's no real bus station in Provincetown, the route just ends at the public restrooms beyond Commercial Street near the entrance to MacMillan Pier. It is the very center of town; clam roll stands, foot-long hot dogs, T-shirt shops, even a traffic cop who seems to be welcoming the anilingus pilgrims flooding into town as if he's one of them. Vaulta and Leepa are liberals of course. Any minority movement is A-OK with them, but they are rendered speechless when a rimmer crusader happily chants, "Eating ass is a gas!" as the bus pulls to a stop. Leepa tries to understand any diversity but worries her shaking derriere may send out the wrong signals to this crowd. Vaulta, well, she's no prude, but at her height, this sexual act is both impractical and out of reach for many, especially while bouncing. Campolina is perhaps the most familiar with the act of rimming. She's at least tried it but soon realized messing up her lipstick just wasn't worth the effort.

"Booty call! Booty call!" yell those hippy-dippy radicals from Providence as they push their way off the bus past Springboard Sam and Double Back Barbara, who hate to be racial profilers but must admit to each other that African Americans have never been at the forefront of rimming activism. Adora thinks she has seen it all but when that man with those weird blisters on his lips whispers, "It's not foreplay, it's a stand-alone act," she fears this is beyond her newly expanded comfort zone and holds Surprize's ears so she doesn't have to overhear such a salty debate.

Billy? Well, if he *wanted* to, he could lick his own asshole, but now he just waits his turn getting off the bus behind that pitiful beauty queen with the "R" crown. Guess he knows what that stands for now! She's Queen of the Rimmers and she actually has subjects waiting to honor her. After her red-carpet-like exit, he gives himself a little aisle space, hurls himself forward, topples down the steps, and lands rolling at the feet of a uniformed nurse who offers "complimentary gamma globulin shots" to all rimmers. He declines politely.

Live and let live, thinks Poppy as her feet touch the ground of the promised land of international anilingus. She looks up to see a whole family wearing I EAT ASS sweatshirts. OK, it's extreme, but the children are teenagers and, with proper parental guidance, old enough to make their own decisions. Vaulta, Leepa, and Campolina have already been welcomed by a rimmer glee club from Plymouth identified as such by the badges they wear proudly pinned to their clothing. And finally, Springboard Sam and Double Back Barbara see another African American couple who obviously have taken the oral-anal plunge. Even Daryl is allowing Richard to feel the love outside his pants coming from the ass cult. Could Daryl rim Marsha? It's a question he must now ask himself.

But what's with Billy and all this rolling, Poppy wonders. He's always been ahead of the curve on stimulation through advanced body movement, so she'd better pay attention to this new relaxation technique. As they pass a packed bakery advertising "Donut Holes" on the way back to Commercial Street, Vaulta and Leepa give somersaults a try, but hey, it hurts. "It *is* a lot of trouble, but it's worth it," Billy cries before calling out to them to try rolling horizontally. As rimmers good-naturedly jump out of the way of these human newly rolling logs, Campolina considers the move from shaking to rolling. Can you roll in a ladylike way, she wonders, hesitating. "Three hundred and sixty degrees!" yells

Billy as they turn the corner to Commercial Street, where some sort of Rimmer Pride Parade is about to begin. What the hell, thinks Campolina as she feels the anal-based cultists' budding joy swelling around her. It's a new world out there. She throws herself down and begins rolling gracefully along with Vaulta and Leepa through the marchers, who move aside in confused acceptance.

"Aim and your trunk will follow," Billy bellows to Springboard Sam and Double Back Barbara, who are shaking and bouncing their way past a club advertising "Rimmer Bingo!" OK, they're game. They hold hands and together hurl themselves to the asphalt, rolling up the parade route lengthwise like a hastily added float. Rimmers cheer them on, thinking their body contortions are all part of the circular tributes of the anal-oriented festivities.

"Heteros do it, too!" yells out a couple of jock-type ass kissers, and Daryl feels relief. See? Not all rimmers are queer. He's so turned on thinking of Marsha's heterosexual behind that he throws himself down and starts rolling, too. Maybe this will crack some sense into Richard's gay head. At each rotation, Richard is getting squished, trapped inside Daryl's hot, tight, itchy underpants, and gravel is chafing his hole. What the fuck? Who wants to roll when you can rim? Let me in! Open up! Wee-ooh, ooh-wee-ooh!

Adora feels a little old to even consider licking butt, but she must admit the Rimmer Folk Dancing Classes held "free of charge" in front of Town Hall are a nice touch. And the "Children of Rimmers" participating in curbside face-painting sessions where they are made up to be happy anuses—well, they're beyond adorable. But rolling? She's got knee issues. She'll have to sit this one out.

A whole group of "Parents of Rimmers" marching with

their anal-oral offspring part like the Red Sea in welcome as all Poppy's cronies roll through them, politely shouting "On your left" and "On your right" for safety, but will Poppy join them? Be the last man bouncing, so to speak? Passing the Unitarian Meeting House with a sermon board out front announcing RIMMING AND THE SCRIPTURES . . . YOU BE THE JUDGE, she can see her rollers' new elevation of bliss, each turn bringing serenity and then the strength to reinvent themselves, just as the rimmers have. Is it not divine intervention? A celestial sign that it is time to move on to rolling? OK, she's game. She takes aim, runs, hits the ground rolling, and rolls and rolls and rolls. It's hard. It's painful, but my God—enlightenment. May she never come to a stop!

29

Dog owners are still screaming in panic as their former pets maul them out front of Lester's doghouse headquarters. Some angry, indoctrinated mongrels have already escaped into town leaving their stunned, bleeding jailers in shock, foolishly calling out the ridiculous "pet" names that these animals will never answer to again. The days of anybody giving them orders have come to an end. "Sit"? Fuck you! No human command will halt this canine insurrection, that's for sure.

Lester takes Marsha's hand, and they walk out into this new world and see firsthand the carnage his reeducation of dogs has ignited. Marsha, like all converts, is filled with zeal, and she accepts the fact that violence such as this is in order if the dramatic truth between master and man's best friend is ever to be exposed. "Maybe dog owners will now take responsibility," Lester barks with authority. "Leash laws!" he scoffs. "Put *them* on a leash and see how they like it! Dog parks? Ha! Did anybody ask the canines if they'd like to go there? And do what? Pose for selfies with two-legged freaks? Climb over man-made obstacle courses that even the worst miniature golf course down Cape would reject? Walk in germ-filled stagnant 'splash pools' and call it 'swimming'? Dogs want to bury their own shit," he continues ranting, "not have human beings pick it up! There's even a rule in dog parks. NO DIGGING, the sign reads. Dig it!" he half growls, half shouts. "That's what dogs do! Dig! Dig! Dig! And today they're gonna bury you!"

Marsha, footloose and freshly fornicated, feels like biting somebody herself. She's no longer paranoid about police presence or her silly fugitive status. With pets attacking their owners, the authorities won't give a shit about a few missing suitcases. Besides, she's fucking the authorities now, so la-di-da! And if that daughter of hers and her freaky followers or that disgruntled employee with his dummy dick catch up with her, well, Lester and she will sic Baxter, Travis, and Draco on them!

Lester opens the truck's door for Marsha, takes out that same tranquilizer gun, and shoots a dart right into an irate pet owner who has somehow managed to get his own attacking dog in a chokehold. The so-called animal lover flies back in stunned paralysis as his dog, hardly a "companion" one anymore, bites off a piece of his ear.

Marsha, standing proudly on her own two hind legs, sees a younger woman wearing a BOW WOW BASH charity T-shirt wrestling with her suddenly vicious lapdog. "I bet you dressed your dog up for Halloween!" she yells accusingly. "I did!" the abuser yells back defensively, horrified to be fighting off her "good dog" who used to be so cuddly. "She was Kesha and she looked really cute!" she adds defiantly as she rolls over on her pet, trying to stop the attack. Just remembering this humiliation is the final straw. Her dog chews her face like a rubber toy. Can dogs laugh? Marsha's not certain, but it sure sounded like this one was. Lester howls back his dogged approval and finally Marsha is ready for the last truth. "My husband's name is Kent Samuels," she seethes in perfect English, "and he's the Town Crier."

He's also King of the Rimmers. And guess what? Kent Samuels is leading the Anilingus Pride Parade. "Hear ye! Hear ye!" he bellows, ringing the damn bell and dressed to the nines in that ridiculous pilgrim outfit he even wears off-duty. "Provincetown welcomes the international rimming community *and* their families!" he continues, beaming at the wild cheers from male and female, gay, straight, and trans anal enthusiasts of all ages, creeds, and colors.

As Marsha Sprinkle joins the parade route with Lester, she freezes in her tracks when she sees her ex-husband. "There he is," she seethes, "the anal-oral intruder who dares to live openly rimming without shame." Lester stares in revulsion. Yes, his three dogs, the only ones still allowed to obey a human command, could be the emasculators. But where are they? He sees bitten and mauled owners being treated by medics, but his elite canine protectors have suddenly vanished.

Marsha feels something below her knees pushing through the crowd. Is it Baxter, Travis, or Draco coming to rip apart her ex? No, it's her daughter! My God! Rolling on the ground. Has she finally lost her last marble? There's what's-her-name. Leepa! Rotating through the crowd like a runaway roll of paper towels. Lester sees them, too. He tries to step on Vaulta, but she's too quick and rolls past him with growing momentum. It pisses him off.

From the ground level, Poppy doesn't even *see* her own mother. She's *just* glad she's "log" rolling rather than "pencil" rolling. It's easier to get through a crowd with your hands down by your waist rather than up over your head, as Campolina is doing to protect her hairdo. Twisted Billy is more to the right of them but she's confident he's keeping up—after all, he's the one who discovered this new mode of travel. Daryl is probably not far behind, with his dickwad buddy Richard. What Poppy can't realize is, now that Richard is gay, he's having second thoughts about Daryl's antiquated sexual views on women, especially Marsha. Richard might be a libertine, but still. A no is a no. He's not a chauvinist pig.

It's exhausting, all this rolling, thinks Poppy. It required *way* more energy than bouncing *or* shaking. And it's dirty, too. Her clothes must be filthy by now, and both Springboard Sam and Double Back Barbara have had to help her pick cigarette butts out of her mouth midrotation on well-synchronized turns. She looks over and sees dogs running at her level, keeping up with the crowd. But what are they doing? Oh my God, they're trying to stick their noses up each other's butts! Is everybody in the world a rimmer but her?

Up above, Adora, shaking traditionally but open to rolling intellectually, if not physically, locks eyes with Marsha, who freezes, unprepared for a family reunion. Lester stares in shock at his onetime guard dog, Travis, who is sniffing the butt of Kent Samuels himself in front of the rimmer crowd like some stupid pet trick out of David Letterman's old TV show. How could this be? How could his loyal guard dogs go from revolution to rimming? Mutiny! That's what it is! Mutiny!

It's the end of the parade route at Flyer's Boat Yard, where the water taxis will take off to hook up to a special Rimmer

Moonlight Cruise that is supposed to set sail later that night. Kent keeps ringing that damn bell on a stage out front, without once swatting away Travis from behind, and announces the entertainment for the event, the Dancing Dingleberries, who come out to sing a little preview. Surprize is so happy to be the center of attention for all the rim-recruit dogs that she struggles out of Adora's arms right when the singing group bursts into a cover version of "Baby Got Back." Adora calls for her, but does a natural-born dog ever listen when she's alone and free to rim?

Poppy stands up vertically, exhausted from all this rolling, bruised physically and maybe even mentally. My God, it's a sea of rimmers out there! And then she sees them. Her parents. Apart as always. Her mother stares back with hatred for her own flesh and blood. And her father, yes, that's him. She'd recognize his features anywhere, after all, some of them are right on her own face. She must accept the fact that, yes, he *is* a rimmer, but she loves him just the way he is. Unconditionally. He sees her, too. Poppy. At first he's not sure, but when Kent looks over and sees his vaginally programmed, tight-ass ex-wife, he knows. His daughter, the seed of a fecal miracle, is here to celebrate her heritage. Can't Marsha see it's a new era?

Kent flicks his tongue to both of them, hoping for a truce. Marsha involuntarily bites her tongue inside her own mouth in traumatic recovered memory. Poppy rolls her tongue in a gesture of peace, but Lester growls his fiercest orders of attack to his dogs. Then he sees Travis and Draco. Their faces are mouth-to-anus with each other *Human Centipede*–style in a line of canines whose loyalty to Lester no longer matters. You can brainwash an animal, but their sexual instinct can never be eradicated. Dogs *are* rimmers. It's just nature's way.

Plain and simple. And Surprize understands this. She's been wanting to lick butt even before the "change." Matter of fact, there's a cute little terrier puckering up right off the parade route. "Grrr-yip" means "grrr-yip," doesn't it? She's no Rover but she rolls over and the terrier lifts his hind legs and Surprize gets her "brown wings." Rolling and rimming. It's a beautiful thing.

Vaulta and Leepa are next to rise, hesitantly peeking out like seals in the ocean. Springboard Sam and Double Back Barbara stand on their own hands first and then resurface in the crowd as they rotate to a standing position. Daryl ascends hesitantly, his body more chiseled and defined from all this rolling, yet guarded because he can feel Richard spinning out of his pants, eager to explore the rimming community. He sees Marsha right away. Oh my God, she's hotter than ever. He wants her more than he wants to breathe. But no, Richard has to be queer now! Uncooperative below. Hey, wait a minute! Who's that guy with his arm around her? She *allows* that?! Marsha sees Daryl's devastated expression and his now-gay, uninterested penis sulking below and smirks. But we'll see who gets the last laugh, Daryl thinks, never giving up. You don't need a hard-on to rim, do you?

Twisted Billy is the last to reveal himself, rolling upward like a small tumbleweed of energy from the ground below he now loves. Kent Samuels is so busy ushering in the merry-making rimmers and the now-unviolent, ass-worshiping dog converts that he misses the revelation. But not Poppy. Is she seeing things or did Billy just . . . just fly? Yes, he did. Even Billy seemed shocked at his new level of weightlessness. He only went up and stayed there for a few seconds. But he was definitely off the ground. An inch? Maybe two? What difference did it make, he had conquered gravity through sheer willpower. Leepa and Vaulta saw it, too. They try, but alas, no go. Campolina's always been light on her feet, but winging it doesn't work for her either.

Billy concentrates. His rising upward may be scientifically unexplainable but it's ideologically righteous. It works. He goes up again, maybe a millisecond longer. Springboard Sam and Double Back Barbara try levitating, too, but they remain earthbound, their magnetic field not yet developed to the fullest extent. Daryl leaps up like the ox he is, trying to imitate the others, and Richard lets out a hoot of derision at his heterosexual owner's complete lack of grace. Adora attempts to follow but she's way past the age for hovering. Poppy's the one. If anybody can do it, it's her. She stares at her mother and feels the mutual hatred pounding in her veins. Up she goes. Nobody could call it soaring, but what do you expect on a first attempt? She's fucking airborne. Lester and Marsha see it, too. Before they can react, Surprize sticks her nose up Marsha's ass. Night must fall.

30

Poppy and her posse wake up in Dick Dock, the public sex area under the Boatslip motel that was once the cruising ground of promiscuous gay men, now abandoned due to the rimmer renaissance. Last night's cruise had been a huge success and Kent had told his daughter where to hide from Marsha. He knew how evil and vengeful his ex-wife was and gave his tacit approval that Poppy and her followers must quietly take the law into their own hands. A police force that allows a rimmer festival is not apt to care about a suitcase thief wanted in another jurisdiction. The cops are under orders to show tolerance this weekend and respect the extremes of this newly celebrated sexual minority. Some of them even flicked their tongues in rimmer esprit de corps. But Kent had to be careful. Yes, Marsha must be eliminated for the good of society, but he was a beloved public figure in town. He couldn't get his hands dirty. They would have to do it themselves.

Rimmers had had enough. They were tired of being looked down on by subcultures in the sexual underground. Tired of being the last unaccepted tribe of oral outlaws. And the rimmer dogs were a welcome addition, their foot soldiers if you will. Once these canines tasted ass, all past allegiances were off. These dogs are now *their* own best friends, not Lester's.

Poppy keeps her new flying ability to herself. Well, flying is maybe exaggerating. OK, rising. Whatever you call it, it's too special and unexplained for normal rimmers to understand. She's not even sure if she understands it herself, like she did bouncing, shaking, and rolling. Are there side effects? She has asked Billy but he's so private—never wanting to "lead," he explains, only "interested in setting an example." He does admit that "floating," as he prefers to call it, is a "burden." She's not sure what he means yet, but she *has* experienced headaches right after and he doesn't deny that he has, too. Weightlessness can bring on nausea, and who wants to regurgitate down on fellow cultists? Since you can barely stand up straight under Dick Dock, the rest of her gang can't wait to hit the streets, where there's more headroom. They can at least *try* to soar, can't they?

Marsha is already awake and unafraid. When she and Lester had retreated to the doghouse after last night's disgusting pageant, they had felt momentarily defeated. Those filthy dogs! All that work. All that training. A lifetime of Lester's extreme dog home schooling wiped out. Canceled by their defiant tongues. He knew dogs had special glands that led them to know another's history by sniffing each other's asses, but he thought he had trained them to conquer such predispositions. Thank God he was still human enough not to share this canine basic instinct. Marsha had suffered enough.

But oh, happy day! Last night Marsha had produced her first adult bowel movement. Not a pellet. Not a cracker compost. A real live turd. She offered to show it to Lester, but he declined and instead cooked them a big dinner: Portuguese stew, garlic bread, even chocolate pie. And then they had front-door sex. Missionary mating, the way it should be. Even though her anus had been fully emptied, it was never entered once. Not by a penis, not by a finger, and *definitely* not by a tongue. Here was the rectal isolation that gave Marsha the final courage for vaginal supremacy. Rimmers must be punished, and the first to feel the pain would be Kent Samuels.

Kent had introduced Poppy to what she guesses you could call her stepmother, except she's not sure they're married. Like it would matter in this world! Rear End Rhonda, apparently that's now her legal name, is nice enough and tactfully ignores Poppy's attempts at being airborne. With the ass Rhonda's got, she knows better than to try and fly. It would take many jet engines to get this butt—a shelf, really— airborne. Rhonda's quite happy here right on the grounds of the Rimmer Carnival set up on the outskirts of town.

Kent has taken the bouncing-shaking-rolling, now want-to-be-hovering crowd of outside agitators (literally) under his wing and introduces them to VIP rimmers (who must go unnamed) who are flooding the midway to ride such attractions as "The Anus Wheel" and "The Mudslide." Rear End Rhonda has heard about the horrors of discrimination that have spewed from Kent's first wife Marsha's lips and understands she is Public Rimmer Enemy Number One. Now that Rhonda has become a sort of mother figure to the anilinguists, she guards her social position with poise and a small dose of suspicion. Kent trusts all rimmers, but Rhonda knows there can be bad apples bobbing beneath the seat of power.

Like these dogs! What the hell's with them? Running in packs, rimming indiscriminately. Where's that nutcase dog-catcher when we finally need him? Next thing you know mongrels will be trying to fly like Kent's long-lost daughter. I mean Poppy is sweet and all, but her friends! Non-rimmers can be tolerated to a point, but Jesus, Rhonda now has to deal with an ex-mother-in-law and her transitioning pet? That one called Leepa just fell flat on her face trying to . . . what? Take off? Come on! You'd think they'd learn by example but no. Can't they see Vaulta and Campolina have skinned their knees badly from aborted takeoffs? They might need stitches! Another one of them, and Christ, his dick is hanging right out of his drawers, runs up like he's on an imaginary skateboard and tries to launch but lands with a thump right in front of the "Dodge-em-Turd" ride. Spring-board Sam and Double Back Barbara are rotating inside, violating the carnival rules with head-on collisions they hope will propel them to midair buoyancy. But instead of hover-ing, they smash into the sparkling metal-mesh ceiling above and crash down to the electrical-contact silver floor below.

Poppy and Twisted Billy are managing to stay afloat at the same time across from "The Log Jam" water flume ride that affords happy rimmers a quick way to wash up between anal dives. But *remaining* up is not easy. Poppy's and Billy's medical reactions are more severe than anything they'd experienced earlier. Just the concentration above is enough to aggravate their already pounding headaches. And now, nosebleeds! Oh great! Are the metaphysical demands of being on the forefront of any visionary movement worth this? Before they can even have this rarefied debate, they see her. Satan herself.

Marsha doesn't see them, but she does see Satan number two, her town crier ex-husband, and hear ye, hear ye, it looks like he's found himself a new bullseye for his evil tongue. But good God, what's the matter with her? No one could have an ass *that* big. Lester sees her, too. There's a moon out tonight! But Kent Samuels is worse! The Pilgrim Pervert! He's the one that will pay for making Marsha live a life scarred with penis prejudice, unable to admit carnal visitors. Lester takes out his trusty, heavy-duty dog nail clippers, the perfect instrument for their planned surgery. If these sharp little babies can hack through a Doberman's infected ingrown toenails, then they sure as hell can slice off any organ this keister-feaster plans on using sexually.

But not if Poppy and her gang get to Marsha first. Collateral damage, that's all Lester is to these supernatural avengers, who are beginning to conquer gravity in the shared psychosis often referred to by psychiatrists as "folie à famille," group madness. Vaulta, Leepa, and Campolina have almost given up trying to soar in combat, but Daryl is still attempting—he does give a flying fuck even if that now can mean only rimming. "Hey," Richard thinks, "I'm gay now, remember? If anybody's ass is gonna get invaded it's Daryl's, not Marsha's, and I'm just the dick to do it."

Poppy's headache is killing her, but she knows it's time.

She must end her mother's life with her own hands while her grandmother watches at the same moment. Poppy's feet will crush Marsha's lying lips as she uses them as a springboard up to freedom and Vaulta and Campolina land back down on her from above and Leepa follows like an atomic bomb. Springboard Sam and Double Back Barbara can then shake Marsha, rattle her and roll her and even yodel about it if they are so moved. And Daryl? Who knows? Maybe Richard can poke Marsha's eyes out with his gay shaft, but hopefully she won't be *totally* blind. She'll need to see their happy faces coming toward her to finish her off, bouncing her to death. Billy? He's so astrally advanced he just stays up there to watch. Yes, there's a little turbulence, but up is still up. Nothing phases him now. Come to think of it, he *is* now.

Marsha sees Kent leading his backdoor bachelorette over to the Anus Wheel to buy tickets. She grabs Lester and they give chase, but these fucking dogs keep jumping out in front of them, rimming each other exhibitionistically in defiance of his unselfish past devotion to their liberation. It's now too late to attack Kent. He's already seated on the ride. With her! Waving to other sex offenders like she was prom queen. You'd think rimmer royalty, as these two imagine themselves, would have something better to do than rotate around in a ride shaped like what they really were—assholes. Shouldn't they be home writing rimmer grant applications or organizing lick-ins at other pervert beach communities like Key West, Fire Island, or Rehoboth Beach, Delaware?

Poppy struggles to continue air-lingering, sometimes falling back to earth with an unmajestic thud. But then all she has to do is look back up at Billy, floating like a locust, disrupting like a bee, and she's off into the rarefied free zone of air they both have managed to semicontrol. Migraines, lavalike nosebleeds, now combined with a sudden skin rash that resembles prickly heat; it's all manageable when you're united in the holistic divinity of payback. Adora has to signal Springboard Sam and Double Back Barbara to help her drag Surprize away from all the dog rimmers to her final offensive-line position in their planned assassinations. Daryl's completely useless now that Richard, ass level in the crowd, is searching for any willing male buns, but how do you rim when you don't have a mouth? These assassins may be damaged but they're ready. They're willing. And they're *more* than able.

But their victims may just die all on their own. There's a scream from above. It's Rear End Rhonda and the car she is riding in with Kent is beginning to come apart due to her morbidly desired ass. Kent calls for help as he sees the bolts on Rhonda's side start to pop out and the whole car begins to separate from the wheel precariously. Marsha looks up in a fury. This man cannot die accidentally, he must perish at her command.

As the rimmer crowd below cries out in fear, Lester slashes the air with his powerful nail cutters in frustration. He sees Poppy and her puppets coming at him and Marsha with a look of intensifying magical hatred beyond his celestial understanding. They were fanatical physical fitness idiots before, but now they're downright scary. Campolina without camp, vibrating with venom, headed straight toward them. Vaulta, shaking not with fear but a desire to annihilate. Leepa, rolling at him like an avalanche from hell. Together they're the airborne Children of the Corn. Springboard Sam and Double Back Barbara, well, maybe they still can't fly, but they sure can plummet, and who wants to be their landing strip? Adora? Even that once-grizzled senior citizen looks like she's possessed with youth serum. And whoa! That yapping dog of hers, or whatever it is, is foaming at the mouth, but the foam is pink! Pretzel-boy—he's all straightened out now, gliding toward Lester like in *The Thief of Bagdad*. And Daryl! Daryl! Daryl! That pitiful excuse of an upper-body hetero is daring to look at Marsha's ass with newfound lust, flicking his tongue all the while. Before Lester can come to her rescue, Richard, a feminist gay man at last, takes over, goes south, and dives under his balls, barreling back toward Daryl's own asshole. "Ow! That fucking hurts!" screams Daryl in shock as Richard jams his head up Daryl's anal opening. "How do *you* like it?" Richard yells back, muffled from inside, giving Daryl a taste of his own medicine and proud to be teaching his master a well-deserved lesson in sexual politics.

Where oh where are Lester's three guard dogs now that he needs them? Surely the lure of rimming is a passing fancy. What could feel better than saving the life of the only man who can still dominate you? In one final attempt at rallying back his troops, Lester howls out the most guttural, ferociously painful battle cry from the pits of dog-pain hell, beyond rabid, over the top of abandonment, beneath the valley of hunger or animal cruelty—a helter-pet-shelter last hurrah against oral-anal human-canine supremacy. At first nothing. But then he sees him. Baxter. His first guard dog. He takes his tongue out of another dog's rear end, looks back at Lester, and barks. Once. Just once.

Kent and Rhonda's car on the Anus Wheel comes completely unattached at one end and hangs on its side vertically. Rhonda slides down and struggles to reach Kent's outstretched arm above as he grabs onto the spoke of the ride, but her oversize posterior is her own worst enemy. The panicked operator, trying to help, mistakenly lurches the wheel forward and Rhonda falls to her death, narrowly missing a floating Poppy below but seriously injuring several of the rimmer faithful on the ground.

Marsha looks up in fury at her ex-husband, who is hanging on for dear life, but suddenly the other end of his car snaps off and Kent comes flying down at a high speed with that rimming tongue screaming right toward her. Lester grabs Marsha out of the way in the nick of time before the body lands on another woman, an anilinguist who they later learned had been in the Witness Protection Program but was now definitely in the wrong place at the wrong time. Lester kneels down, slices out Kent's protruding tongue, and tosses it to Marsha, who flips it like a hot potato into her own vengeful mouth and scarfs it down. There, she's finally divorced for real. "Thelp," gurgles Kent before his blood strangles him inside his own rimmer throat. But who can understand him now with this speech impediment? Nobody, that's who.

As rescue squads and ambulances move onto the accident scene, Lester reaches into the dead rimmer's purse, grabs her fictitious government-supplied passport, and replaces it with Marsha's ID out of his pocket. Marsha and Lester lock eyes. "Liarmouth," he whispers in code. She knows what that means. Time to invent an alternative reality. A reinvented truth. Marsha pockets the new identification and quickly throws herself into the pile of injured bodies, covering herself with the carnival ground's dirt and gravel and playing dead like the liarmouth she once was. Lester cradles her "lifeless" body in his arms and screams, "No! No! No!" for Poppy and her brain-dead followers to see.

It works. Finally, Marsha is gone, Poppy thinks. Her

father had to give up his life to complete the vicious circle of generational vengeance, but what a gift! So selfless. So loving. Such a beautiful thing to do for his daughter. Poppy abruptly falls down from "hovering" to the ground, but what does she care? Her burden has ended. She can finally sit still. Forget her futile attempts at uninterrupted movement that will lead only to mental frustration, physical exhaustion, and possibly death. Her followers can have their own lives back, too. Be unburdened people who don't have to prove anything. Vaulta and Leepa can be stationary for once. Campolina can be light on her feet because of gayness, not some otherworldly passion for upward mobility. Springboard Sam and Double Back Barbara will never have to bounce, shake, or roll again. They can concentrate on soaring metaphorically into well-deserved yodeling fame. Daryl, well, now that Marsha's dead he can't have sex with her. He's not *that* fucked-up! Maybe he'll find another domineering woman who will treat him badly while he stands still. Richard? Can he go back to the everyday joys of urination and learn his place, gay *or* straight, in the natural order of things? Her own grandmother Adora can finally retire and pretend she never heard of rolling, rimming, *or* rising. Once she stops shaking, Surprize will be totally accepted in the extreme pet world by all breeds and finally free to live in harmony with domesticity, away from the anarchy of the rimming outlaw lifestyle. And Twisted Billy? So humble. So lovely. So peaceful. Maybe now that he no longer carries the heavy responsibility of spiritual discovery, he can live free and just be himself. Not Twisted Billy. Just Billy. Plain ol' Billy.

Yes, the journey to rise above, below, and beyond the human condition that began on a trampoline and ended at a rimmer festival has at last come to an end. Poppy, Vaulta,

Leepa, Campolina, Springboard Sam, Double Back Barbara, Billy, Adora, Surprize, Daryl, and Richard can be content right here on earth. Terra firma. Feet planted on solid ground, with *no* powers. Look at them. Can they be happy? Happy at last?

31

It was a beautiful spring day for a funeral in Moreland Memorial Park Cemetery, the closest one they could find to Dutch Village. Calling it a funeral might be pushing it. A "gloating" was more like it. Around the freshly dug grave stood the celebrants, hardly mourning, eager to shout out their curses on the deceased. A "hate funeral" like no other.

They waited six months to bury her. To make sure she was really dead. After all, in real life several of them had actually been able to fly, if you could call it that. Who knew what deep, dark magic this witch could pull from the other side of the grave? They burned her up of course. Cremated the body right there in Provincetown. From the ambulance to the dead-on-arrival emergency room right to the furnace. Alone, just what she deserved. Now if the resurrection did happen, she'd still be screwed. Ashes can't walk, can they?

There was no press present. They had originally covered

her death from the "freak accident at an anal-swinger festival" angle. Much juicier than the "most wanted" suitcase thief one, and besides, the insurance companies had settled those old baggage claims long ago. Nobody "wanted" her now. Not the FBI. Not the media. And least of all her family and their friends. Even the reverend they had found on Craigslist to lead the services loathed the legacy of Marsha Sprinkle once he did his research. "We are gathered here," he begins, "to spit on the grave of this terrible harridan and to take a time of healing to judge, condemn, and destroy the reputation of such a horrible human being.

"Everyone hated her," he continues. "Her employees, her poor deceased ex-husband, her own daughter, and yes, her mother, too. Even God thought she was a cunt," he thunders to the heavens above. Harsh? Maybe not. Even one of the uniformed gravediggers, waiting patiently for the signal to throw in the first shovelful of dirt, laughs out loud. So does the other one. Then they both hop. Twice.

"Let me read from the scriptures," the minister intones. "Revelation chapter twenty-one, verse eight. 'All liars shall have their part in the lake which burneth with fire and crimson which is a second death.'" "Hallelujah!" Poppy and her onetime followers shout out like the normal people they are trying to become. "Proverbs chapter six, verses sixteen through nineteen," he announces piously. "'There are six things that the Lord hates, seven that are detestable to Him; haughty eyes, a lying tongue, hands that shed innocent blood, a heart that desires wicked plans, feet that are quick to run to evil, a false witness who pours out lies, and a person who stirs up conflict in the community.' Is this not Marsha Sprinkle herself?" The graveside crowd knows they are not supposed to cheer at a funeral, but they do anyway.

When the murmurs of approval die down, the reverend asks in a holy voice, "Would the family like to share?" knowing full well the volcano of hatred that will follow. "Yes, Father," answers Adora, standing up ramrod straight without the slightest bit of shaking, now content to just sit home in New York City, drama-free watching *Dog Whisperer* reruns on the National Geographic channel. "I want to apologize to the world," she volunteers, "for giving birth to such an evil creature." Surprize, now purring in the cutest way possible, fully identifying as a cat, mews lovingly in support as the other gravedigger, possibly a woman, sneaks away shaking sideways with her male fellow funeral groundskeeper. He's doing it, too!

Poppy, now content to stand despite the excess weight she's put on due to lack of exercise, adds in a loud, clear voice, "Finally I'm over the trauma of being born from inside the poisonous vessel known as Marsha Sprinkle!" She doesn't even hear the shattering of her car's windows in the parking lot. "Right on!" shouts out Vaulta, still standing tall but now active in the world of American women's basketball, where she can finally jump in a way that society can better understand. Is that her vehicle's burglar alarm she hears in the distance? Of course not! Who would break into her car at a funeral? "She was a complete psycho," witnesses Leepa, no longer a big girl, so exhausted from all those Overeaters Anonymous meetings that she thinks she's seeing things when that other weird gravedigger grabs a gasoline can from a tool shed and runs up the hill to the parking lot. Does she know this fool? He *does* look familiar.

"A viper," adds Campolina, real name Harold Atkins, now such an upscale gay guy who's left his drag persona behind to become a real estate agent that he doesn't even wonder why all that smoke is billowing from right where he left his new truck. Let other queens worry about it. Not him. He's through with all that diva shit. "A fucking witch," accuses Sam, as he's now known since he's not springing anywhere anymore except to his job repairing the karaoke machine up at the corner bar near the old trampoline park. "A kleptomaniac," chimes in Barbara, who, if she's double backing to anywhere since their Grand Ole Opry plans tanked, it's to an honest day's work selling her old Jimmie Rodgers CDs up at the North Point Plaza Flea Market. *Boom!* What the fuck was that explosion? Whatever it was, she and Sam sure aren't yodeling about it.

"Marsha Sprinkle had no soul!" blurts out Billy, surprising his own self now that he's given up the spiritual life for a more mundane one as a chiropractor's receptionist. Imagine his shock when he sees the roof of his heavily financed red Hyundai land with a crash not twenty feet away. *Now* how's he supposed to get home? He's certainly not walking with the new back pain that's come on since he's been static.

"She was frigid, too!" hollers Daryl in one last blast of bitter, leftover horniness. Yes, he's pled guilty to third-degree burglary for the suitcase crap and served two months of home detention, and he's single now to boot. But that's not a problem because Richard down below has turned over a new leaf—celibacy. Both have accepted the calmer life of an incel. It's just easier that way. But what they both want to do together is the perfect finale for this character assassination funeral. "Burn in hell," the pastor cries, and Richard, taking his cue from Daryl, pisses on Marsha's grave. "Burn, witch, burn!" the antimourners begin chanting, over and over, building in intensity.

Suddenly dogs are heard howling in the distance. The crowd freezes. Did the earth just shake a little or is that their new nonmovement paranoia? Oh, my God, he's not a grave-digger! He's that horrible dogcatcher from Provincetown and he's rising above them in the air of the parking lot just like they used to be able to do. His angry guard dogs pour into the cemetery, aimed directly for their service. Poppy re-alizes she's made a mistake. She blinked. She should have known never to walk away from her special powers, because there are always enemies waiting to steal what is magically yours, and that is what happened. The other one's not some gravedigger either. It's her. Her mother, Marsha Sprinkle. A little heavier but still alive. Partially revealed through a cloud of explosive gasoline smoke like a bad Hallmark Easter card. Rising up in the air farther than Poppy had ever been able to reach, possessing the same powers she once ridiculed and refused to understand in others. Worse yet, dogs seem to like her now. Will there ever be justice?

Poppy tries with all her might to bounce, shake, roll, or rise—any way to escape the charging dogs, but she's not a defier of gravity anymore. None of them are. Miraculous powers are not retrievable once abandoned. There's no sec-ond chance at divinity. They all miss the boat. Baxter, Les-ter's favorite guard dog, attacks Daryl and bites off Richard. Connected or not connected, impotency is now forever. Tra-vis, the large boxer, lunges toward the pastor and begins mauling him while Draco rips apart the pages of the Bible with his teeth. "Run!" Poppy screams to her onetime follow-ers, and even though they now have wills of their own, all obey. Yet Poppy has never had to run—she knew how to move upward with both of her feet on the ground but never forward with one after the other. Vaulta and Leepa ape Poppy's uncoordinated gait, but they trip over Campolina, excuse me, Harold, who has clumsily fallen, too, unused to running in men's shoes. The dogs attack all with a new vengeance. Sam and Barbara's shaking *without* benefits only slows them down, and poor Adora quivers now with fear, not aggression. Surprize is no fool, though. She may have been trapped in the wrong animal body, but in times of war, one must adapt, switch loyalties to the winning side. Traitor? No, survivor! Surprize bites Adora right on her reconstructed belly button and returns her "outie" to an "innie." Like the dog Surprize must be again, she runs to the welcoming growls of Baxter, Travis, and Draco and takes her new position in the animal kingdom. It's been a journey. Lord, it's been a journey.

Billy can't fly anymore, and he's accepted that fact, but when Draco takes to the air toward him and stays up just a few seconds longer than possible for *any* dog, he ducks and thinks fast. Spotting a motorized handicapped cemetery cart left behind from an earlier funeral, he jumps on, revs the motor, and signals to his gang to leap aboard, and they do, just like in that famous photograph of the last helicopter leaving South Vietnam. Piled on and hanging on to each other for dear life, they beg Billy to stop and pick up Richard, who is writhing on the ground, cut off and abandoned. Last man down! Billy, ever the hero, does so with his last remaining drop of dexterity, and the chewed up, mauled, bitten, and castrated speed away, looking back at the burial plot.

Marsha and Lester, surrounded by Baxter, Travis, Draco, and the newly feral Surprize, watch the losers fade in the distance. Marsha steps forward as Lester joins the dogs in a howling chorus of barked victory. She turns sideways and smiles. All can now see her bump. Yes, Marsha Sprinkle is with child. She's pregnant and that's the God's honest truth. Poppy starts to scream. And scream. And scream. And to this day, she's never been able to stop.

ACKNOWLEDGMENTS

Thanks to Trish Schweers, Jen Berg, and Caitlin Billard in my office for being top-notch researchers and copy editors. As they typed each draft of this novel from my handwritten original, they teetered on the literary edge of taste with me, hopefully protecting my cockeyed balance. My agent, Bill Clegg, is a voice of reason through the damaged strains of my narratives and can point out impossibilities even in the midst of fictitious anarchy. Jonathan Galassi, my editor, is graceful in his suggestions, understands my perverse morality, and gets my jokes with seeming delight and glee. Deferring to his judgment always feels as if it's the right choice.

This is my fourth book with Farrar, Straus and Giroux and working with the team (Lottchen Shivers, Katharine Liptak, Logan Hill, Janine Barlow, and Na Kim) remains a privilege. Oh yes, also thanks to Michael Goldstein for his book *Ear Masturbation*. I have no idea how it ended up in my library but this slim volume certainly was inspirational.